# Aristocrat Wives

## A novel
## by Ekene Onu

NOUVEAU
Africana

This is a work of fiction. Names, characters, places and incidents are either the product of the author's imagination or are used fictitiously, and any resemblance to any actual persons, living or dead, event or locales is entirely coincidental.

Published by Nouveau Africana Media,
A division of Refresh with Ekene LLC
741 Monroe St, Atlanta, GA 30308

ISBN: 978-0-578-20222-8

**For my sisters across the diaspora**

Let us not search without
**for that which we carry within.**

# Chapter 1

# Karen
# Even mansions burn down

Karen swirled her wine, breathed in deep and appreciated the bouquet. It was a good Cabernet Sauvignon. She detected strawberries, oak and a hint of florals in the aroma. It felt silky in her mouth as she sipped it and she enjoyed the lingering finish from the tannins. She sat there deliberately focusing on the wine, trying to relax as she waited out the traffic. After thirty minutes trapped in one spot, the plush interior of her Range Rover felt like a padded cell, so as soon as the driver could move she asked him to pull into the nearby, just opened and stunning Casa Bella Hotel. It was right by the ocean and had been decorated to mimic one of the luxurious boutique hotels in South Beach, Miami. She could hear the blaring of the horns as the traffic persisted and she turned her attention to the serene view of the Atlantic Ocean and took in the beauty of the waves. There were worse ways to spend one's time Karen thought and smiled to herself.

A girl caught Karen's eye as she walked into the raised bar area from the hotel lobby. She remembered that the same woman had been right behind her as she entered the hotel but she sat in the lobby as Karen walked up to the bar area. She was wearing a too tight, short skirt that showed her too large stomach and too big butt. Her weave was cheap and tangled at the back. Her bargain basement blouse was fraying at the bottom and her worn down heels clicked noisily on the marble floor. Karen watched her through the safety of her oversize designer sunglasses and smoothed her own tailored skirt with deliberation, as if doing so would avert the disaster that she felt was coming.

She got up and walked to the bathroom. Almost as soon as she pushed past the door into the pristine, white marble room, she heard quick, hollow steps, the same woman had followed after. Karen turned towards the mirror and pulled out her compact, pretending not to notice the strange woman standing there in front of the sink, motionless except for her glaring.

"You may not know who I am, but your husband is in love with me!" The woman said, looking right at Karen's reflection in the mirror. She stood behind Karen with her hands on her hips.

Karen kept her gaze on the mirror and kept dabbing at her face with her powder puff. She stole another glance at the woman and a thought flew into her head - she had poor taste in lipstick. Nude would suit her better than red and matte better than gloss.

"Didn't you hear what I said?" The woman said with so much force that she spit a little.

Karen side stepped the spray of saliva that settled on the mirrored glass, and then she flicked off an imaginary piece of lint from her blouse. She thought about her husband, Dele. He had started getting careless. How could he choose this sort of woman as a mistress?

Finally she turned around and faced the woman. She took her time before responding, shaking out her long, enhanced but natural looking hair. She lifted her manicured fingers to her face and took off her sunglasses, pausing just long enough for the woman to notice her flawless and oversize diamond, and only when she saw the woman's lips quiver a bit, did she speak.

"Surely you aren't speaking to me?" she inquired in her upper crust unspecified Euro accent, carefully cultivated through years at English boarding schools and courses in European universities.

The woman didn't speak.

"Darling, has a cat got your tongue?" Karen took advantage of her moment of intimidation and moved closer to the woman. Then she stopped, placed her hand on her hip and surveyed her slowly.

Karen continued to watch her as if she was a circus curiosity on display and the woman finally gathered her wits. "I know you have heard my name. I am Gia. Dele screams it out loud whenever I am on top of him," she said, pushing her chest out, feeling bolder.

Karen threw her head back and laughed in response, it was a rich throaty sound. By the time she spoke, the woman who called herself Gia, was breathing hard and fidgeting, "Sweetheart, your name is of no consequence to me. My husband changes whores like he changes his boxer shorts and he does that sometimes twice a day. You see he can't stand to be in anything dirty and once he is done with them that is what they are," she said, looking the girl right in the eye.

"I presume that's why you are here. Let me guess, first he stopped taking your calls, then the phone number is no longer in service. You think that by approaching me, you can get him back." Karen smiled as the girl's mouth dropped open. Chewing gum chick! She thought. She wants to swim in the ocean and she is still wearing inflatable wings.

"My darling, the best advice I can give you is to get on with your life. Dele doesn't remember your name, no matter how many times you think he called it out because at the end of the day the only name that really matters to him is Mrs. Karen Thompson." With that Karen turned on her heel and walked out of the bathroom, leaving the girl standing there.

Hours later, Karen walked into her bedroom. Her head was pounding. She lifted the receiver by her bed.

"Yes ma?" the steward answered.

"Have the girl bring up my medicine and send a glass of Chardonnay with it," she said.

"Excuse me ma, you don't want me to send up water?" Karen frowned a little, irritated at his presumption and she would have chastised him immediately, but she found herself silent, realizing that the idea that this man with whom she had no kinship, cared whether she drank alcohol with her medication was a little comforting.

"Of course" She acquiesced, "Send up a glass of cold water."
The girl was up within minutes and after swallowing the pills,
Karen lay down on her bed with her shoes still on and her handbag
still on her shoulder and found herself drifting away within
seconds.

She was walking on the beach, marveling at how wonderful
the sand felt between her toes. She was a different person,
laughing, feeling free. She heard someone calling her voice in the
distance, but she had no desire to respond. Then she felt strong
hands on her shaking her shoulders. Her eyes jolted open, and she
saw her husband's face. Dele was home and sitting on the bed next
to her with a worried expression on his face. "Are you alright?"
he asked. She struggled to collect herself. Her hair was askew and
her lipstick smeared, it was particularly strange as she was always
impeccably put together. She tried to sit up, but felt dizzy and a
wave of nausea overtook her and she brought her hand to her
mouth.

Dele held her and put his hand on her forehead. "Are you
alright?" he repeated, watching her attempt to collect herself. She
was disconcerted by her physical symptoms, but even more so by
his affection. He looked into her eyes with a questioning gaze and
she began to shiver.

"I am fine," Karen replied, "just tired."

Dele looked at her like he did not believe her.

"Are you sure?" he prodded. The look on his face was
inscrutable: a mix of worry, frustration and endearment. In the
entire period of their relationship, Karen had never seen him look
at her like this.

"I'm fine, Dele. Are you, alright? You hardly come into my
bedroom, what's wrong?" she asked with a quizzical look on her
face. She waited for him to respond. She raised herself up, settling
more comfortably on her pillows. His eyes followed every move
she made and when he saw her lean back into the pillows, he

sighed. "I guess I am just tired as well," he said, leaning back on to the pillow next to her. He put his arm over his face.

"Karen, do you ever wish you could start things over?" he asked, letting his leg touch hers ever so slightly.

Karen raised one eyebrow, but she did not respond. What did this mean? She wondered. She felt a strange urge to reach out to him and hold him for a moment, but she could not will herself to move and she was not sure how Dele would react. It would be so out of character for her, but this too, was out of character for him. Then just as suddenly as it happened, he moved his arm and Karen saw his expression and knew the moment of opportunity had passed. Dele turned and smiled at her, a tight grin that was familiar and yet distancing. "Don't mind me! I probably just need a hot shower and maybe I'll go to the club," he said, getting up from the bed.

Karen felt a sudden sadness overcome her, but pushed it away. Her moment had passed as well. "Do what you must" she said, "But remember if you visit every rundown, easy to get into club, in time it will diminish you." He looked at her and Karen knew he understood what she was saying.

He walked out of the room towards his own lavish master suite. Karen watched him go. She could see the form of his back through his shirt and soon she was imagining his body in the shower. He was still as strong and muscular as the first day they met and despite herself, she was still attracted to him. Her thoughts were interrupted by a persistent sound. A phone was buzzing; It was Dele's, he must have dropped it without knowing. Karen did not pick it up. She didn't need to, she knew what it was, probably a text from some woman who wanted to be his warm space tonight and depending on his mood, she probably would get her wish granted.

Now it was Karen's turn to sigh. She picked up the receiver again.

"Yes Ma." The steward responded, ever ready to serve.

"Bring me up some more Valium and that glass of wine!" she ordered, this time leaving no room for debate.

# Chapter 2

# Lola
# Every hot bowl of soup will eventually cool

The bedroom was quiet except for the relentless humming of the generator in the back of the house. It created a background beat for the words that were bouncing around like an aggressive rap verse in Lola's head.

*"Why couldn't he get it up?"* she asked herself.

The words had been swirling around all night, accusing her in every syllable. *It's your fault! You are not sexy! You are so boring in bed!* "What is happening?" she screamed in her head, exhausted from anxiety and lack of sleep. Her husband lay next to her and her head was on his chest. His arms were around her, assuring her of his affection, but still she found herself contemplating the worst case scenarios and it made her feel more desperate. She was lost in her thoughts. *Is this how it starts, the beginning of the end? Was this a sign of their bodies yielding to the ravages of age or their marriage yielding to the ways of society?*

She lifted her head and kissed his chest. He was hairy and the curls on his chest tickled her nose. She moved up to his neck, moaning as she did. She caressed his arms and moaned even louder. She was hoping to reconnect, she wanted a deeper level of intimacy, but her husband shifted his position on the bed and inched away from her.

She did not need a crystal ball to tell her that something was very wrong. Her heart had started racing and her mouth was dry, but it was not for the reasons one would expect in this sort of situation. The irony did not escape her as she considered her nakedness. She remembered how they used to make love and how he would take charge in bed and pull her close, his grip just shy of uncomfortable. She had a flashback to one of the many times when he kissed her, sucking gently on her bottom lip. Parts of her body ached in remembrance and she shuddered. The memory was vivid, but it was marked by age. Like a beautiful photo covered with dust. She could not remember the last time he touched her with such passion. She took a deep breath and was still for a moment wondering what to do next. She did not want her marriage to slowly fall away into nothingness, like a road that has suffered under the pressures of the traffic, climate and a lack of maintenance, slowly deteriorating until a sink hole appears without warning and swallows the car whole. She had watched so many marriages around her seem to spontaneously combust, but upon further investigation, the signs had been there all along.

She had always said that she would not be a statistic; she had always said her marriage would be forever. Remembering her convictions, she became energized and she decided to take the lead and be the aggressor, thinking that maybe he would find that exciting enough and so like a weary runner who had found her second wind, she unleashed her passion in her mind and planned to straddle him, determined to turn things around.

She reached for him again under the covers, but he moved his hips away as if frightened. She was mortified. She knew what he was trying to hide but it was too late, she could already tell that he was soft. She could not stop herself from sighing in sadness when he pushed her away gently and moved towards the edge of the bed muttering something about having to get to the office.

Finally she gave up. She felt tears welling up behind her eyes as she watched her husband rise from the bed, rigid and tense in every other part of his body, except the one place that mattered.

She exhaled again and asked him what was wrong. "Nothing," he responded, evading her stare. "Look," he said tersely, "I have to get to work," and with that he got up and walked into the bathroom. Lola sat on the bed and watched the goose bumps rise up on her arms from the cool of the air-conditioner. She rubbed her arms to warm up and then willed herself to get up as she swung her legs over the side of the bed. She paused for a moment and sighed yet again. She pressed her lips together and blinked repeatedly, commanding back the tears and then she reached for her long silk robe, a gift from John's latest business trip to Singapore. The robe felt delicious on her skin, but when he presented it to her, she was more grateful for the limited edition Vuitton bag that accompanied it. Whenever she thought about that bag it made her smile. There was only one other woman in Lagos who had a similar one, fortunately this particular style never caught on with the counterfeiters. However today, even the thought of being a fashion do in the society pages was not enough to pull her out of the mood she was descending into.

She pulled the robe tight around her naked body and walked into the bathroom. He was in the shower already and Lola touched her hair from reflex. Like many Nigerian society women, her hair maintenance routine was involved and tedious, so getting it wet was always a factor to be considered before any activity. *Too bad*, she thought ending her internal debate, she would risk messing up her hair that took three hours at the salon to style yesterday, if it meant getting to the bottom of this new disconnect between she and her husband.

She got to the door of the shower and stood there for a few minutes, watching her husband through the steamed up glass walls. She stared at the flexing muscles in his arms and followed the sinewy lines across his shoulders and down his back, watching the soapy water run down to his legs as he washed himself. He was in good shape from his weekly squash games, his stomach was flat and other than a few grey flecks in his hair, he didn't look like many men his age, who were already sporting substantial potbellies. They had always been very attracted to each other and once upon a time, she would have simply dropped her robe and joined him in the shower, but these days she felt more and more insecure in their relationship and mornings like this made her even more so.

He had his back to her, but she knew he knew she was there. She could not bring herself to join him. After a while, she coughed aloud and asked "John, is everything okay?" The pitch of her voice was higher than usual.

He did not turn, but stuck his head under the water cascading from the waterfall shower head, that Lola took pains to order from a particular bathroom company in Italy. She watched the rivulets of water run down over his head. He stood there for a long time and so did she. Finally he stepped back from the water and Lola realized that it must have been getting colder because the water heater only dispensed so much hot water at a time. It was an irritating limitation, considering how much they had spent on plumbing. However this was Lagos where so many workers and companies operate under the motto of "idea la need (we just need the general idea, the details are unimportant)" and as such, substandard work was not uncommon. When she queried the building contractor, he had simply shrugged his shoulders and shook his head saying, "Pele, ma! We have to manage abi?" Lola knew many madams who would have berated the man so bitterly, that he would have felt like he was being flogged, just for having the audacity to flaunt his incompetence, but she had no such inclinations, so they managed with barely hot water.

"I know you can hear me!" she shouted, determined to get his attention. She started to say something more but her voice cracked, so she just stood there with her arms folded across her chest watching him. He finished rinsing himself, turned off the water and stepped out naked. Lola was again taken aback for a moment by his physique. She so adored her husband. She tried to look into his eyes, but he looked away as he wrapped the plush white towel around himself still dripping water everywhere. Lola looked down at her white bath mats that were getting soaked. He continued toweling off and their silence persisted as he put on deodorant and moisturized his skin. Then he stopped and looked at her. She met his eyes but she could not comprehend what was in them. She wanted him to explain away those past awkward minutes. She wanted to hear words that would reassure her, but even as she waited for him to speak, she knew nothing he could say could quell the fear that was rising in her heart.

Suddenly he pulled her to him and kissed her. It was not a passionate kiss, but it was a strong kiss and the message it sent was simple. Then he held her away from him and drove the point home, "Everything is fine" he said. There was a warning in his words. She was not to bring it up again. She was to submit. Everything is fine, she thought and pressed the words into her heart. "Everything is fine", "Everything is fine." She repeated the mantra, smiled at her husband and thought about her life with him and how she did not want it to change. She hugged him, burying her head into his chest and he kissed the top of her head.

She really had no business complaining. She had a good life. She was attractive, her kids were in the best schools and she did not have to work, so she could be active with various charities and help out a lot at church. She did a lot at church and often patted herself on the back for it. She was not like those women who were just socialites without a cause. They attended The Lord's House. It was a large church and she was one of the notable women there and she was working her way up into the Pastor and first lady's inner circle. They knew who she was already, but Lola craved more recognition, so she made sure she always gave generously, participated in several ministries and looked wonderful at church. After all, she thought, image is everything, isn't that what they say? The thought of becoming the ultimate high society wife operating at the highest levels was so seductive that it pulled her away from the drama of the moment.

She was determined to be happy. They were an enviable couple. She was the wife of a rich and powerful man and she knew many women envied her. He was a good husband. He provided, he was caring. As she continued thinking, her brow furrowed and she reminded herself that he had flaws. Even as the imperfect images in her memory banks imprinted on her inner eye, she forced her mind to make the edges a little less sharp. Yes, he was a little controlling, but that came with being such a powerful man, didn't it? Sometimes he scared her when he shouted; when he lost his temper, but he was often sweet and only loud when he was under stress. She had learned how to manage his stress at home. She looked at him and chose to only recall the good, to remind herself of everything she fell in love with when she first saw him. He was so handsome, so charming. Her thoughts were rewarded when he came close and kissed her; his hand ran through her long and wavy hair. This morning, it fell around her shoulders. She was still in her robe. When they first got married she used to wear these sexy see through lingerie affairs, but after many years of marriage and the after effects of two children, these days, she favored long silk robes.

She was not so young anymore; her once full and perky breasts now sagged a bit and her waist was a little thicker. She had researched plastic surgery and even considered flying out to Los Angeles at a friend's recommendation, but she could not bring herself to do it. She knew she was not model thin like her husband preferred but she knew she was still not fat and besides her husband loved her, so she swallowed her fear, looked up at him, took his hands from her shoulders and placed them on the curve of her butt. She encouraged him to squeeze. He raised an eyebrow and smiled as he did.

"I love you," She said as she moved closer to him. Finally she felt a firm sensation pressing against her and led him back to the bedroom. This time, he finished what she had started.

# Chapter 3

# Chika
## Single ladies, put your head down.

Chika looked around her new nicely furnished flat with plush sofas and chairs, terra cotta painted accent walls and vibrant Nigerian art. She had left everything she knew behind in London. Her tiny flat, cold floors and matchbox kitchen had been her home for so long that in this space, with the ever present heat, she felt ill at ease. Even though Nigeria was her ancestral home, she felt like a stranger, especially since she had no close family members living in this bustling city called Lagos. So much had changed since she lived here as a child. Gone were the carefree days of skipping home from school and buying roasted plantain from the roadside. Today, she had battled traffic, dealt with electricity and water issues in her supposedly serviced apartment and for the umpteenth time, she asked herself, if the move back home to Nigeria was right thing.

Her new maid came in to tell her that she had finished making dinner. Chika waved her away because even though the maid had cooked her favorite Egusi stew as she had requested, her stomach turned at the thought of eating. She sighed and her shoulder length braids swept across her face. She had made a plan and she was going to stick with it and see it through. Living in London had its perks, but it had become a lonely existence. All her friends were married off and having children, and while her work as a presenter, author and inspirational speaker kept her fulfilled, she could not push aside her fears. What if she never found the one? What if she never got married? She was already thirty-eight and if her parents were still alive, they would have despaired for her future. The truth was that she hoped to meet someone when she came back home. She always worried that perhaps the issue was that she could not relate to the British and Nigerians in London. She had not been lucky with any. She thought that maybe being home, she might meet a different class of men, or at least that one man who would get her and connect with her. So far that had not happened. She received attention from men, but no one that she could consider. The crazy thing was that despite the population density, Lagos was even lonelier than London. Everyone was paired off. Well, her contemporaries at least and the married women here were not just smug, they were paranoid and insufferable. She was sick of going solo to functions and enduring the salacious comments from married men who assumed just because she was single that she was desperate and shielding herself emotionally from the energy of some of the wives in the room. If looks could kill, she would be in the hospital from the glares of the women who were determined to make sure that what was theirs remained theirs. Even old high school friends, acted strange when she came around them and their husbands. She thought about how black men in London complained when white women grasped their purses tighter when they saw them. Well, even that snub could not compare to the grip some of these women had on their husbands when a single woman came into the room. She felt tears pressing behind her eyes. She blinked and felt at the brink of despair. She was tired.

"Ngozi!" she called out.

"Ma?" the young girl responded, running out from the kitchen.

"Please bring me some cold water and Paracetamol, I have a bad headache," Chika said.

Once the maid brought them, she took the pills and let the cool glass linger against her cheek.

"Ma?" The maid stood there waiting.

Chika looked up and smiled, "Thank you Ngozi," she said handing her the glass. She got up and adjusted her blouse. "Please put away the food, I am going to bed."

"Yes ma," Ngozi said, curtsying a little.

"Good night." Walking towards her bedroom, she walked past her bookcase and thought she should read a little before bed. Her eyes fell on two titles, *God's Promises to Singles,* and *Sex and the City.* She chose *Sex and the City* because she wanted to laugh her troubles away.

# Chapter 4

# Karen
## Pass the champagne please

Karen surveyed her sitting room, an ornately designed room; it was not her taste with the heavy draperies and luxurious copies of Victorian furniture. Her mother-in-law had insisted that it be done up in this way. "The queen of England sits in a chair much like this one!" she exclaimed. When they first got married, Karen was so invested in being the perfect daughter-in-law and creating a meaningful relationship with her, hoping that it would help her relations with her husband. But soon she realized that no matter what she did, her mother-in-law would never consider her a daughter, rather a rival for her son's affection and as such, their relationship became a war of wills as Karen stepped into her role as Mrs Thompson. Karen looked around the only room in her house that she couldn't stand to be in and she conceded that she had lost that battle, but the war was still yet to be won.

The grandfather clock chimed. Karen looked at her watch and took a deep breath to calm herself. It was her turn to host the High Society Ladies Luncheon and everything had to be perfect. The social group had existed for as long as she could remember. It had been exclusive and sought after, long before she was even born. Karen was a legacy member from the moment she was conceived because her grandmother was a founding member and her mother was active in the group when she was alive. In the beginning, it was created at the prompting of a husband who needed to keep his pretty wife occupied, but over the years it had become quite the force formidable. They did a fair amount of charity work around

Lagos and a tremendous amount of strategic influence was wielded by the elite members.

They got together every month to discuss the various philanthropic pursuits of the group, but sometimes it just felt like a keeping up appearances contest. Everything was up for competition. The size of your diamond, the ethnicity of your weave, car model, the kind of work your husband did—everything was important. Naturally, Karen was usually the de facto winner; she couldn't imagine it being any other way. Her husband was the heir apparent to one of Nigeria's largest fortunes and he had made a small fortune on his own. Recently, he acquired an oil block and to celebrate he bought a Bentley. She came from a moneyed family as well. In fact, their marriage was arranged by their grandmothers who were close from their years attending luncheons much like the one she was preparing for today.

"Madam, the entrees and appetizers are ready for your approval."

Sammy, the chef from the luxurious Palazzo Hotel in Lagos of which they owned a thirty-five percent share, was catering the event. The last host, Funke had wowed the crowd with gruyere crusted popovers, specially brought in from Paris just for the luncheon. Today Karen was determined to outdo her with caviar blinis and she had hand carried the caviar from Budapest just yesterday morning. The chef had also prepared traditional fried rice accompanied by perfectly golden fried plantains, chicken lollipops and rack of lamb and sauteed wild mushrooms to make sure that the menu was not purely continental. As Karen bit into the chicken lollipops, they were moist on the inside and crispy on the outside and just on the right side of spicy. *Funke eat your heart out,* she thought, feeling a delightful shiver run over her at the notion of destroying all memory of the woman's luncheon.

Funke was Karen's classmate in secondary school; the prerequisite year that all the Omoruyi's spent in Nigeria before being shipped off to boarding schools in England and finishing programs in Switzerland. Then Funke was just a very thin nonentity. She looked like the poster child for famine in Africa. At first Karen pitied her because she came from such a poor family; she couldn't even afford the modest school fees of Queens Academy, so she was on a scholarship. Karen took her under her wing, until she found out that Funke had been stealing from her and pretending to be rich. She didn't cut her loose as a friend, but the nature of their relationship changed.

She lost touch with her after she went off to England. Years later, Funke was discovered in some sort of look of Africa search and became a successful model. After that she met her current husband, a French born and bred Lebanese man whom she met in first class when he came to Nigeria to negotiate an oil deal that kept him in Nigeria indefinitely and turned him into a multi millionaire many times over. Now they shuttled between Paris and Lagos. So, almost twenty years after secondary school, Funke went from being a penniless nobody to one of the most recognizable faces in the world and she never let Karen forget it. "Karen darling", she would say as she air kissed each cheek, laughing. "I know, so many kisses, but what can I say, European influences." She had a strange accent because her thick Nigerian words were always at war with her attempt at French refined English, but she was so at ease with herself, everyone called it exotic. Everyone except Karen. The last time Karen saw Funke, it was at a fundraising gala in London. Funke screamed her name across the room and Karen was disgusted. She was not bothered because everyone turned to look at her, but the fact that they turned away from her immediately to look at Funke and didn't stop staring burned her inside. Funke returned their adoration with glee and that rubbed Karen the wrong way.

When she got to where Karen stood, she exclaimed, "It's so lovely to see you, Karen. I missed the last luncheon; I was in Monaco you see. Have you been? You should totally go. It's marvelous"

Karen said nothing. It took all her energy to keep from rolling her eyes. She had been visiting Monaco since she was a child. That's the problem with new money, Karen thought, it is like wearing designer clothes with the tag still on.

Funke prattled on, ignoring Karen's cool reception. "Oh my God, we have come so far, haven't we?" She said smiling and patting Karen's hand. "I mean, just look at us now. Me, an international supermodel and you, well, you are, well... married to Dele Thompson!" As her life was being summed up to the circumference of her wedding ring, Karen's palms itched to smack the flesh off Funke's cheeks. Life was funny. Once upon a time, Funke used to beg just to be able to borrow Karen's rhinestone studded pencils, and now she was always in some international magazine or the other; slim and elegant, dripping in gemstones and draped in couture. As irritating as she was, Karen had to admit that she had done well for herself.

"Madam, is it to your satisfaction?" Sammy asked, drawing her back to the present moment.

She looked Sammy over, appreciating him for the umpteenth time. She didn't request him frequently just because of his delicious food. He was so beautiful to behold with his dark skinned Senegalese good looks and properly French accented English that tinkled like music in Karen's ears. He smiled at her and Karen had to collect herself quickly. "Yes, Sammy, it will do." She forced herself to focus on the impending lunch and her social politicking. Funke might be an international supermodel, she thought, but here and now, she was still the queen bee. Karen reminded Sammy that perfection was the only option for this event. "Please get ready to plate the courses and have the wait staff assembled." After confirming all the small details like the centerpieces for the twenty-five tables set in her garden, she went up to her room to get dressed.

\*\*\*\*\*\*\*\*\*\*

Karen's quarters were large and luxurious. To get to the mistress bedroom, you had to walk through the gorgeous living room designed for she and Dele to lounge privately; however, she was the only one who used it. There were two doors on the other side of the room. The left door lead into the master bedroom and the right one led to hers. Karen's room was her sanctuary and the crowning piece of her room was her bed. It was large and comfortable. The beddings were the highest thread count possible and the Persian throw rug felt plush under Karen's well manicured feet. She walked past her bedroom into her dressing room and the small alcove that housed her desk and computer. She noticed that the icon on her screen was blinking. She had mail. She sat down at the small ornate black lacquered desk and clicked it open. It was from Dele. Dele Thompson was a very busy man. She hadn't spoken to him in a week. He sent periodic texts or emails detailing his itinerary. Today he was in Bordeaux, yesterday he had been in New York discussing a possible partnership with an old associate who had made a killing in entertainment and now, was interested in making wines. He had sent his next week's itinerary. He wasn't back in the country until the end of the month, but Karen would meet him in New York in another week to see the specialist. He included a short note with the only term of affection being "My dear" but he referred to every woman in his life that way. "My dear, will be delayed in France. Grapes are very interesting, may really consider this venture. Sorry haven't called. Been busy. Meetings, meetings! See you in New York."

Automatically, Karen checked his platinum card statement online. She had discovered the password before they even got married. The first charge was two weeks ago at Victoria's Secret, $100 for a mid-priced lingerie. Karen relaxed. It was just a time pass chick. However the next couple of entries caused her to sit up, four entries in one day from La Petite Coquette. She raised her eyebrows because this was her favorite lingerie store, then Gucci, Louis Vuitton and Chanel in quick succession. Since Dele rarely did his own shopping, Karen wondered if his time pass chick had become a serious contender.

She pondered it for just a moment more because she had to get ready for her party. She signed out of her email and went to have a shower. The heat of Lagos could be so oppressive that in spite of the installed central air conditioners in their home, she sometimes had to shower several times a day just to feel normal. After her shower, she put on a pair of green silk and linen blend trousers with a matching kimono style blouse. Her naturally reddish hair, enhanced by a celebrity colorist in Beverly Hills was nicely set off by the green fabric, which brought out the faint emerald flecks in her eyes. She smiled at her own image. She took after her grandmother's exotic looks with recessive genes from the Portuguese sailors way back in their history. She completed her outfit with gold jewelry that she purchased in Dubai, including a ruby and gold ring.

"Madam, the people have started arriving." Her maid materialized at the door.

"Alright." She said, without turning around. "Make sure that the servers start passing around the hor d'oeuvres" The maid nodded, backed out and walked away.

Karen took one more look at the mirror and then went down to greet her guests.

All her friends were there, even her frenemy Funke, who walked in looking like she had just come from a runway show. She was wearing a stunning, full sleeved sheer white chiffon blouse with white hot pants, which made for a striking contrast against her dark, well oiled and well shaped legs that went on forever. Karen air kissed her with a tight smile. She was just about to utter something catty to Funke when she noticed her friend Chika walking in. All of a sudden she felt calm and relaxed. She excused herself and went over to give Chika a hug. She really liked Chika. She was the one person she could let her guard down with. Even though she found Chika's christianity and her overt way of sharing her faith in God a little over the top and preachy, she always found some wisdom in her words once she filtered through the Bible verses. They had met in secondary school a year before she traveled abroad, and they became fast friends. It was an unlikely alliance. Even then, Chika was religious. She often invited her to fellowship and Karen always refused, but they lived on the same street and often carpooled so they still found many areas of commonality. Over the years, even though they always lived in different continents as Chika had moved to London just as Karen returned home to Nigeria, they still kept in touch. Now that Chika had moved back from London, Karen was sure they would pick up where they left off. She was grateful to have at least one real friend whom she could trust, who was good and drama free. She smiled as walked towards her. She was wearing an inexpensive but beautiful Adire maxi dress with an elegant cut.

"Chika!" Karen exclaimed, embracing her. "How long has it been?" she said.

"Too long, Karen, too long" Chika responded. She took off her sunglasses and smiled, exposing her bright white teeth. Between that and her glowing brown skin, Karen couldn't understand why she was still single. She was quite beautiful. Even Dele had noticed and commented on it from time to time. Karen shook off her irritation. Of course he had noticed.

"Your home is lovely, Karen," Chika gushed. She looked around at the home and her gaze settled on a larger than life portrait of Karen and Dele that welcomed guests in the foyer. "Gosh, I don't think I have seen you since your wedding," Chika remarked. Karen nodded and smiled, Chika was right, and it was amazing how they had gotten so caught up in their own lives and didn't have time to catch up with each other.

"Oh my, it really has been too long if the last time you saw me was in that fabulous white gown. We just celebrated another anniversary actually. We went to Maldives, it was heavenly!"

"It must have been wonderful!" Chika said, nodding. "I can just imagine! You and Dele make such a striking couple, it is like you came out of a magazine," Karen grinned. "Oh do go on!" she said laughing and then she noticed Lola walking towards them and waved her over. As she approached, Karen pointed her out to Chika.

"I want you to meet my friend Lola," she said, introducing the slim and shapely woman walking up to them, dressed in trouser jeans, with the seemingly prerequisite H for Hermes belt and a silk gold hued button down shirt. "Lola and I met when our husbands worked on a long term project together."

"Hello " Lola said, extending out her hand. Karen noticed the extra glint on Lola's hand and grabbed it before Chika could accept it and her eyebrows rose in an inquiring way.

"Ah, Ah! Lola, what's this… a new ring? C'est formidable!" Karen said peering at the stone with the scrutiny of a jeweler.

Lola smiled. "Thank you. It is a nice ring, isn't it? It was my anniversary gift from John, and he had my old ring turned into a pendant!" she said, fingering her necklace.

"It's quite beautiful" Chika said.

"Indeed it is… I wonder what he is trying to make up for?" Karen said in her usual blasé way.

"What do you mean by that, Karen?" Lola asked, pulling her hand back and lifting her head up; a hard expression coming over her face as she looked at Karen.

"Oh, pay me no mind Lola, I didn't mean anything at all… you know how I get sometimes. I must have had a slice of cynical with my coffee this morning. Besides, I forgot my manners! I should have introduced you two properly," Karen said. "Chika is the new host of a *New You*, the soon to be hottest talk show on TV, and this is Lola, well she is also Mrs John Amadi."

"John Amadi of Amadi holdings?" Chika queried.

"Yes, that's my husband," she said looking like the cat that got the cream. "I am really proud of him."

Chika smiled. "I can understand that. Didn't he just win a big award from the business community?"

Lola beamed. "Yes, he did." Lola stood a little straighter and tossed her hair extensions back a little. Chika started talking to Lola and soon she asked, "So what do you do?"

Lola looked flummoxed, "I just told you, I am John's wife." Chika looked confused by the answer. She looked at Lola and tried to understand her response.

Karen intervened quickly. "Why, yes! Being a wife can be a full time job sometimes! But, what Lola is not telling you is that she is a wonderful singer. I keep telling her that she missed her calling. She should be singing on Broadway, instead she just sings in church." Karen ended with an exasperated sigh.

"Don't be silly Karen, I sing in church because I have a gift and I want to use it to serve God. Can you see me in the music scene in Nigeria, no way! I am way too...well, let's just say it's not my scene."

"Now I know why you look familiar! You sing at The Lord's House right?" Chika said. "You sang a beautiful solo last Sunday! I couldn't stop crying."

Lola smiled broadly. "Thank you. That was one of my favorite songs"

Chika continued. "Oh, You really do have a gift!" Chika then turned to Karen. "I had no idea you had started going to church, Karen."

Karen retorted, "Who me? No, not at all! No offense to you guys, but I find church folk, present company excepted, quite hypocritical! Lola, has shown me some videos, that's all."

Chika said. "I know what you mean Karen. Unfortunately in or out of church, we are still all human and we all make mistakes. All the same we should all strive to be better people. That being said, you should really think about coming to service with me one

Sunday."

Just then Funke walked over and inserted herself into the conversation. "Bonsoir ladies!" she trilled.

"It's not quite evening, Funke," Karen said.

"Of course it is darling! Somewhere in the world!" she said with a sweet saccharin smile, ignoring Karen's glare.

"Lola dear, you look lovely. I love the way you have allowed yourself to fill out a little. I wish I could just relax and gain a couple of kilos like you, but I am just too much of a control freak."

Karen interrupted, feeling the need to defend her friend. "Lola, I think you look sensational."

Funke shrugged, "Of course you do darling."

"Anyway Funke, we were discussing going to church, would you care to join us?" Karen said, smirking.

"Err, not today, maybe next time. I have to run ladies. Chika, it was nice seeing you. I haven't seen you since boarding school, but I've been watching your career. Well done! I hear your show will be like Oprah for Nigerian TV. You should have me on your show some time."

Chika perked up. Funke was an international celebrity and it would be great to get her on the show.

"Would you really? Wonderful, let's talk scheduling right now. Chika said whipping out her smart phone.

"Oh no, dear, I don't handle stuff like that. Have your assistant, call my assistant. Now I really must go, Ciao!

"Aren't you staying for lunch?" Karen asked, wondering why Funke was leaving.

"I can't dear. I have to fly to Rome tonight. Italian *Vogue* called. You girls have fun here and keep the home fires burning, after all someone has to do it while the rest of us travel and conquer the world. Kisses ladies!"

Chika and Karen stood there shocked at her rudeness, but Lola recovered enough to distract them as they stared after Funke with a look of disbelief. "So Karen, when are you coming to church?

Karen looked at her and grinned, "Lola, you have jokes abi? Thanks! I was moments away from throwing my shoe at her."

"So you'll come?" Chika asked again.

Church is never going to happen, Karen thought. Chika smiled, and Karen realized that her resistance was written all over her face, but the sparkle in Chika's beautifully made up eyes showed that she took no offense. Relieved that her unspoken message was received well, Karen laughed out loud and linked her arm through Chika's and Lola's. "Come, ladies, let's go join the festivities!".

Chika had certainly come a long way from days in boarding school, Karen thought. She was now much more polished and stylish. Back then she was such an odd duck. Queen's Academy social scene was already an uphill battle, and Chika made it worse by being known as a Jesus freak. It seemed she still hadn't changed. She used to try to convert Karen almost every Saturday, but over the years they had learned to agree to disagree. As far as Karen was concerned, she was just being polite; her grandmother always told her that if people acted as if they didn't want to deal with you, it would be unseemly to try to force them into relationship and from Karen's perspective God had turned his back on her a long time ago.

"This is such a lovely luncheon," Chika said, as they walked outside and found their table. She sat down and Karen and Lola joined her. A waiter materialized and poured wine into their glasses. Chika covered her glass. Karen shook her head. "What is it Chika? Don't tell me you don't drink? Or are you still doing holy, holy?" she asked.

Chika rolled her eyes. "If by holy, holy, you mean do I still live by my moral code? Then the answer is yes, of course, especially since I have authored a few books on living as a single Christian. I don't want to be the cause of anyone stumbling. However, I do have a glass of wine on occasion but this is not one of them," Chika said with indignation.

"Okay O! Calm down, Pastor Chika, I didn't mean to offend," Karen said chuckling. "It's just that with your new TV persona, I wasn't sure if you had changed."

"Wow, I would never have pegged you as a church girl, you look so cosmopolitan," Lola added, pulling her shirt down to make sure her butt wasn't exposed by her wretched low rise jeans. She suffered in them because they were considered fashionable and had the right logo well placed to draw attention. In spite of the pride that Lola felt from being able to wear such high end jeans, she hated the fact that she couldn't sit down in peace without worrying if she was showing more than she planned to.

Chika watched her tug at her clothes and she and Karen exchanged a look of amusement.

"My faith has less to do with how I look and more to do with what I feel and believe. I am more spiritual than religious, so I guess I may not fit into your stereotype, but there you have it and as a matter of fact, my show, *A New You*, has a strong emphasis on faith," Chika said.

"Well, good for you Chika. I'll be tuning in for the sermons on TV because I am still yet to set foot inside a church, and I don't plan on it either," Karen said.

Chika laughed. "Well clearly not much has really changed!"

"Why mess with perfection?" Karen said. "Now where are the wait staff when you need them! Forget wine, I need champagne! I have to toast to Diamonds, Divas and the Divine!"

# Chapter 5

# Lola
# There's a fly in my life!

Lola watched Karen and Chika laugh and toast like they were best of friends. She felt a slight pang of jealousy and didn't understand why. She was friends with Karen already and it wasn't as if Karen couldn't have other friends. She took a deep breath, sipped her wine and crossed her legs, leaning back into the chair. She hated feeling unsure of herself. For some reason, ever since she moved back to Lagos, she never felt like she really fit in and the sad thing was, she didn't feel at home in America either.

She always felt as if she was behind the curve. When she first became acquainted with the ways of Lagos society, she felt a great deal of pressure to be recognized as a full-fledged high society wife and so she worked hard to look the part. As soon as John was able to afford to take them to Europe on holiday; she started shopping designer stores as if from a list. She remembered one day when they met up with John's friend in New York. The friend's new wife prattled on and on about some new sushi place that they had to try for lunch, but she had only two things on her mind: a Dior and MiuMiu bag to add to her collection. She told them to go without her because she was stuck in the store trying to identify which bag would give her the biggest logo for her buck. She remembered feeling triumphant only for a second, because right after she counted out the crisp euro bills and paid for her new handbag, she saw how unimpressed the sales lady was and felt two feet tall.

The only time she could remember feeling good was in the

early days of her marriage, when it was just she and John in their small apartment. Back then, they were like a jigsaw puzzle, they made sense when they were together. Now it felt as if they only made sense when they were apart. She looked at her phone for the hundredth time that day. She checked her email and her text messages. Nothing from John. How busy could he be on a Saturday in Port Harcourt that he had no time to call or even text his wife? She took another deep breath and sipped her champagne. She was so wrapped up in her own head that she didn't notice the two women who had joined the table at the other end.

She looked up when she heard them talking in hushed tones. It became apparent to her that they didn't realize or care that anyone was there. She recognized one of the women. She was one of the Otunba's wives. Otunba was a favored son of one of the established royal families of Lagos and unlike many, this family still had the wealth that went along with the title. She was his latest wife—he already had three. Although his second wife divorced him and moved to London, according to rumor, she had a thriving business supplying exotic prostitutes to wealthy Nigerian politicians.

Lola kept trying to remember her name; it was Bukky or Bimpe or something. She couldn't quite recall. Considering the fact that the woman was barely over thirty and had done nothing remarkable in her life except to marry Otunba, it was fitting that she was only referred to as Otunba's new Iyawo. Lola noticed that she and her companion were dripping in gold, and both carried handbags from Chanel's current season. Again, she felt that slight sense of unease. The women were oblivious to her surveillance and they kept talking, getting less quiet. Lola began to make out what they were saying.

"I don't believe it!" Otunba's wife retorted. "No, that's not right! Not at all!"

"Whether you believe it or not is irrelevant, the truth is the truth!" her companion responded. "Why would I make up something like that?"

"No, now! I know you are not lying. I just can't believe that the marriage ended over something like that," Otunba's wife said.

"Ah, you know how some of these hot headed, liberated women are. Everything is do or die." Her companion picked up her drink to sip. Lola noticed it was beer and not champagne. Karen would be horrified. She felt no woman with any sense of decorum should be caught drinking a beer, and certainly not at one of her luncheons.

Otunba's wife exclaimed suddenly. "Kai! Women…this life is not easy. So just like that she left and had nothing?"

Her friend shrugged in response.

"So after all those years of marriage, now that the money is flowing in like hot water, she is out in the cold." Otunba's wife said.

"Well, it's her fault," the friend countered, "after all, does she think her husband was the first man to have a mistress? After all, if you found Otunba with some other woman, would you lose your mind?"

"Please, if I found Otunba with someone else, I would beg the girl to make sure she holds him well, well. In fact, if I can find someone to be doing him for me on the regular, no problem, just as long as she no wan snatch am! Ah beg! Do you think it is easy, sleeping with that old man? His potbelly alone can suffocate someone, and as for his, you know... Well it is so tiny, you can barely see it and his balls just...Ugh. In fact, please find someone for me now. I need a break!"

She and her friend laughed and high fived each other, letting their hands linger in mid-air for more seconds than usual. Lola noticed that they played with each other's fingers. After some time Otunba's wife spoke again.

"The woman's problem was that she loved that man too much."

"Abi!" Her friend agreed. "If you want to be happy, you

cannot love a man. Let him love you, but keep your own heart for other things."

"Yes o!" Otunba's wife said, nodding. "Look at it now, the woman is in her forties, divorced and she is in America now because Lagos had become too hard for her."

"My dear, she is in one small apartment like this. Shebi, I was in her house, last month when I visited Washington DC, it was so sad. She had these cheap looking imitation leather chairs and she has to scrub her own floors and empty her own rubbish. Chai, what a life!", her friend concurred.

"What is she doing? How is she providing for herself? Or is her ex-husband supporting her?" Otunba's wife asked.

"Ex-husband *ko*, ex-husband *ni*," the friend said hissing. "You know how some men can be once they divorce you. It is like you and your children don't exist. I hear the woman is working in a hospital. You know, cleaning bed pans and such."

"What! Oyibo shit! Haba!" Otunba's wife shook her head. "How the mighty have fallen! I remember when she used to ride around here with her designer sunglasses, balancing in the owner's corner of that Mercedes wagon her husband bought her."

"Well, he collected that car sharp, sharp. These days, the woman is riding the bus." Her friend hissed. "Anyway my dear, you see how things happen. Bottom line, once you marry and if you marry well, no matter what, you manage. After all, now she is suffering and it is the mistress that is enjoying the money now."

"Na lie!" Otunba's wife cried out. "Women o! Why must we suffer! I hate stories like this."

"Come o, why are you making noise? Weren't you Otunba's mistress before you became his wife?" Her friend threw back with a raised eyebrow.

"Fi mi le jo! Don't harass me o! Otunba is polygamous so his wives were prepared. This man was a Christian abi, one woman for life, no be so?"

"Na so o!" Her friend responded. The rhythm of bass drums

and guitars burst forth from the live band that had just started to perform at another part of the garden. This drew the women's attention and they got up and left the table. Lola watched them leave and noticed the red bottomed soles they were both wearing. She found herself dialing her husband, but the automated voice responded: *the party you are trying to reach is not available at this time, please call again later.* Lola almost threw the phone in frustration. Where the hell was he that he couldn't pick up his phone? She thought, allowing herself to descend into an abyss of dark thoughts of other women and sad visions of taking out her own trash.

# Chapter 6

# Chika
## Money may miss the road, but it can pave a new path

After the luncheon at Karen's, Chika and Karen had been spending a lot of time together. The interesting thing was that Karen had planned to help Chika get settled in Lagos, but it was Chika who seemed to be introducing Karen to most of the things and places they were encountering. They were at the Good Stuff supermarket browsing the aisles as Chika stocked up for the week. She was shocked at the prices for some of the basic items that she bought for next to nothing at her local Tesco's, but Karen seemed surprised that they stocked certain items at all. After her third exclamation upon finding a certain type of cheese, Chika said sharply, "Karen, why are you the one acting as if you just moved back? How can you not know what is available in your own local stores? Don't you notice when you go grocery shopping?" Chika watched Karen's eyes glaze over. Then it occurred to her. "Oh my goodness, do not tell me that you don't even buy your own groceries?"

Karen shrugged in response with an unconcerned look on her face, "Not even when I am in London on holiday." Chika shook her head. She couldn't imagine that sort of life where the day to day basics were done by someone else. Karen lived like a pampered princess whose feet never touched the ground.

As they rounded the corner, Chika asked with a hint of sarcasm, "So are you bathed as well? Do you have ladies in waiting?" Karen threw her head back and laughed out loud, indifferent to judgment about her decadent lifestyle. "Sweetheart, what do you want to hear? That I bathe in milk and rose petals too?" Karen was so amused by her own thoughts that she almost ran into a woman. The woman in question almost fell out of her six-inch platform heels. Karen was wearing bejeweled flat leather sandals from Morocco, so her footing was sure. All the same, Karen immediately launched into the offensive. "I beg your pardon," she started to say, making sure to enunciate her words. The woman steadied herself and also started to yell. Karen took a step back and put on her sunglasses and while Chika, stepped even further back. In scenarios like that, she had learned it was wise to create some physical and emotional distance because you never want to be too close to crazy, and from the look of things the woman could have been close to a mental overload.

When Karen covered her eyes behind the oversize fashion forward spectacles, the woman seemed to recognize her all of a sudden. "Oh. My. God!" she squealed in staccato fashion, which startled Karen even further. "You are Karen Thompson! Finally we meet!" the woman said and extended her hand. Chika watched as Karen let it hang there for several minutes, but before she could nudge her to do the right thing, Karen extended her hand, not moving forward, while the woman closed the gap and grabbed Karen's hand; beaming like Cheshire cat.

Chika watched the whole exchange with amusement. It looked as if the woman might kiss Karen's ring. She couldn't get over the way the rich in Lagos were treated by some people. The way the woman oohed and aahed, you would think that Karen was a walking winning lottery ticket or better still a Las Vegas slot machine, and if she said just the right thing, a million gold coins would fly out.

Karen let the woman pay her respects before she spoke up. "I don't recall your name or your face. Are we social acquaintances?" The woman shook her head and said, "Not really.

I am a friend of Tina Dewumni, the designer, if you recall, she sent you a dress for the Nigerian Star award show" Karen looked like she hadn't heard of the designer, but she simply said, "Oh". The woman continued gushing. "I have always loved your style Karen." When *Today's Style* did a feature of your home, I wanted to call you and compliment you on your great taste, but for some reason I didn't have your phone number, so odd since we practically are in the same circles."

Karen nodded and said thank you. "Well, we really must be going, so sorry to have bumped into..." She didn't complete her sentence because the woman started to shake her head and interrupted, "No, no, no! I should be the one to apologize. It's no problem at all. In fact, it is God that said we should collide today." Chika tried to keep from laughing because she was sure that behind the dark lenses Karen was rolling her eyes, and true to form Karen continued with her dismissal. "Well, be that as it may, I really must take my leave. Do have a nice day." Chika gave the woman, who was struck mute by Karen's brush-off, a weak smile. She walked away only after Karen had already taken a few large strides away from that spot.

They were a few feet away when the woman hurried over to them, shouting as she struggled to move as fast as she could in her platforms. "Karen! Karen!" she shouted so loudly that people were starting to look. Karen muttered under her breath and took a deep breath. She stopped and turned around. The woman looked a sight teetering towards them in her high heels. Chika held her breath and prayed that she would not fall. Karen shifted her weight onto her other hip, crossed her arms in front of her. The woman got close enough to reach out to her, but this time she had something in her hand. "I just wanted to give you my business card. I do events and public relations. I know that we can probably help each other." Karen nodded and accepted the card.

"Thank you," she said.

The woman stood there, and Karen cocked her head in a

questioning manner. "May I have your card please?"

Karen was quiet for a beat longer before she responded to her question. "You are very kind," she said, "but no. Have a lovely day."

She turned away with an air of finality and said to Chika who still had things in her basket. "My dear, please meet me in the car. I have some calls to make." She walked out of the supermarket with quick strides. Chika watched her and shook her head. She thought that Karen was such an interesting piece of work and that was putting it nicely. When people found out they were friends, they sometimes asked her how she could be close to her because of her hard reputation. But Chika had known her for years and knew all the soft spots that Karen rarely let the public see. At the register, Chika was still so lost in her thoughts that the cashier had to repeat the total sum twice. The second time, she repeated the figure with a curt tone. Chika smiled to calm her, fished out what seemed like too many Naira notes and paid the bill. She walked out to the car and Karen's driver quickly jumped out, grabbed her bags and opened the car door for her to enter the sleek black Range Rover with tinted windows. Chika, leaned back into the seat, and looked over at Karen who was busy typing away on her smart phone. She spoke as soon as Chika entered, "Sorry to abandon you darling, I just couldn't bear it for one more minute." Chika shrugged it off. "No worries, must be flattering, sort of, at least?" she asked in response.

Karen took off her sunglasses so Chika could have an unobstructed view of her facial expression.

"Flattering? Not at all. Quite frankly, it's a bit creepy. I meet so many women like that. They don't know me, don't even like me, but they would give their first born to be around me. For one reason and one reason only, because I am rich. Tell you the truth, you are probably one of the few women I can call a friend because you see me. Just me. And maybe Lola as well, because even though she also has traces of sycophancy, she occasionally shows backbone and I see glimpses of authenticity. She used to be so much more refreshing to be around before her husband started doing government contracts. I keep telling her to watch it because she is a step away from becoming one of these Guccified Lekki stepford wives types and God knows that is so not a good look.

Chika eyes widened, "I really had never thought about it like that!"

This time Karen shrugged. "Why would you? No offense, but you have never really had the kind of money I grew up with. You have had the opportunity to really pull yourself up from middle-class. Don't get me wrong, I think that's great! But you could never know the life I lead."

Chika scrunched her nose up and her forehead wrinkled as she considered her friend's words, and just when she decided that she was offended, Karen spoke up again. "Darling, don't be mad. Aargh! It's the limitations of this blasted language! I honestly didn't mean to sound insulting. It's just irritating the way people don't see me. They see what I represent, what they want. There was a woman who followed me around so much that I began to fear that she would kill me and wear my skin."

"I think you are being a bit dramatic Karen," Chika said, still smarting a bit from Karen's previous statement. "Well, that being said, let's move on shall we?" Karen continued "Perhaps we can listen to the radio, I heard one of the radio personalities talk yesterday, and while I have no idea what she was talking about, it was so interesting to hear her accent switch from English to Irish to American to goodness knows what accent. It's a wonder she didn't swallow her own tongue."

Chika laughed at Karen's straight faced comment. Karen smiled also. "That's what I was looking for! Those wonderful white teeth." Then she grabbed Chika's hand between hers, in a way uncharacteristic of her nature. "My friend, you can't be mad at me! You are all I have in this world o!" And then she grinned and just as suddenly dropped her hand and picked up the newspaper, losing herself in the black and white print. Chika turned and looked out of the window, and though the view was rich with detail from the wiry men hawking every possible item to the sandy haired Arab looking children begging for alms, she couldn't be distracted from the thoughts of her enigmatic friend and her decision to make her new life in this land of juxtapositions; a city so crowded with people, yet the divide between the haves and the have nots was large enough to fit whole planets.

# City Life Magazine
# The Gossip Page
# Guess who?

She looks like your everyday silly and shallow rich man's wife. Her husband has been known to brag that when he says "jump", she asks "how high" as she readies herself to leap. Some people think she epitomizes submission; others call her a *mumu* of the highest order because she lives quietly and stays out of the spotlight, while her husband is known to cavort with various women in the city.

However, *City Life* has gathered information that proves that Madam jumper is a master manipulator; that her subservience is really a subversive move. This woman is apparently trained in the ancient arts of war because while her fool of a husband thinks he has a fool for a wife, she has been quietly amassing wealth on the side. It is said that she owns several properties in Lagos and has used a shell company to hide her identity. She has also siphoned tens of millions from her husband. Apparently, while he was being distracted by her "how high?", she was calling the banks and transferring dollars to accounts in the Cayman Islands.

The proverb states that a hippopotamus can be made invisible in dark water. Well, this lady has proven that because we have also heard that after twenty-five years of marriage, this woman, who is about to celebrate her forty-eighth birthday, is actually going to celebrate her emancipation. She plans to serve her husband with divorce papers at her party, now that her children are practically done with their education in America.

Watch this space and watch o! Remember you heard it here first. High society marriages are not for the faint of heart. Live and learn.

# Chapter 7

# Karen
## Yes, money can't buy love, but last I checked, it was never on sale

Karen stirred in her sleigh bed, custom made in Italy and specially shipped from her favorite furniture store in Los Angeles. She stretched and leaned against her overstuffed pillows encased in her eight hundred thread count Egyptian cotton pillowcases. She reached over to the other side of the bed and felt the cool smoothness of the sheets. She looked around her bedroom, the large flat screen television, the beveled glass mirror in a carved frame, the nine drawer dresser with a hazelnut finish. Though surrounded by all this luxury, she still felt a sense of angst and that irritated her. She didn't like feeling out of sorts, she preferred her emotions in neat little boxes that were labeled and organized, so she got out of bed and tried to get past her emotional state.

She hopped on the treadmill that was next to her and switched on the television. She watched as CNN reported on some natural disaster on the other side of the world. Usually, once she started to run, she felt a release, it was as if the nervous energy was trapped in a pressure cooker and running opened the valve. However this morning, the release would not come. So she increased her speed and let her mind drift. She started to think about her father. She never really knew him. He was always traveling when she was younger. Her memories of him were connected to the gifts he showered her with. She was the last born and only girl in her family. Her mother always called her a desperate blessing. Her closest brother was almost twelve years older than her, and it was because she was born that her father didn't move his mistress into the house as a second wife. She wished she had more memories of her parents, but her mother died when she was young and, she and her father had been estranged for a long time. She didn't remember much about the funeral, but she did remember that her father's mistress tried to cause some drama but was silenced and put in her place. It was that day that she found out that she had two sisters, both older than her. Her father didn't acknowledge them and neither did the rest of the family but financially they were taken care of. Karen heard her father's mistress still lived in Ikoyi with her daughters who had followed their mother's path of being the consorts of wealthy men who desired cheaper interactions.

The calorie counter on the treadmill read 412, and Karen blinked at the number. She was twelve when she had last seen her half sisters, her own flesh and blood. She released a deep intake of breath as she hit the cool down button and slowed to a walk. Finally, she stopped and got off the treadmill and the newspapers on the tray caught her attention, the steward sent them up every morning with her morning coffee and one perfectly boiled egg. The society pages were peeking out. Memories of last week's blind item insinuating Dele's latest indiscretion intruded into her thoughts. She hissed in spite of herself. The writer had speculated that he was sleeping around because she, Karen, his wife, was cold and barren. In Nigeria, a man's weaknesses were always a woman's fault. She stood up and tried to stretch out her quadriceps. She lost her balance and fell into a chair. She leaned back and closed her eyes, her breath heavy. She would not cry. She could not. She had been well trained from her youth not to do so. Her grandmother would chide her when she cried as a girl. "Stop that this instant, Karen," she would say firmly in her clipped British accent. Her grandmother was old school: educated in Swiss boarding schools, but with strong Yoruba sensibilities.

"Crying is for commoners, what will tears do for you?"

Still her grandmother had not experienced this pain—the pain of longing for a child and not being able to have one. She had been to many doctors and no one could give her a reason why. She almost wished for tears to wash these thoughts away, but they would not come. Her hands fell over her belly. Was she so hardened that the soft parts of her womanhood had become brittle and broken apart? Was that why her husband refused to come to her at night, instead pursuing every woman he came in contact with? Or was it that her unacknowledged pain had become a tumor blocking the growth of anything good within her. And what if Dele got tired of waiting and trying with her? What if he made a baby with one of these random women, what then? Her sadness gave way to anger. Dele had better not try her, she thought, her eyes darkening in tandem with her thoughts. She would never tolerate him having a child outside their marriage; one little girl removed from her family was enough for a lifetime.

# Chapter 8

# Lola
## Love me jare! By fire, by force

Lola stood in the mirror and frowned as she studied her body's imperfections. She knew that she couldn't be called fat, but her body had certainly changed from her bikini days in her twenties. She was irritated with herself, every week she swore she would start going to the gym and eat less, but she couldn't help bingeing on chin chin and buttered bread. As a result, she was now up one more dress size and her husband was mentioning it all the time. Even worse, her body was morphing into a different shape as she creeped closer to middle age. It was as if it was insisting that she recognize that she was aging. She pushed up her boobs that had started to sag quite a bit. She worried that they were inching closer to becoming intimate with her belly button. She sucked in her stomach and held her shoulders back, but the sag was still evident. She had tried to avoid it by choosing not to breastfeed, but still, gravity took its toll.

She adjusted the straps of her see through chiffon baby doll negligee, trying to make her cleavage look better. She walked away from the mirror and turned towards the bed. She spritzed it lightly with perfume and then lit the candles all around the room. She was determined to seduce her husband that night. It had been a while since they had made love and she was feeling less and less connected to him. He had promised to come straight home after work, no stopping for drinks with the boys this time and she was going to be ready for him.

She had been waiting for some time, and finally heard the

main gate being pulled open by the guard. After a few minutes, she heard his measured steps as he came up the stairs. She fiddled with the pillows and tried to find the right position as she listened to the strange accent of the nanny greeting him and his relaxed jovial response to her. She smiled and relaxed a little herself because it sounded like he was in a good mood which should help everything flow smoother.

"Lola!" She heard him call out as he entered the anteroom to the master bedroom and then his footsteps just outside the door. She fluffed out her hair and tried to get a sexy expression on her face. "Lola!" he called out, opening the door. He stopped and smiled. "Ah, what's this?" he said, raising an eyebrow. "It's whatever you want it to be," Lola said, trying to sound throaty and channel Angelina Jolie.

"Hmm, well…hmm," he said as he sat on the edge of the bed furthest away from her and began to take off his shoes. He seemed a little put off and Lola started to feel unsure of herself, but she gathered her wits and decided to push through with her plan of seduction. So she crawled over to him and started to massage his shoulders. He leaned back into her and smiled as he closed his eyes. "That feels good," he said. She felt emboldened by his reaction, so she leaned around him and started to take off his tie. He opened his eyes and watched her with a half smile as she did this.

"What's going on Lola?" he asked, stopping her by cupping her face, he looked around and commenting on the lit candles, the perfumed air and her lingerie, said, "It looks like you have gone to so much trouble" he said, looking around as she attempted to undress him. Again she tried to be the courtesan she thought every man wanted. "Why wouldn't I, aren't you my man?"

John didn't respond, but he smiled and kissed her on the lips. Then he put his hands around her waist and pushed her away with care. "Lola, this is great and I appreciate the effort, truly... but I had a really crazy day, and all I really want is a hot bath and to go to sleep." He kissed her again on the cheek and stood up and walked away from the bed.

Lola was devastated. "What the hell!" She thought. She couldn't believe he rejected her. It had been quite some time since they had been together. She couldn't believe he was turning her down. Didn't they say that guys always wanted sex? What the hell was happening? She swore to herself. She felt defeated for a moment, but she refused to give up. This wasn't just about this one night, this was about their marriage. She wouldn't let things remain this way. She loved him and he loved her, surely that love could overcome any tiredness or weariness he must be feeling. She would not let their marriage become a sexual cliché. She got off the bed, walked over to her dressing table, looked at her body in the mirror and gave herself a little pep talk. She was still sexy and desirable. She was still getting hit on by men and so he should be happy to have her. She said to herself even as she heard the shower turn on. "I am his wife and I will make sure that after tonight, every part of his body knows it!" And then she walked into the bathroom after him.

He was already in the shower and steam was beginning to fill the air, when she entered the room. "I thought I would join you baby," Lola said, taking off her lingerie and pulling her hair into a quick bun.

"Err okay," John replied.

"I can wash your back and you can wash mine," Lola said, standing in a suggestive pose.

John laughed. "Okay sweetheart," He responded, moving back to make room for her. Lola got into the shower and began to soap his back. She thought he stiffened a little and wondered why he was so tense. "Have I told you today that I love you?" she said.

"I love you too," He said. Then he turned her around and began to soap her back. Lola arched her back in delight. She felt shivers in every place that counted. He washed her neck and soon the sponge was dropped and he let his hands roam all over her body. She turned around to face him and they explored each other more. They stood there for a while kissing and touching each other, and Lola felt like she was in heaven. She loved John Amadi. She loved her husband. She returned his kisses with fervor and took them to the next level. He usually loved it when she took the lead, but this time he wasn't following. He just wanted to keep kissing. Lola was getting impatient. She enjoyed the foreplay, but she wanted to go further, but when she reached down and touched him, she could feel that he was completely soft.

She looked at him in shock. He looked away. "What's wrong?" she asked.

"Nothing is wrong, Lola." He said and tried to start kissing her again.

She pushed him away. "How can you tell me nothing is wrong? I am standing here naked and we have been making out for how long and you are not even remotely aroused? What is going on?" Lola said, her voice rising in agitation.

"Lola, will you calm down?" John said. "It's no big deal. I've had a very stressful day. I am just tired. You should have listened to me. I told you tonight was a bad night." He reached over and pulled the shower head towards him and dunked his head under it. Lola stood there as if oblivious to the fact that she was covered in soapsuds; her arms folded across her chest. She was aghast when he got out of the shower and toweled himself dry, leaving her behind dripping wet. Finally, she stood under the shower thinking about how messed up her hair was going to be in the morning and that made her even more enraged.

"You must be out of your mind, John! Tonight was a bad night? When was the last time you touched me?" Lola screeched as she exited the bathroom and followed him to the bedroom, dripping water everywhere although she was holding a towel. "Eh? I'll tell you, a whole month! And then you were so drunk, it was a bloody wham bam session." Lola said and began to dry herself. She walked up close to where John was sitting on the side of the bed and resting his head in his arms.

Lola took a deep breath. Then she walked and stood in front of him. "John, talk to me. What is really going on?" she said, putting her hand on his shoulder. "Don't I do it for you anymore? Or are you sleeping with someone else?" she asked, scared, but needing to hear the answer.

John didn't answer. He was in his pajamas. He leaned back onto the bed, adjusted the pillow and closed his eyes. Lola watched him in silence. They were both silent for a time, then she walked back over to her side of the bed, stopping at her wardrobe to grab a nightshirt.

Lola didn't know when the tears started to roll down her cheeks. She was sitting on her side of the bed, and the air conditioner was blowing so cold that she began to shiver, but she couldn't will herself up to get a robe to cover up and she couldn't get in bed under the covers.

"Don't cry babe," John said, sitting up, he moved across the bed and came behind her and covered her shoulders with a blanket. He kissed the top of her head. "Nothing is wrong, I love you. Let's not talk about it okay, this stuff happens. We are just not as young as we used to be."

Lola turned to stare at him. He seemed to think that she would be satisfied by that answer."You can't be serious John. We are only in our early forties, are you suggesting that by fifty, we'll be back to being celibate? Lola said, taking a breath after each phrase. She waited for a few minutes watching for a reaction. She was frustrated by his lack of concern about his situation. He just shrugged his shoulders and laid back on the bed. "Tell me the truth. What is going on? She became hysterical and started screaming, "Tell me! Tell me!"

John looked up at the ceiling and took a deep breath. "Why can't a man have peace in his own house!" What kind of rubbish is this?" He shouted in exasperation.

"So your wife needing affection is rubbish abi?" Lola

sneered.

"Lola stop... Please, leave it alone!" he pleaded, "I am so tired. Please!"

"I will not!" she exclaimed. "This is not normal. Look at me. I am a full blooded African woman and I didn't get married not to be touched!" Her voice had turned into a scream.

Suddenly John jumped out of bed, and he appeared enraged. "Look at you!" John shouted. "Yes, just look at you!" He gesticulated wildly at her body. "You want the truth?" John asked.

"Yes! I want the truth," Lola said, but right after she responded, she realized that the energy had changed and she suddenly wanted to quiet him, worried that they had both said too much and even more harm could be done if they didn't stop now. So she rushed up to him and tried to hold him, but it was too late; the proverbial genie had shattered the bottle.

"Just get out of my way!" he said, and this time he was rough when he pushed her aside and he started walking out of the room.

Lola knew that she should leave him alone, but she couldn't. What was the truth? The questions hanging over her head drove her to follow him into their personal living room. He put the television on and started fiddling with the remote control. He too was trying to find quiet, but the same energy that caused him to push her aside when she sought peace now seized her and Lola found herself snatching the remote control out of his hand.

He looked at her and threw up his hands and growled. "Lola! What is it? Look I don't want to talk anymore" he said looking at the TV screen. A football match had come on.

Lola stood in front of the TV. "John! Talk to me! What did you mean by did I want the truth?"

John sighed and Lola felt as if his breath carried the weight of their marriage, but she couldn't just watch as everything she had worked for float away into nothingness. John was still talking as she contemplated the demise of their relationship. "I didn't mean anything. Look, Lola I am tired. I told you, I have had a long day. Why are you making something out of nothing?" he said looking at her and Lola felt him willing her to believe the words he was saying.

Lola heard his plea, but the words didn't connect with her. She knew there was something more that was left unsaid. "John, is there something I need to know? Do you need to see the doctors? Are you impotent?" As Lola questioned his manhood, her voice dropped in volume with every syllable.

"What? You think I am the problem?" John sat up straight as he repeated her question slowly, enunciating every syllable. Lola knew that his ego had taken over and she stepped back from the force of his emotion. "Am I impotent? You are asking me if I am impotent?" Lola was startled when he looked at her because his rage was evident in his expression. "I will have you know I am a complete man!" He said,, then he got up and walked past her. "I am done talking now. I am going to sleep."

Lola knew that pushing the matter any further might agitate him further, but she also felt that it she didn't address it, things would go from bad to worse.

She put her hand on his arm.

"Stop, John, you have to talk to me." She stood in front of him trying to appear soft in her defiance. He flung her hand off as if it were a snake attempting to bite him.

"What the hell is wrong with you? Don't put your hands on me!" John snarled.

"No!" Lola said, but this time her voice was quieter and she wondered how this night had turned so poisonous. She was still thinking when she saw him raise his hand.

The slap came quickly and startled her by its sheer force. It knocked her back on to the chair. Her eyes started watering immediately. She couldn't look at him. "Aargh!" he shouted. "You see what you caused! Is this what you wanted?" he screamed at her.

He started to pace the room.

"Okay! Fine. You want to know my problem?" he asked.

Lola kept looking at him. He looked away.

"You are my problem," he said. "You are disgusting. I can't stand the woman you have become. When I married you, you were so sexy and now you have just let yourself go. And to top it all, you don't do anything. You used to have so much going on, now what do you do? What do you do everyday? Just spend the money that I make? You want the truth, Lola, the truth is that you repulse me."

The force of the slap couldn't compare to the violence embedded in his words. She felt as if she was gutted and her entrails exposed. She lay in the position frozen with pain, it was as if someone had poured ice water over her and she couldn't move.

She didn't even realize how hard she was crying, until the tears started to drip onto her cleavage. She became self conscious and she knew her crying would aggravate him further, but a low wail had already escaped from deep within her and like that genie, it too refused to be stuffed back into its place of imprisonment. So she sobbed and cried. She had never wanted to die before, but his words wounded her more than anyone had hurt her before.

"Aww, shit...Lola...I am so sorry!" John said, standing looking defeated as he realized how venomous his words were. "I didn't mean that!" "I am sorry baby. So sorry. I didn't mean it okay. Don't cry." He got down on the floor and held her as whispered the words over and over, but the room still held the echo of his earlier tirade.

Lola allowed him to pull her close, but his embrace gave her no comfort as she felt numb with pain. She let her mind drift away and leave only her body present as he kissed her neck. She felt as she were floating and she watched with sadness as he caressed her breasts, and kissed her on the lips and when he finally entered her and moved and grunted over her, she returned to herself and cried out in anguish and shame. She lay there feeling his weight on her as he slept, and then she pushed him off and walked over to the bathroom. She barely got to the toilet when she started to throw up.

# Chapter 9

# Chika
# The ties that bind

Chika had been beaten down by the day to day frustration of Lagos. It had been a crazy day. She had gotten sucked into the vortex of mismanagement that plagued everything in Lagos. For the fiftieth time that day, she wondered if she had made the right decision to move back to Nigeria. Chika blinked and shook her head. She had too much to do and no time to spend wallowing, so she told herself to pull it together. Right then, her phone started to ring, saving her from the brink of despair.

"Hello," she said.

"Chika! How are you?" Lola said

"Hello, " she said.

"Chika! How are you?" Lola said in a singsongy voice. "It's me Lola, remember we met at Karen's?"

"Of course. How are you Lola?" Chika responded, she was happy to hear from her, especially because she didn't know many people here and Lola had been nice so far.

"Just fine dear! Just fine! No problem at all," Lola replied. "I hope you are keeping busy and not getting into any trouble?" Lola said, laughing at her own joke, and then there was an awkward silence as Chika didn't respond. She felt like the statement was judgmental. Why would she get into trouble? Was it because she was single? She started thinking that Lola was probably just as irritating as so many of the wives she had met.

"Well, I guess you are wondering why I am calling," Lola said breaking the silence.

Chika noticed that despite her tone, Lola's voice sounded a bit subdued and she started to soften towards her. Maybe it was a simple faux pas, she thought. She decided not to take it personally.

"Not really, but it's nice of you to keep in touch," Chika said, attempting to be cordial.

"Well, I was actually calling to invite you to lunch, I thought we could get to know one another," Lola said.

"Lunch sounds okay, when would you like to meet?" Chika asked.

"Oh, I am free whenever, you tell me, my schedule is wide open," Lola prattled away.

Chika rolled her eyes. Of course her schedule was wide open. She had met so many ridiculous housewives since she moved back. So many women who had nothing better to do but gossip and groom themselves like cats. She found them so annoying. Mrs Money miss road!

"That sounds nice, but I have to get back to you tomorrow, I have a few things pending, you know some of us have to work for a living," Chika said, regretting the barb as soon as it came out of her mouth.

"Oh," Lola said, clearly hurt.

Chika remained silent because she was slightly irritated with herself. Why did she say that? Lola had been nothing but polite to her. She started checking herself and her motives. Was she actually jealous about her being a Mrs Somebody?

"Chika, you know what, just forget it, I was just trying to be nice," Lola said her voice screeching a little.

Chika felt bad. "I'm sorry Lola. That didn't come out right. I am just stressed out, you know I am still learning the ropes here and work is so hectic."

"Well, I guess I understand. But I want you to know that I don't sit around all day doing nothing. I have a very full schedule actually!" Lola said sharply.

"I am really sorry. I had no business saying that" Chika said.

"It's okay. I am just sick of being discounted" Lola responded.

Chika was surprised at how quickly Lola accepted her apology. She expected her to be more aggressive because the last time they met, she thought she came off a bit haughty. She wondered why she settled on being just a housewife. Chika remembered how beautifully Lola sang. A few Sundays back, Lola did a solo at church and there wasn't a dry eye in the house. Chika thought. Why do so many women settle for just being mousy wives? Then again, Chika had to admit that Lola and her husband made for a handsome couple. She wished she could walk into a room on her lover's arm. And just like that she was sad again.

"You know what Lola, lunch would be great. Can I call you tomorrow?" Suddenly, Chika couldn't get off the phone fast enough.

"Oh, that would be fine. We could go to this restaurant I know for sushi? Do you like sushi?".

"Pardon me... Hello?" Chika said.

"Ah ah, can't you hear me?" Lola asked. "I don't hear any static?"

"Hello? If you can hear me, it must be a bad connection," Chika said

"Must be network...Chika can you hear me?" Lola said.

Chika hung up the phone and leaned her head back on the sofa. She was tired, maybe Lagos was really not good for her. Already she was resorting to lying over little matters like ending conversations.

"So sorry Father, I'll do better I promise," She thought, praying for forgiveness as she switched on the do not disturb button on her phone.

# Chapter 10

## Karen
## Love is for suckers, marriage is for life

Karen declined the offer of the self-described celebrity photographer to stand in front of the step to have her photo taken and hastened her steps into the over decorated, crowded space. She loathed seeing herself in the papers and it didn't matter whether the words accompanying the photo were glowingly positive or not. She almost didn't attend this wedding, but her great aunt had called to remind her of how important it was that she "show face" at least. It would be considered a significant offense, if she didn't attend. She had tried to hint that she might be out of the country, but her aunt would have none of it. "Karen" she said, "that excuse might fly for common folks, but for people like us, that simply isn't good enough, if we need to make arrangements for Uncle's private jet, let me know, but kindly make yourself available and be sure to wear the Aso Ebi I am sending you. I sent it to that young designer you like. She had your measurements on file. Have a wonderful day." And she clicked off.

Karen wore a one sleeved modern take of Iro and Buba, the traditional attire for Yoruba women, and her hair was carefully gathered under the elaborately tied gele on her head. She looked around the room and thought it was a good thing that she didn't come trying to compete, because there were so many women wearing fabulous vibrantly colored and jeweled and shiny geles that it was hard to see the officiant and the bride and groom at the front of the room, even though they were seated on throne-like chairs and the backdrop behind them was covered completely in white roses and crystals. At every corner of the venue, there was something to see, from the stunning women perched upon pillars and draped with fabric as if they were the illegitimate offspring of greek gods and Nigerian women to the many intricately constructed rose and crystal chandeliers hanging from the ceiling of this massive venue. There had to be over a thousand people in the room. The bride was the daughter of one of world's richest men, at least according to this year's Forbes list and the groom was the son of one of the former heads of state. It was obvious there was no expense spared. The whole room was lush with flowers, Tulips flown in from the Netherlands and Peonies from New Zealand. The linens sparkled from the gold threads woven specially into the cloth that was commissioned just for this occasion. Karen spotted the celebrity event planner, Funke in the crowd. She made a mental note to call her for the next luncheon she was hosting, as Funke had a reputation for excellence and it showed in this wedding.

While she enjoyed the decor, she was already feeling weary and the evening had only just started. How was she going to get through the night, she thought as the usher in a purple satin dress, welcomed her and started to walk her to her seat in the VIP section. They passed a wedding guest in a body con dress, and Karen noticed her with amusement. She wondered how such a thin woman came to have such a distended stomach. Was it adult onset kwashiokor or perhaps just a love of beer?

She was seated next to Chief Mrs O. C Njoku. As the woman rose to greet her, kissing her on both cheeks, Karen was almost suffocated by her perfume; a heavy, spicy oriental scent. It was almost as if the whole bottle had broken over her body.

"Hello Mrs Njoku, How are you?" Karen gasped in greeting. "What an interesting scent you are wearing!"

Mrs Njoku clapped her hands in delight as they both took their seats. "You like it? Well of course you would, you have such discerning taste. I bought it from an exclusive perfumier in Paris. If you like, I'll give you his number, but only if you promise not to share it with anyone. Exclusive things aren't meant for everyone," she whispered in a conspiratorial tone. Karen smiled graciously and changed the subject.

Their attention was caught by another woman across the table, Nike Johnson. She waved gaily. "Hello," she said, just loud enough to be heard over the din. "We'll catch up later." She mouthed to Karen, who flashed her whites in return. She had no interest in catching up with Nike. She was the wife of one of Dele's distant cousins from the poorer side of the Thompson family. However, Nike and her husband did not intend to stay on the wrong side of the family tree. No one knew exactly how they got their money, but everything from drugs to 419 fraud had been insinuated. Nike herself was even said to dabble in the prostitution import and export business. The gossip was that she exported Nigerian girls to places like Italy and even as far away as Scandinavia where African girls were part of erotic exotica, and that she procured Indonesian, Filipino and even some African American video vixens for her well placed political clients. Judging from the amount of gold and diamond jewelry she was wearing, business seemed to be going quite well.

Karen did a modified pranayama, a yoga breathing technique that helped her feel a little less stressed but she couldn't wait for this evening to be over. As the waiter came over with glasses of champagne reserved for the VIP tables, Karen took one gratefully and fished around in her purse for her bejeweled pill case, but before she could find it, she was accosted by yet another specimen of Nigerian high society. It was Janet Anozie.

"Karen darling!" she said at the top of her voice as she approached the table. Janet was a double barreled type of woman, her voice was loud and her clothing was louder. She was dressed head to toe in some sort of atrocious designer logoed trouser suit and she had the audacity to further the fashion crime by wearing a matching pair of shoes and purse. Karen was flabbergasted. She wondered where in the world she had purchased such an ugly outfit. Karen's stare was so obvious that Janet noticed, but she took it as positive feedback. "You like my outfit?" Karen said nothing, but kept a smile on her face. Janet continued, assuming her fashion do had stunned Karen into silence. "It is ripped from the runway!" I got it when I attended the fashion shows in Milan. Karen nodded in understanding, thinking that perhaps this is one of those avant-garde pieces that were put together for show with no expectations that anyone would wear it exactly as shown. Yet, here she was, miles away in hot Lagos, looking not so hot, or cool for that matter.

Before Janet could tell her more about her sojourn in Milan, Chika and Lola walked up. Chika looked lovely in knee length red ombre dress that hugged her body in the right places, creating the illusion of perfect curves and Lola looked resplendent in her green chiffon gown. Standing up, she quickly excused herself from Janet's presence and turning to them, hugged each one tightly.

Lola said, "Here you are! I should have known you would be on the VIP table." She seemed a little wistful as she ended her statement.

Karen just shrugged. "Where are you guys sitting?" Chika nodded in the direction of the back of the room. "Do you have any space on your table?" Karen asked.

Chika responded, "Yes, actually it's just us. Why? Do you want to come and sit with us?"

Karen smile and said yes.

Lola looked confused. "Why would you want to come to the back, you won't be able to see anything!" she exclaimed. I would love to sit where you are seated! It's the perfect vantage point. Karen was nonplussed, "I think I have actually seen quite a bit for one night already," Karen said as she grabbed her purse and sunglasses and walked towards the back with her friends.

# City Life Magazine
# Gossip Page
# Guess who?

We all know that just because something looks good on the outside, doesn't mean it's not rotten on the inside, but here at the *City Life* offices, we have discovered that not only are some things rotten, they also smell like rotten eggs.

Apparently one of our esteemed Aristocrats has a serious problem. You wouldn't believe it if we told you who. But let's give you a hint. He is a tall, handsome, British educated, French speaking, world traveled, and cultured man.

We have heard that he often forces his wife and children to endure hours of classical music and insists on a particular French wine with dinner every night. And perhaps that very wine is the source of the problem.

You see, we have learned that his poor wife is really suffering. Actually, she has suffered every night of their marriage, for years, and she is so ashamed. She only recently shared her plight with someone, who of course shared it with someone else, who shared it with us.

It seems this refined man has a major flatulence problem. That's right, you read right! At night, all he does is pass gas.

Potent, smelly, practically life threatening gas! The poor woman has to import a particular British air freshener by the container full because it is the only thing that will neutralize the smell. She has to spray it several times at night, just to survive till morning!

Oh dear! Our editors are asking each other over a steaming cup of Earl Grey, what would you do if you were in this situation?

# Chapter 11

## Lola
## Writing a check is one thing, making sure it doesn't bounce, is another

Lola and her old schoolmate Mimi were having lunch at the J Spot, the trendy new café that was the place to see and be seen. Mimi was picking at her salad, alternating between talking and staring at the people who walked into the restaurant, while Lola stared into space and listened in between small bites of her dry chicken sandwich. *I would rather be eating Ofada rice*, she thought to herself when she was interrupted by Mimi's outcry.

"It's a fake!" Mimi declared.

"What?" Lola asked.

"It's a fake!" Mimi said, gesturing at the woman who just walked by their table looking nondescript in a pair of no name jeans and a simple white t-shirt. The only thing noticeable about her was her Celine purse; the same one that Mimi had slung over her chair a little while earlier.

"Her bag isn't real! This purse cost me well over two thousand dollars! Just look at her, hers can't be real!" Mimi exclaimed.

"I don't believe this!" Lola said.

"I know! It's awful how all these fakes have pervaded the market," Mimi said.

"Are you well at all?" Lola almost shouted. "You were just telling me that your husband, Yomi, no longer sleeps in the house and now you are talking about bags! What is wrong with you?"

Lola exclaimed. Lola was irritated, because she had spent the last hour listening to Mimi vent about her husband's awful behavior. And from what Mimi had said, her husband had gone from bad to worse in the two years they had been married. It was as if she was stuck in a bad Nollywood movie.

Lola knew that Mimi and Yomi had never had the kind of romance that she and John had. In fact, it was Mimi who had pursued Yomi. Lola crinkled her nose when she remembered it. It was so crass. It was on one of those first weekends just after they had moved back to Lagos. Mimi had come over and asked her to come to what she called the party of the year. She was somewhat ambivalent because Mimi was a little crazy at social events. She was that girl who might be found dancing on tables or something, but they had been friends since secondary school and though she rarely agreed with her ideas or behavior, she didn't believe in dumping old friends, but as the events of that night unfolded, she came very close to disowning her.

They had been standing in a corner, sipping champagne and people watching, when Mimi said that she noticed Yomi's eyes lingering on her for a moment, but not long enough for her to hold his gaze. Yomi Pedro was considered quite a catch in Lagos society. He was from a well established political family and was extremely good looking, so there were many women trying to catch his eye and from all reports, he liked to keep his gaze and his other parts constantly moving.

Lola was bored and missing her own husband. A few random men came up to try and chat her up, and she would constantly refer to her husband or point out her ring, but that only deterred a few, so she stuck close to Mimi, so she wouldn't have to put up with any more ridiculous pick up lines. However, Mimi tried to abandon her in her quest to get Yomi. Lola wrinkled her brow in a futile attempt to get her friend to change course by showing her disapproval. Mimi ignored her and whispered, "I'll be right back". She was determined to win her prize that night. Defeated, Lola looked around for a place to sit and watch because she knew Mimi would be gone for some time. She knew that based on Mimi's history, she was going to act out in some way that evening. When she finally found an armchair within view of her friend, she leaned against the plush cushions. A man sauntered up almost immediately and asked if he could sit on the arms. She gave him such an emphatic no, that he was taken aback. In the past, Lola would feel bad about her behavior, but she didn't care at the moment. Her feet hurt and she was tired and sick of playing nursemaid to her crazy friend. She chastised herself, and concluded that this would be her last outing with Mimi. Just as she thought that, she saw Mimi cross the room in hot pursuit of Yomi. Lola watched Mimi attempt to talk to him, but he shunned her by acting as if he was engaged with other people. Lola wished she could telepathically advise her friend to give it up. She felt Yomi had insulted her already and hooking up with him would not be worth it. "A man who doesn't respect you will never treat you well" She would have counseled, but Mimi was too far gone; it wouldn't have made a difference, she wouldn't have listened. It had become like a game for her and she was going to be declared the victor, no matter the personal cost. So Lola watched in dismay as Mimi pranced around the room vying for his attention.

At the end of the night, fortified with liquid confidence, Mimi marched up to him and said aloud, "It's too bad we didn't get the chance to talk because getting to know me would so be worth your while." Lola shook her head in disbelief, but she was in utter shock when she watched Mimi's next move. Yomi was standing with a couple of guys and they snickered, but Mimi didn't seem to care.

He appeared amused as he responded, "Please remind me… have we met?" Lola knew it was an insult, but Mimi brushed it aside and persevered.

"My name is Mimi. We were introduced a few hours ago," she said.

"Of course," he said. "Well, I am sure, like you say, it would have been worth my while, but I've run out of time to talk tonight," he said as he began to turn away. Lola sighed. It was both an expression of shame and relief, now that the guy had given her the final insult, maybe Mimi would give up and they could leave, but it was not to be and Lola's mouth fell open when she saw Mimi's next move.

"No problem," Mimi said in response to Yomi's brush off. "I have to get going anyway. Here is my card. Call me," she said as she pushed the card into his hand that still lay wooden at his side. He shook his head while his friends could barely keep their laughter in. They turned back to the bar where they were standing. Then Mimi dropped her keys on the floor and they clanged loudly and when she knew the men had turned in response to the noise, she bent over very slowly with her back to them, picked up her keys and walked away. When got into the car, she told Lola that she knew he would call. When Lola asked why, she said that the combination of a mini skirt and a g-string had never failed her before and Lola lost for words, could only snort in disgust.

Mimi had been right; he called her the next morning and picked her up that evening. She confessed to Lola that she used every single move she had to keep him hooked for the next six weeks. After a while, she started scouring the internet for more ammunition. He thought he had her just where he wanted her, but she planned on being more than a dial-a-freak, she planned on being a wife. So during the next couple of sessions, she suggested they use her condoms that the manufacturer had tweaked for increased pleasure and that Mimi had tweaked for inefficiency and soon enough she tested positive on her home pregnancy kit.

Lola knew being pregnant was not enough to get one married these days, but she had to admit that Mimi had done her homework. Yomi was the son of a prominent senator who had presidential ambitions and who was also a very vocal Catholic, who pushed for more morality in Nigeria. He introduced a decency bill requiring women to dress more conservative ways, but the bill got thrown out. Lola thought of her low rise jeans and was thankful that her fashion sense would not become reason for some corrupt and morally bankrupt police officers to extort even more bribes than usual.

When Mimi told her she was pregnant and going to tell Yomi's father, Lola was not surprised, Mimi was a schemer and she knew her business well. Lola knew she would put on a show, and Mimi roped her into escorting her to see Yomi's father. "I know it was wrong to fornicate." Lola watched as Mimi performed her lines so well, acting as if she spent every Sunday in church and had just happened to have found herself at the wrong party. "But I love your son so much." She had on her most nun-like outfit and was so convincing that her soon to be father-in-law informed his son that unless he didn't want to be cut off without a dime, he had better do the right thing and marry this nice young lady and make his grandchild legitimate.

Yomi did what he was told, but he did not go quietly into it. At first, the heaven Mimi expected became a hell of sorts. Lola suffered through the many phone conversations when Mimi would call her crying. Lola had no advice to give; after all she had warned her, plus she had no experience in this arena, when she married John, she married him because she was in love with him.

Mimi said Yomi wouldn't speak to her for the most part and when he did he cursed her out, calling her a gold digger in not so nice language. In spite of her emotional distress, Mimi was determined to be his wife though and Lola was amazed at her resilience because Mimi soon started taking it all in stride and became immune to his taunts. She refocused her energies and started planning the wedding of her dreams. Soon Lola was no longer listening to cries and wails, but squeals of delight as Mimi described shopping for her dress in London and booking the most expensive reception hall in Lagos.

Lola felt like she was getting an education in the art of being a courtesan, just listening to Mimi describe the things she did to make things work with Yomi. The week before the wedding, Mimi decided to seal the deal with Yomi because as she said, she "didn't want him acting crazy at the wedding" and spoiling her perfectly planned day. So she picked up a couple of "girls" from University of Ikoyi. They were known for the favors they exchanged for money. She took them to Yomi's apartment and together, they all indulged one of his secret fantasies. After when they left, she told him how she would be the perfect wife. She painted a picture of a perfect babe who knew how to be an acceptable wife and mother, while fulfilling every sexual fantasy that he had. Lola listened in amazement to the story thinking that once again, Mimi's powers of persuasion were proven because she bore witness to the fact that Yomi walked down the aisle, in a cravat and a morning coat and married her friend a week later, beaming like the cat that got the cream.

For a while after that, she kept him satisfied by cooking all day and working all night. She kept up with current affairs so she could wow his friends with her intellect when they came over. More than one of them retracted their statement about turning a "ho" into a housewife. But Lola wondered what her friend had gotten into, what kind of marriage it was, when she overheard Yomi recounting a bedroom move with his wife to his friends at a respectable dinner party. Lola knew that Mimi was exhausted all the time and terribly nauseous, yet she had to cater to him just to keep the peace.

And the pattern would have continued, if Mimi had not put her foot down one day, when she was past six months pregnant and exhausted. His baby was secure in her belly and her position as wife had been established with everyone, so all the kitchen and bedroom acrobatics had to stop. That day, she hired a steward. She reported that Yomi grumbled a little when he came back from work, but dinner was so good he accepted it. That night though was when the real trouble began. He started to make moves in the bedroom, but Mimi was tired and not in the mood. "I can't Yomi, the baby," she whined. "Too much pressure." She placed her hand on her swelling stomach for emphasis. Yomi contemplated this for a while, and then pulled her to him and kissed her. Mimi smiled. He had never been tender with her. Sexual yes, but never tender. She told Lola that she thought that things would be better than she had imagined. But then he started pushing her head down. It took a minute before she understood what he wanted. She angrily pushed his hand away. "What!" Yomi shouted.

"What do you mean what?" she shouted back. "I told you, I am tired, abi you don't see I am carrying your baby?" He looked at her and hissed. He jumped on his feet, put on his jeans, grabbed his keys and left. She heard the gate open and his BMW zoom out a few minutes later. He didn't return till morning to get ready for work. He didn't speak to her or eat the breakfast she had made herself. She was distraught. So she once again came to her friend Lola for advice.

"I told you that the payment on this loan might be too much for you to handle, but you wouldn't listen," Lola said

Lola watched Mimi try to save her marriage. For a while, things seemed back to normal but after she left for London to have the baby, Yomi never came, or even called. She had been gone for almost two months, and all that she could get out of him when she finally got him on the phone was a grudging, "How is the baby?" When she told him that his son was fine, he said, "Okay, good, I have to go now, I have a meeting." And he hung up. Lola was the one who had to inform her friend that her husband had started hot and heavy with another woman, so Mimi packed up her son at barely two weeks and headed home to put out the fire in her marriage yet again.

And here they were again, Lola thought, just two years later, back at the same place, sitting at a café, wondering what advice to give Mimi, who distracted herself from her farce of a marriage with spotting authentic designer products. Lola eventually said, "Don't worry dear, it will work out." But even as she said it, she knew it was not true. She couldn't help thinking about her own marriage to John. God forbid that she would ever be in the same situation, she thought. What would she do? If John decided to leave her, she had no money, nothing of her own. People saw her living a lavish lifestyle, but it was all John's money. If she left him, she would be starting from ground zero. And what would she do, if he turned into the sort of man that would take her sons away from her? She started to get anxious. This was not happening to her. It was happening to Mimi and even though she was her friend, deep down inside, Lola believed Mimi deserved what she got. She was not like Mimi. Sure, she occasionally went a little crazy shopping and who wouldn't want to be more relevant in society, but she was decent, a good person, after all, she even went to church regularly. *Anyway*, she thought, shaking her head a little. No matter what it seemed like, she chose to focus on her belief that she and John were okay. "We are okay," she said in her head again, over and over, like a mantra as she ended the tedious meeting with Mimi, hugged her and walked to her car.

"Take me home and hurry up!" Lola commanded, once she entered the Mercedes G-wagon. The driver pulled out of the restaurant parking lot and inched forward into Lagos' legendary traffic. "Can't you find a different way?!" Lola shouted, urging the driver to get her home faster. She chose to ignore his insolent expression that asked wordlessly if she wanted him to perform magic and make the car fly. Finally she gave up and tried to relax as she reclined in the back seat of the large SUV truck. Sitting on the side of the car, commonly known as the owner's corner, she looked out at the sea of non-moving cars in front of them, and felt frustrated. And when there was an opportunity to move, it seemed to her that her driver was deliberately moving at a snail's pace. She was so stressed out because she had to get home in less than fifteen minutes after her meeting with Mimi.

"Madam, na check point," Innocent, the driver announced. Lola squinted to see the men in uniform up ahead. She rolled her eyes and hissed. "Such nuisances!" she thought aloud. These ridiculous police stops served no other purpose except to extort money. Today was so not the day for these asinine disturbances, she had to get home. Finally, the car moved through the checkpoint, and Lola sent up a silent prayer of thanks because they didn't bother her, but waved her through when they recognized her car—one of the perks of being among the elite—besides they were not far from home, so there was hope yet.

"*Oya*, Innocent, hurry up!" No sooner than she said it did the two cars in front of her have an accident. Nothing serious just a fender bender, but from the way one of the drivers jumped out of the car, blocking traffic, and rolled up his sleeves, Lola knew it would be more than half an hour before she left this spot. She resigned herself to the fact that she was not going to make it. She chastised herself, "Why did she eat that damn meat pie at that restaurant? And the Jollof rice and the slice of chocolate cake?" she thought. "Why!" As she was stuffing her face with the delicious goodness, she felt bad but decided to simply purge herself of them when she got home. But it looked like that was not going to happen and soon the carbs, sugar and fat would add to her expanding girth.

Lola had learned how to purge from her roommate in college. It was a disgusting but necessary habit, Leah had told her. Leah was a typical American princess. Her father was very wealthy and his money served to fix Leah's imperfections. She had fixed her nose, lipo'd her stomach and hips and even had cheek implants. Based on her body type and appetite, she might have been closer to a slim size six, but she was a rail thin size zero who gorged on cakes and sweets and then stuck her finger down her throat to throw it all up. "Gross, but no calories this way," she explained when Lola saw her and was horrified. Within a month, she became like Leah, mostly living on cigarettes and diet coke, and occasionally gorging and then purging right after.

"No longer than 15 minutes," Leah would say, after that it's too late, and the fat will settle right here" she would say pointing to her nonexistent hips and butt. When she was still in her twenties, she adhered to this rule, so she was a slim size four when John met her. However over the years, she binged more often, and in spite of her occasional purging, she gained a little bit of weight. Many people would have considered her weight gain inconsequential and considered her quite slim, but in the aristocrat circles she ran in, where Eurocentric standards of beauty were the order of the day; even a modest gain of two pounds was considered terrible. So of late when she found herself struggling to fit into her size six jeans, sometimes, she felt like disappearing into the ground. And it didn't help that John commented that her stomach was now beginning to bulge and she was becoming unshapely. His words made her feel so bad, she felt like she was going crazy. She felt like a candidate for the mental health ward. Every month she vowed to concentrate on eating healthily, and then she would live on vegetables and salads for a few days, but without fail, something would stress her out like John locking his phone and taking late night meetings. And whenever she got anxious she binged on carbs of every kind and the pounds piled on.

She hissed and shook her head trying to banish the images of cellulite that were filling up her brain. In exasperation, she bought a gossip magazine from a vendor in the street and flipped to the society pages. She was surprised to see John on the main page. *Big Boys and Girls Storm CEO's Funeral*, the headline read. She was curious and irritated at the same time. When would these so called journalists come up with some decent copy? He looked handsome in a black lace caftan. His designer sunglasses almost hid his face creating an air of mystery. He was smiling and handsome, but Lola was looking at the woman next to him. She was glad she looked good in that shot. They looked perfect like a power couple ready to take on the world. From the way she had her face turned to him, and him looking down at her, they looked very much in love. As Lola stared at the glossy picture, she became filled with apprehension. Just then she saw a hawker selling plantain chips and she bought four bags, which she tore open and began to munch them, allowing the spicy sweetness to soothe her.

"Madam," Innocent said, interrupting her thoughts, "E be like say, we need petrol."

"Crap," Lola thought.

By the time the driver pulled into the driveway of the mansion in Lekki Island, she could feel the fat making itself at home on her already too full hips. Lola was more irritated to see that John's car was gone. These days, he was never home. He was always at some function or another. In the early days, she used to insist on going with him, but while they were there he would always disappear with his boys and she would be left alone or in the company of someone she didn't care for. So now, she preferred to do quiet lunches with her friends and to spend time with their kids.

She tried to do more with them because she knew that their father never made out time. He was always in the society pages with his crew, laughing and posing for a photo op. When she complained, he insisted that socializing that way allowed him to finance their lavish lifestyle. "Laugh together at night, sign the contract in the morning," he said. He ran with a pretty powerful set. It was always the same guys. Ahmed Gota, the heir to the Gota fortune. His father had recently been listed on the Forbes 100 list of wealthiest men. Lekan Johnson, special assistant to the governor and Jimmy Okeke, self-made millionaire, and Chairman of the Board of True National. They were rich and powerful, but Lola couldn't stand them. When they came by, they acted like she wasn't even there and made every effort to exclude her. They were all married, but even though her husband had been friends with them for quite a while, she had only met their wives once or twice at functions. They were probably like her—lonely. She read an article about how some American women were referring to themselves as golf widows because their husbands were always off playing golf. Well, she was a society widow. For a while she tried to be like Karen and take her mind of things by buying expensive things, but the euphoria of the purchases never lasted. Instead, she often found herself wishing for the early days when they first returned from New York, when things were simpler. When they both went to work and came home together because they only had one car. They would share war stories about Lagos life on the way home. They were closer then, real partners. Living in a two bedroom flat in the mainland because that was all they could afford. He still thought she looked beautiful in the clothes she bought at the designer discount stores in America before they moved back. Then, they were still so in love. They hadn't conceived any children, but they had fun trying, often waking up in each other's arms. These days, when they slept in the same bed, John was far away on the other side of it, holding a pillow in between his legs for company.

She broke into a smile when she saw her son Kevin bounding towards her, shouting "Mummy, Mummy!" Their Filipino nanny was right behind him with a disapproving look on her face. "He wouldn't go to bed until you came home. James is already sleeping," she said. Lola enveloped him into a hug. She hadn't meant to be out late. "No problem," she said in response, "please bring up my things; I'll put him in bed," she said walking away with her son in her arms. He was heavy, but the strain brought her comfort. At the end of it all, it was worth it, she thought, but just as she began to feel at ease, a stray thought crossed her mind that replaced every period with a question mark.

# Chapter 12

# Chika
## Successful women delegate...

It was a cool night in the rooftop lounge and the jazz singer's voice was deep and throaty, and the way she sang was seductive. Chika was enjoying both the music and the show. She was sipping her glass of cabernet and feeling relaxed for the first time in months. She looked over at Gbenga, who gave her a smile and a wink. He was the one that insisted she join them for a drink after they had finished taping some promo clips for her new show. She wanted to say no, but Gbenga was her executive producer and every other person on the show's production was going. She thought it would be bad for morale if she blew them off.

Soon she found herself sitting with her boss and some of his friends, enjoying the scent of the sea, carried by the ocean breezes. The other team members had left to go to an afterparty, and this time Chika felt safe to decline their offer to join them. Gbenga did as well, saying clubbing was not his scene. They stayed and soon they were joined by Gbenga's friends, a very sweet and doting couple, who walked in with their arms intertwined and a very glamorous woman, with long wavy hair with blonde highlights who wore a wedding ring with a huge diamond. Gbenga introduced the couple as his oldest friends, Didi and Peter. He went to high school with them and they had been together since then. Didi kissed Peter on the cheek as Gbenga introduced them and giggled as Peter blushed, while the glamourista rolled her eyes.

"This troublemaker is my cousin, Nina," he said, pinching

her slim and toned arm. Chika took a long look at her. The woman was carefully coiffed, with mink lash extensions and as Chika looked at her cheekbones and the slant of her nose, she was willing to bet that it was the work of a good plastic surgeon.

Nina swatted Gbenga away playfully. "Mind yourself o!" she exclaimed, half smiling and rolling her eyes seductively. "Hello Chika, nice to meet you" she said, extending her hand.

The vocalist had taken a break in between sets so they started conversing quickly after placing their orders with the waiter sporting a black T-shirt and black jeans. Wine for Didi and Peter and a Grey Goose classic martini for Nina. And a large bowl of asun, peppered goat meat for the table.

"Where is your Oga tonight?" Gbenga asked Nina.

"Who knows, who cares!" she said in response. Leaning back into artfully shaped rattan chairs with mud cloth cushions.

Didi and Peter looked at each other and both raised their eyebrows in response to her statement.

She back tracked quickly. "I'm just kidding. He had to travel to Port Harcourt."

The waiter brought their drinks. Didi took a quick sip of her wine and Nina popped the olive from her drink into her mouth.

There was a momentary lull in conversation as everyone spooned the asun into their small plates and took bites of the tender, flavorful meat. Chika savored the taste, in between sips of her chapman drink. Suddenly Peter cleared his throat with a strange expression on his face. When everyone looked at him, he started to speak, "Nina, can I ask you something?" he said.

Nina shrugged in response. "Sure."

Peter nodded and kept his lips pursed as if he were about to deliver bad news. "Do you ever worry that your husband might be cheating?" Peter asked, not meeting her eyes and looking down at his drink. Chika wondered what he knew that brought up this line of questioning.

Nina smiled slowly, "I don't worry about him cheating

because I know he does."

Everyone fell silent. Unsure of what to say. Chika wondered if the night was going to become a sad one. But Nina continued to smile and even started to chuckle a bit. "Oh, please don't look at me with those big pitiful eyes!" she chastened Didi. "I don't need your pity because it's not a problem for me. I consider it outsourcing," she said, smiling and reaching for her drink, then she lifted the martini glass up to her glossy lips.

Chika just stared at her as she was dumbstruck. Gbenga however, was not. He laughed. "That's a good one Nina! Outsourcing, I think I may just have heard it all!" he said chuckling.

Didi was not amused. "I don't believe you Nina! How can you say something like that?" she said, gesticulating with a great deal of passion.

Nina raised her brows in response. "Oh come off it please, Didi. You think life is a fairytale? I'm just telling you the truth, and for your information, my husband and I actually have a pretty good relationship. Look, when we first got married, I wanted to be his everything: his confidant, his partner, his lady and his freak. And now we have both risen to prominent positions in our careers and we are raising three beautiful children, and still enjoy each other's company. Life is really good!"

Well, except for the sex right? Peter asked, holding his wife's hand.

"We have sex! Just not all day and all night. Look I am tired! Plus it takes him so much longer to start and finish now that he is older, and I just can't do it for hours anymore. I mean come on! I can't be blowing grammar in the boardroom, then in the bedroom, I will be working my mouth double time! I tire *bo*. So if he gets some random chick to do it and get the physical reaction he needs no *yawa*. I mean it's just sex; it's not love," Nina said, downing the rest of her drinking quickly and signaling the waiter for another one.

"So are you telling us that you don't mind if he has a dalliance or two?" Gbenga asked.

"Honestly I don't. Quite frankly I don't care. As long as it's random and purely physical," Nina responded.

"What if he falls in love?" Chika finally recovered enough to ask.

"With what, her mouth?" Nina retorted.

"Don't act like it's not possible, Nina," Gbenga said. "I think it's a recipe for disaster."

"No it's not. He would have to see her as a whole woman for that to happen and I won't let that happen."

"How are you so sure it won't?" Gbenga prodded.

"I just know," Nina said, sipping the new drink the waiter brought by.

"Really?" Gbenga continued his line of questioning.

"Really," Nina said firmly. "Plus I would break her legs before I let that happen. She can open her mouth and open her legs, but the day she tries to open her mind and think she can go higher, that is when she will understand that blowing grammar trumps giving head any day, period, full stop."

Everyone laughed and the tension was released.

"Well, all I know is I could never be involved in an adulterous affair. I don't know how these women do it; they must have no standards whatsoever," Chika said in irritation.

"Well, I find that it is best not to judge people, sometimes they are pushed against a wall," Gbenga said as he pulled out a cigarette and lit it.

"I don't know about that, everything is a choice," Didi said.

"Exactly," Chika agreed, looked directly at Gbenga and his cigarette.

"What do you think Nina?" Peter asked. Nina was looking up at the night sky, rolling her glass around gently, causing the ice to clink against the glass.

"Honestly, I couldn't give a damn. To each his own, just

know when you make your bed; you are the one who will have to sleep in it," she responded.

The vocalist walked back on stage and the band started up again. "Thanks for your patience ladies and gentlemen. I am going to sing you one of my favorite songs from the incredible Nina Simone. "I want a little sugar in my bowl."

People started clapping as the band started playing and the conversation was forgotten as Chika enjoyed the music and the cool ocean breeze.

## Chapter 13

# Karen
# Wishful thinking is an expensive
# indulgence

Karen stepped onto the plane and looked for her seat. "Bienvenue" the pilot greeted them. The flight attendant ushered them to their seats, offering juice, water or wine. Karen chose white wine and settled back in her roomy seat to drink it. The girls in the seats in front of her giggled. Their demeanor suggested that they were not used to traveling in luxury. Traveling first class had become so routine for her that she no longer noticed the perks. Rather, she often found fault. The seats could be plusher and the pillows softer. The flight attendant appeared again, this time offering cookies. Karen shook her head; the flight attendant kept smiling, unfazed.

As the plane taxied for takeoff, Karen looked out of the window. She always got a window seat, ever since she was a child and traveled to London on her family's yearly pilgrimage. She would visit the usual tourist attractions. She always loved Madame Tussauds—all those wax figures. She would seek out her star of the moment and pretend that the wax figure was alive, and she was in charge of his speech. It was always a wonderful trip. She and her mother would visit Harrods and buy clothes and accessories as if style was going to be embargoed. Her father rarely traveled with them. By the time she was old enough to understand why, her mother had taught her how to shop herself numb. Karen's mother, Ronke's anesthesia of choice was jewelry.

Fortunately, there was more than enough money to keep her permanently on drip. Ronke had loved precious stones, and now Karen had no need to buy them because she had inherited all of her mother's gems since she had no other sisters.

Karen thought back to when her mother would hold her and call her a pearl. "My darling, an oyster only has room for one perfect pearl and you are mine." Karen closed her eyes and drifted deeper into the memory, thinking about the days when she and her mom would giggle with delight, sharing a bowl of ice cream or some other forbidden treat. Karen missed her mum so much, they were very close. Her brothers identified with her dad and they treated her mother, Karen and indeed all women as if they were of no consequence. Karen and her mother were kind of their own miniature family. Even though she had her own lavish pink princess bedroom, filled with beautiful dolls and plush soft toys. At night, she would often leave her room for the comfort of her mother's warmth and her mother allowed her this indulgence, even though she was no longer a little girl. She did this right up until the time of her death.

She recalled the night she lost her mother. She wandered into the room in a sleep filled haze. She was twelve going on thirteen and her mother had started half heartedly banishing her to her own bed, but despite her protests, she would pull back the covers and allow her to crawl into bed with her and immediately Karen would fall asleep to the sound of her mother's breathing. But on this night, when Karen entered the room, her mother didn't stir and when she crawled into the bed, there was no warmth to be felt. Karen blinked away a tear as she recalled how she ran to her father's room banging on the heavy ornate door. He was awake. He had just returned home a short time before the incident. He rushed to her mother's room and took her in his arms as he bellowed for the housemaids to get his driver and car ready. He looked at the pill bottle on her bed stand and sat on the floor, pulling her body with him. She was limp, but still beautiful. Karen remembered her delicate features, small pointed nose and again that red hair juxtaposed against her brown skin. She was a unique beauty. Her father spoke quietly to the doctor, who had been collected from his nearby home by the driver. He took her pulse and shook his head. They laid the body in the bed and covered it. Shortly after funeral arrangements were made, Karen was sent to live with her grandmother and she never really spoke to her father again.

Another memory flitted through her mind like the wisp of cloud outside her window that looked like it had been pulled apart by a hand. It was Valentine's Day at her boarding school and the excitement was thick and choking those who had nothing to celebrate. Karen looked over at the gifts on her table. Three different boys had sent elaborate gift baskets complete with teddy bears and chocolate. She was not moved. They would get thank you notes on her special stationery, but no more. She couldn't be bothered with the frivolities of teenage romance. After her mother died, she did not find emotional concerns relevant. Her grandmother believed in luxury when it came to her surroundings and her things, but she practiced emotional austerity. The facts of her mother's death were hidden from the press. A short press release was sent stating that she had been taken by a sudden illness. Karen carried the weight of her mother's suicide, which made her decide to adopt her grandmother's approach to life.

Karen stared out of the window again. The sky had darkened and she couldn't really see the clouds. These days nothing pleased her, nothing seemed to elicit that feeling of joy that she saw so many people so freely express. She looked over at the girls in front of her. They were fiddling with the personal video screens and giggling. Karen watched them attempting to understand their excitement. What must that feel like? To experience a bit of luxury for the first time, she wondered. It was if she was trapped in the black and white world of a twilight zone episode, where genuine joy and happiness was inaccessible to her, and all the while the world around her marched forward, pushing through into colorful manifestations of love and life. The couple on the other side of the aisle clinked their glasses, toasting to something that tickled them. They were whispering to each other as they laughed and linked their fingers together. Karen turned and watched them in the reflection on her window. She swallowed a lump. She wondered if she and Dele would ever be like that; she wondered why they had never been like that. No longer satisfied with her reflection, she turned and looked right at the couple who were so engrossed in each other they didn't even notice her staring. She tried to remember how it was when she and Dele first met, tried to remember if her lip had ever quivered like the girl's was doing now and if he had ever looked at her with such naked desire.

The flight attendant interrupted her again this time asking her what she would like to eat for dinner. This time Karen was pleased with the disruption because the road she had been on didn't lead to flowery memories of romance and passion. Dele and Karen had been a product of high society matchmaking and when they met, they knew it was just a formality. Chemistry, while it would have been a perk, was simply of no consequence to their future together. She perused the menu and ordered the chicken in the white wine sauce. While the attendant went away to bring her meal, she picked up the remote to watch a film. She chose an action flick—nothing like gunfire and up tempo background music to change your mood. By the time the attendant returned with a tray carefully arranged, with a starter salad and dessert of chocolate croissant, Karen's mood had changed and she rewarded the attendant with a sincere smile and a kind thank you.

After she picked at the salad and sampled a bit of the chicken, she allowed herself to bite into the warm chocolate pastry. She asked the flight attendant for some warm milk and some cognac, which she used to spike the milk. What was better than a pastry and milk? She thought, dessert was really one of the main components of the charm of the West. She heard more giggling and couldn't help herself, even though she chided herself for looking again at the couple, who were now licking chocolate off each other's lips. She bit her tongue and put the croissant down. Terrible for the figure anyway, she thought as she picked up her mug of milk. Sweet and heady, just what she needed, and with the help of her favorite nightcap, that small green valium tablet, she drifted into oblivion.

# Chapter 14

# Lola
# Love is not complicated, it's loving that is

Lola had started working out in earnest; even hiring a personal trainer. She barely ate and in the last week, she had already lost eight pounds. John noticed and she felt like things might get better between them. They hadn't made love again since that incident because she couldn't bear to be with him that way. She always made sure to be asleep by the time he came to bed, although sleep could only be found in the hands of a double dose of sleeping tablets. There were many thoughts that kept her up at night and John was at the center of all of them. So much had changed between them, and with him. He wasn't the same man she knew when they got married. His values had changed. She knew that living as part of Lagos society had changed them both, but he seemed to have embraced the vices that society living had to offer. She knew he did government work, and had heard how some men compromised themselves in order to make money. Once upon a time, she would have chastised him and reminded him of all their noble ideas to be part of Nigeria's change for the better. She knew that chances were that he had to give kickbacks as part of his business, but she hoped, though she never asked, that it didn't go much further than that.

While she was concerned about his business practices, she was more consumed with wondering what really happened at the late night meetings he was always attending. She had heard rumors about the kinds of night activities many of the government officials got into, and how so many business men got caught up in them as they curried their favor. Lola wondered if John was one of those compromised business men. The thought both scared her and disgusted her, but it also paralyzed her. What could she do? She felt so frustrated when she thought about her marriage. Her mind went back to the words he said that she did nothing. Those words stung, but it wasn't just what he said, it was also what she heard, because even though she understood the difference, she felt as if he said she was nothing.

She always thought they were different, that he was different. The truth was that most of the wives she knew had experienced infidelity before. For some like Karen it was an ongoing issue, but she never thought she would feel the pain of that particular betrayal. John had integrity or so she thought. He was active in church. He used to be a leader in the business development department. She just couldn't understand. She thought she should pray. Funny thing was she went to church regularly, but she rarely prayed beyond the cursory few words she said in the morning and at night. But she prayed now because God had to help her, after all she had tried to be a good wife: she was submissive, never questioned him, she made sure the house ran well.

She didn't realize that she was crying until her make-up began to run. Sure she had allowed herself to fill out a little like many housewives do after children, but it wasn't as if she was fat and even if she was out of shape, surely that wasn't enough reason for John to start cheating. She closed her eyes, thinking that she had to get the thoughts out of her head. She was being negative, she should focus on positive thoughts, plus she had no reason to believe that there was anyone else in their lives. John was a jerk perhaps, but he was a faithful jerk. She decided to have a long shower and then go to sleep.

In spite of her vigorous workout and usual sleeping pills, Lola slept fitfully. She woke up wrapped in the blanket and looked at the clock. It was past two o'clock and John wasn't in the room. Normally, Lola would turnover and go back to sleep because insomnia was not uncommon with John; however, for some reason, Lola got up, then pulled on her robe. She walked quietly to the living room looking for him, but he wasn't there. She looked out of the window and saw his car still parked where the driver left it. Then she remembered that he might be in his home office on the other side of the house, so she crept down the hallway. The marble flooring was cold against her feet, but slippers would have made noise. As she approached the office, the heavy wood-paneled door was ajar and she could see John's back in the chair, he had swiveled around facing the wall. He was on the phone. She heard him say, "I care about you deeply. You know that. Why are you doing this? Don't push this. It's not like you didn't know I was married from the start? I can't. I can't. Look, I can't and I won't!" Lola froze. She felt as if all the blood was draining from her body, and she could feel her heart thumping in her chest even as pain pushed at the sides of her forehead. "Baby, I'm sorry. I am. I know it's difficult for you, but please understand. She is my wife. I know, baby, I know. I can't lose you." Lola felt the tears threatening again as she backed away and quietly went back the way she had come.

Lola didn't breathe till she got back to her room. She crawled under the covers and fought back tears. She was right, but she didn't want to believe it. She couldn't believe it. How could this be her life? She thought as the tears dripped onto the pillow. How could this be her John? Suddenly she sat up enraged. John was a bastard! The thought contorted her pretty features into a grotesque mask of anger. All this time he made her think that the problems in their marriage were about her, when really it was about him. He was cheating. No wonder he was always too tired. And then he tried to hurt her, to make her feel small. He called her repulsive. In all her years on earth, she had never been called that. She had stared in the mirror for weeks after that, and while it hurt, she could never make the word fit. Sure, her butt was a little bigger than it needed to be and her stomach a little rounder, but she was far from repulsive. As she lay there, she tried to picture the other woman. Was she some stick insect? Some model?

Lola was still awake when he came to bed shortly after. She was drained of energy from contemplating their lives and trying to discern his lies and his truths. She had decided to table the matter and hide the fact that she knew until she had more to go on, so she lay there with her eyes closed. He kissed her on the forehead and tried to spoon her. Lola pulled away feigning sleep. He didn't persist. Soon he was snoring and she lay awake listening to the hum of the generator. Her emotions washed over her, threatening to drown her in pain. She looked over at him. He was sleeping so peacefully. She had slept next to him all these years. She was with him when he was nothing, and it was her encouragement that had brought him this far. *I deserve better*! She thought angrily. She went through two difficult pregnancies and deliveries just to bring their children into the world. How could they have shared all that and still he would deceive and betray her so easily. How could this happen? *Abi na juju?* She banished the thought. This wasn't a local movie, this was real life and these bastard men just did what they pleased. After all, her own father cheated on her mother without mercy. She thought she had made sure that she married a different kind of man. How could she have been so blind? He rolled over and she could see the beginnings of a spare tire around his middle. He was even getting fat. Stupid bastard! She hated him in that moment. She thought about how she could kill him. She could cook his breakfast with rat poison, or she could hold a pillow over his head right now and he wouldn't be able to stop her, at least then the extra flesh on her arms would be put to good use. At that moment she caught herself. No matter what he had done, she was a Christian and she shouldn't be thinking about killing him. But she could still think about maiming him, maybe she could cut off the offending penis! After all if your eye offends you...*abi?*

A mosquito bit her and she slapped it away. Her mind warned her to make sure they sprayed the room with insecticide tomorrow. Just like that, she was brought back to reality. If she killed him, how would that help? Her sons would be without a father. Maybe she would even go to prison, if she got caught. If she divorced him, how would she live? She had no real money of her own. She would lose everything that made her who she had become. It wasn't even just the money, it was the prestige! She sighed as she faced the truth—she couldn't leave him. "Who was she kidding," she thought filled with bitterness, John's name opened doors. It was because of him that her sons got admission into their exclusive elementary school. He had become so well connected that she got several perks just for being Mrs Amadi. I can't stop being Mrs Amadi, she thought. She couldn't give up being married. I can't. I can't lose him. I have to win him back. I'll find the bitch and win him back. We have been through too much just to throw the marriage away, she thought.

Maybe she should pray, she thought. Surely God would fight for her. She felt a nagging in her spirit, questions she wasn't willing to answer. She felt guilty about calling on God now because she really never prayed as such, just a quick few words before eating and bedtime. Funny thing was, she had been around women who prayed like Jesus himself was in the room and she always thought they were a little bit strange and they *too do!* Now as she contemplated praying in the hopes of changing her situation, she felt as if she could pray till her sweat turned to blood as well. She leaned back weary against the pillow. What was she going to do? For the first time, she understood the saying between a rock and a hard place.

She was angry and sad at the same time. She was angry at John, but she was angrier at herself. When did she become this sad, pathetic woman, who was nothing without her husband? When did she stop dreaming and achieving? Even as the questions fired through her mind, she knew the answers: when he became more to her than just a partner, when he became a provider, when she gave up her career to stay home after her first son was born. She debated inside of her. What was wrong with focusing on your child, choosing to be home with him? But she knew it was more than that, he didn't lose respect for her because of her change of work status; he lost respect for her because her values changed. When she started staying home, she found herself trying to prove her worth; trying to prove her relevance, so she started to compete.

She didn't even notice the changes in her thinking. It was so subtle at first. In the beginning, it was about getting the best for Kevin. From the best mommy and me playgroups in Lekki, to the best party spaces for his birthdays. However she kept meeting these fashionista moms decked out in their mom chic uniforms: Designer jeans and Chanel bags to boot. She started to feel self conscious and uncoordinated. She felt out of place, and the women around her seemed to think so as well, between the stares and cold shoulders. Someone finally told her outright, that she was a mess. It didn't take long before she started striving to fit in and pushing John to do better in his business more and more.

She could remember the turning point. One night she lay in bed and John came in and cradled her in his arms. For a while they lay there together. It was a hot night and NEPA had once again failed to provide electricity. They could not afford to run the generator all the time, especially that time of the year when Kevin's exclusive preschool fees had just been paid. So as they lay and sweat formed little pools of water beneath them, making the sheets wet and their bodies sticky.

She still remembered each sensation as if she were still lying in that room on that lumpy mattress, with the windows wide open to invite what little breeze there was in. She was so hot that she wanted to push away from him and let her body breathe a little, but she could sense that he was troubled and needed her close. She was right because he began to talk as he rubbed her arm gently but continuously with his thumb. She endured the irritating, repetitive nature of that particular touch because she understood that he only did it when nervous. He kept starting and stopping and each time, Lola held her breath and forced herself to be quiet in order to give him the space he needed to speak.

Her patience was rewarded that night because he spoke for a long time. He told her about his concern about the business dealings he was venturing into. He was worried about partnering with this particular man and also the specifics of the deal were disturbing. It required a significant compromise of his integrity. He described it as feeling like selling part of his soul. He didn't know what to do because the payoff was so huge. It would be enough to rent a bigger house in Lekki and even buy land, upgrade their cars and raise their standard of living, but he was worried that it would not just change the way they lived, he worried that it would really change their lives.

Lola held her breath the whole time, trying to make sense of the dilemma, she knew he wanted her advice, but she didn't know what to say. Life changing opportunities didn't come around every day. Nigeria was corrupt, she rationalized in her mind. You had to do what you had to do. When he finally asked her what she thought. She had no words, instead she pretended to be asleep, snoring lightly, but from the way his body stiffened, she knew her deception had failed. He knew she was awake. And he knew the answer in her heart and he followed it.

Her eyes filled with tears. She sat in the bed, reeling from the discovery but still very mindful about the realities of her life. Even though she was still angry with John, she felt as if she had no choice but to try to win him back. Besides, she rationalized, deep down inside she knew she loved him, and so she was not just fighting to keep the life he gave to her, she was fighting for her vows. She shored herself up with the knowledge that many women before her had done the same and she determined that she would win him back whatever the cost, but as she made her decision, she knew even if she won him away from this temptress, things would never be the same; she would always hate him a little and herself a little more.

"Love is complicated and grown-ups have to make hard decisions." She remembered her mother's words the day she chose to stay with her father even after he confessed that he had a pregnant mistress. Her mother never even shed a tear; she simply packed her things into the guest bedroom without a word. Later, she sat on the comfortable bed reading her bible. That night, was an awakening for Lola, it was then she decided to marry for love. It was as if the awareness of her mother's weakness had forced womanhood upon her, because in the space of one week, she had her first period and her father had broken her heart for the first time. As Lola lay on her own bed, contemplating her mother's lot, she wondered about the state of her own guest room. She snapped her fingers over her head immediately, "God forbid! It would never come to that." She prayed as she closed her eyes and tried to sleep, but like a defiant child, it refused to come and so she lay there while fears for her future and accusations of her more recent past assaulted her.

In the morning, she felt like a crazy woman. Her actions confused her. She couldn't explain her decisions, couldn't explain her behavior, her moods swung from one end of the pendulum to the other. She finally understood that verse in the Bible that said, a double minded man is unstable in all he does. Lola tried to return to a sense of normalcy as she pondered what to do, but she struggled with her internal conflict. Who was she? The woman who stayed and tolerated or the woman who left. She wondered if there were any other options.

\*\*\*\*\*\*\*\*\*

A week had passed since she learnt of his affair, and she was yet to confront him. Instead she felt the need to seduce him again and this time she was successful, in fact it was one of the most passionate nights they had together, but shortly after, when he had fallen asleep with his head on her stomach, she pulled away from him and ran to the toilet to throw up. Throwing up the disgusting mess from her inside was the only thing that soothed her. It felt as if she was removing the rubbish from her life. She threw up until her stomach hurt from the exertion, and then she brushed her teeth and showered and scrubbed herself clean. While the water ran over her chest, she battled with contempt for herself. What was she trying to prove, she thought to herself. She knew she didn't need to compete with this girl whoever she was. She had never fought for a man in her life and she couldn't believe that she was about to start now. She grit her teeth as she let the water flow over her. She turned the faucet to hot as she washed her most intimate parts. It burned her skin a little, but she didn't care. She couldn't get clean enough.

At that moment, she wanted to leave him. What was she doing here with this man who couldn't be faithful to her? This man who at this point had no integrity. But she knew what she was doing: building a life, building hope. She knew women who divorced their husbands and she had seen how quickly they fell from grace. One moment they were the toast of the town and the next, social pariahs. "No!" she insisted out loud. She would get over her ambivalence and make her marriage work and if not, so be it, she continued in her head, there were several women in a love hate affair with their own husbands.

John on the other hand had become very attentive, coming home early on most nights and even being more romantic. Lola couldn't rejoice in it though, she knew it was out of guilt. She also knew he was still seeing the other woman, whoever she was. She had started checking his phone, after a few tries, she figured out his code, after so many years of marriage, it was easy to crack it, she knew everything that was important to him after all. She read text after text from Natalie. Lying there thinking about the black letters on the white background, it made her skin crawl. She read about how her husband touched some woman named Natalie, she read about how he kissed her. She read the thank you text that Natalie sent her husband after he gave her "such a wonderful birthday present". Just thinking about it made Lola's heart drop. Reading Natalie's texts to her husband was bad, but when she read John's texts to her, she felt as if she was falling into a black hole. It devastated her so much that the following morning, she feigned malaria and stayed in bed for the whole day. She had read about how John said, he lived for certain parts of Natalie's body. He said he loved the way she tasted. That part wounded her deeply. She wondered if John had ever said the same to her. When they were first together he would whisper feverishly into her ear, but now their lovemaking was quiet and all John uttered were occasional grunts. Now she wondered if he had become quiet because he had given all his words to someone else. She also read the text where he had typed "I miss you so much, I can't think. There are millions at stake, yet all I can think about is the softness of your lips." This same man that claimed to be so busy sometimes when she called, and yet he clearly made out time to tell this stranger that he missed her.

Every morning she woke up, feeling as if she didn't know what to do, even though every night she went to bed feeling certain that she should not confront him, but work on being the only woman he needed. She yielded to him whenever he reached for her, but it was not easy. When John touched her, her skin burned. Sometimes when he slept, she didn't know if she wanted him to wake up. Yet through all of this madness, she loved him. She was always repentant when she found herself wondering what coffin she would use to bury him, and did penance by praying extra hard for his protection and forgiveness. Through it all, she kept going to church, hoping for a miracle, hoping for a word from the pulpit that would somehow give her clarity. That would somehow give her hope.

If only she could just start life all over. She dreamed about returning to the US, but she couldn't fathom how she would do it. Everything was in John's name, all the money was his and in divorce, the laws in Nigeria rarely favored the wife. As much as she contemplated leaving Lagos, she couldn't imagine stepping down from her position in society and becoming anonymous again. In America, the blessing and the curse for most people was that for the most part, no one knew or cared who you were, even if you were a millionaire, chances are, you could go a whole year without anyone ever giving you any deferential treatment; in America, every man was an everyman. So in spite of the fact that every time she thought about him, it caused her pain, she resolved to let it be because she couldn't imagine leaving him. And so every night she watched him sleep and the soft hum of his breathing and occasional snore might as well have been the clink, clink sound of a prison doors being locked because she felt so trapped and sad that she just lay there next to him and let the tears soak through her pillows.

She had married John for love. Even though she had circled back around to allow money to become a factor in her relationship, she loved him as best as she knew how and yet, here he was, loving someone else. And what was worse, she had nothing to show for all her years of marriage. On those dark nights, though she would be loathe to admit it, she allowed herself to fantasize about what life would be like if he was no longer alive. For many in Nigerian society, being a widow is still more acceptable than a divorcee.

Her feelings were complicated, like most women who never had thought they would ever be in this situation and as such, never knew what to do, or even how to feel, when confronted with such a problem. It was like a seesaw: hate one moment and love the next. Despite the images of the texts firmly imprinted in her mind, right down to the font, sometimes, when they spent time together, it was as if they fell into old ways. There were weekends, when he stayed home and played with the kids and then they made dinner together. Once he made rice and stew that was too salty, but she ate it anyway and they laughed like they had before. That night, he remarked on how much weight she had lost and when he led her to the bedroom that night, she allowed him to make love to her. She responded to his kisses, but her eyes stayed closed and she faked the sounds of pleasure because all she could see was an image of him touching another woman.

She constantly replayed what she had overheard over and over in her mind and every time she found herself slipping into a comfortable place with him, like a pebble in her shoe, it reminded her that he was lying, cheating bastard who wasn't worthy of her love. So her pendulum swings continued, and on good days she felt only a little bit crazy.

Finally in the middle of the darkest part of one night, when she couldn't sleep despite taking a near overdose of sleeping pills, she decided to fight for her sanity as well as her marriage. She would no longer play the part of the silent, praying, wounded wife. She was going to scream. She decided that she had to confront him and tell him all she knew. She would take advantage of his guilt and shame and demand that he stopped seeing that Natalie person and they would rebuild their marriage. She knew he would beg and she hoped that as she heard his words and witnessed his contrition that then maybe she would be able to forgive him, but whether she did or not, she would have to make him pay first and then they would move forward.

Chapter 15

# Chika
## Fine boy, no pimples

Lagos was very hot. Chika sat in the vinyl covered chair in the customer service office at her bank agitated by more than the weather, sweat was pooling at the small of her back and her shirt was sticking to her skin. The dull ticking sound of the ceiling fan irritated her and she was two steps away from being irate. She had been dealing with the same issue over and over again. Her ATM card kept giving her problems and the fact that she had to keep coming in to sort things out had become a major inconvenience.

"Sorry ma," Her banker said, leaning back in a casual way in his chair, further infuriating her. She watched as he twirled a pen in his fingers and half listened to his weak explanations and apologies for the problems with her account.

She interrupted him saying, "You know what Alade, no offense, but I need to talk to your manager." Chika clasped her fingers together and placed them in her lap trying to keep her cool.

"Ah, ah madam, it has not come to that now," Alade said. He dropped the pen and sat up straight. He had become flustered and Chika knew that he was probably trying to avoid a reprimand. Customer service was important in banking especially with account holders with significant balances. However, at this point, Chika could care less about the man before her. She looked at him in disbelief as she listened to his words. He had promised her for more than a week that he would fix the problem and she had found herself stranded on more than one occasion because she rarely traveled around with cash. She was just irritated enough to lose her temper, but she not only didn't want to waste energy on this little man who was inconsequential to her, she also knew that it was important to protect her brand as a coach and guru of sorts, so she closed her eyes and used a calming technique that she had learned. She thought of a beach and imagined birds chirping as she took a deep breath, and then she pictured the waves crashing against the shore as she let out her breath, only then did she speak; her words, measured and heavy.

"Alade, I don't want to get upset. Please go and get your manager." Alade was not to be deterred, so he pleaded his case once more, "Madam, please, if you can just bear with me…"

Chika groaned because she couldn't stand to hear another word. She stood up and got her purse. Alade jumped up too in response. "Okay, Madam, it's alright, it's alright, please calm down and take your seat," Alade quickly said, at the same time gesturing to a female assistant and saying to her, "please bring Madam some refreshments quick, quick! Madam, please wait, I am coming, please," he said, backing out of the room, still pleading. "Just wait, let me bring my manager."

Chika started to nod as she watched him, but at the door he bumped into a handsome man. Chika became so distracted and she couldn't take her eyes off the intruder. She watched how Alade responded to him and realized that he wasn't a customer like herself.

"Sorry sir," Alade said to the man, bowing in deference. The man barely acknowledged him, looking right at Chika. Chika met his gaze and their eyes were locked in it for a few seconds.

"What seems to be the problem here?" he asked. His voice was smooth and deep, it reminded Chika of her favorite crooners from times long past. She had forgotten her irritation as she took this beautiful specimen of manhood in through all of her senses. He was dressed in a navy pinstripe European cut suit that showed off his broad shoulders and narrow waist in a perfect way. He filled the air with a delicate balance of musk and citrus. She began to wonder how his hands, which were large with long fingers devoid of any jewelry, would feel around her waist. She was so involved in her thoughts that she barely heard Alade respond to him.

"No problem sir, I am just helping Madam," Alade said, still doing some cross between bowing and prostrating. Being a petite man, he looked even smaller next to the tall, broad-chested man. The man looked at her, staring into her eyes. Chika struggled to find her voice.

"You must be the manager," she said, covering up her discomposure by sticking out her hand in greeting.

He smiled as he took her hand with one hand and covered it with the other. "Sort of," he said and his lips curled into a smile, his eyes never leaving hers. He lifted her hand to his mouth and with full, well shaped lips, kissed the skin just above her fingers. Chika shuddered as an image of him sucking on her fingers flashed through her mind. She shook her head in shock and tried to focus on the matter at hand. Alade reminded them both that he was still in the room by speaking. Again Chika compared him, thinking that his voice was more of a squeak in contrast to smooth baritone from the man before her.

"Madam, this is not my manager. This is Mr Collins Obaru, he is actually our MD," Alade asserted. Collins raised his eyebrows in acknowledgment of the introduction and his smile was a cross between naughty and nice.

"Oh," Chika said, retrieving her hand, noting that Collins took his time to release her hand to ensure maximum skin to skin contact. Again, Chika was distracted by thoughts in her head.

"Alade is it?" Collins said, turning his attention to the young man before him. Chika felt the energy shift. It was as if she had been basking in the sun and a cloud had covered its glow. Alade seemed to grow in response to Collins focused attention.

"Yes sir," he responded. Collins rewarded him with a patient smile, then spoke in a curt tone, "Go and see Abdul and tell him to do whatever it takes to make Ms…?" He stopped turning to her, his eyes teasing her as he watched her respond.

"Okoye, Chika Okoye," she said feeling feverish at the way he gazed at her.

"Ms Okoye. Alade, go and tell Abdul to sort out whatever the problem is immediately. I want it resolved before Ms Okoye and I come back from lunch, we must keep all our customers happy."

Chika knew she should be irritated at his presumption that she would have lunch with him, but as she watched Alade fly out of the room like a frightened moth, she found herself nodding in agreement when Collins turned to her to ask, "If that's alright with you of course?" They walked out of the office building, his hand was at the small of her back guiding her to his car. Her whole body tingled and she felt so out of control.

She had read about sensations like this in romance novels, but she always felt the writers exaggerated because she had never experienced it before. She sat back in the leather seat of his Mercedes sedan and watched as he filled the space next to her. When his knee casually touched hers as he leaned forward to tell the driver to take them to a well known Chinese restaurant, the currents that washed over her were so intense, that she felt as if she was vibrating.

"I am sorry that I commandeered you like that in there," Collins spoke softly, sounding almost shy. "I don't know what came over me, but I was on my way to lunch when I saw you in that office and I had to stop and talk to you," he said, putting his hand on his head. "At the risk of sounding like every other man you meet, you are very, very, beautiful. I guess I lost my head. Thank you for agreeing to share a meal with me, I must say you have made my week." He smiled. Chika felt heat rising through her face, causing her cheeks to redden. She raised her hand to her face, self conscious. Collins continued talking in that voice that could be on late night radio. "You must be quite something," he said, "from the way you are dressed, it's easy to see that you are quite sophisticated and probably a powerful career woman right? But somehow you are still demure enough to blush." He grinned as she blushed even more and smiled a little. His chest rose as he spoke again. "I feel quite fortunate to have met you today. I can tell already that you are quite a special lady. Next I'll find out you are still a virgin." At that statement, Chika tried to look out of the window to hide her feelings. Collins who was watching her closely didn't miss her embarrassment, then he exclaimed "No way! You must be kidding me?" he said, clapping his hands together and laughing aloud. "Unbelievable!"

Chika felt a flash of anger. "Excuse me. I thought I was invited to lunch and not an interrogation!" she retorted feeling indignant. She had been laughed at before and while she was not a virgin, having had an unfortunate night with her long standing boyfriend at university who attended church and fellowship with her daily, but dumped her like month old rank trash after she gave into his pressures, she had been abstinent for many years and was not going to let this man, suave though he may be, denigrate her decision.

"Oh, please, don't be offended. I apologize, really," he said contrite, looking at her with an expression that was a mix of alarm and amusement. "I am just amazed that women like you still exist," he said putting his hand on his heart. "I meant no disrespect honestly. Please forgive me," he said, flashing that butter melting smile again. Chika couldn't help but smile in response and nod even before she had decided to forgive him. He was quite charismatic, she realized.

"It's alright," she said, smiling and leaning back into the seat. "I have always had a problem wearing my emotions on my sleeve," she said. Then she cut her eyes at him and started feeling flirtatious. "Plus, you must know you have a powerful effect on women, I mean you are no plain Jane yourself!" she said stroking his ego a little.

He laughed again and with that, they fell into an easy rapport that lasted the two hours of traffic to the restaurant and an hour and a half spent enjoying a wonderful meal and even a glass of wine or two against her better judgment. They talked about culture and politics and his youth spent in London and France and her recent return and fear of okadas. By the time they drove back to her office, Chika felt such a connection that she wondered if God had finally sent her the man she had been waiting for.

"I have really enjoyed my day with you, I don't remember a time when I laughed so much while gazing at such an exquisite face," he said as they pulled into his parking space at the bank. He instructed the driver to go and get Alade, while they lingered in the car. When the driver left, he leaned in for a kiss and she met his lips without question. As they kissed, she luxuriated in the physical and emotional feelings she experienced. She felt dizzy when he finally pulled away. When he placed his hands on her shoulders and asked, "May I see you tomorrow?", Chika's stomach churned with delight. She nodded, handing him her card. He smiled like a player who had just scored a touchdown. "I'll call you tonight okay?" he said. All she could do was nod like a parrot because her tongue was still caught up in the memory of the taste of his mouth.

He opened the car door and got out first, reaching back to help her out. As she came out of the car, trying not to let her skirt ride up, she felt a bit embarrassed because she noticed that Alade stood there with a large envelope and a knowing look on his face. She pushed away the feeling of alarm that rose up within her, it was if someone had turned the lights on in a late night party and she began questioning her recent actions. What had she just done? She asked herself even as she watched Collins settle with Alade and kiss her gently on the cheek. She went from feeling elated to slightly ill in the time it took for him to say goodbye. She didn't even know this man. She thanked Alade and turned just in time to see Collins wave to her as he strode away quickly, mouthing "I'll call you". She retreated quickly to the sanctuary of her car and sank into the seat, responding home to the driver's queries of where to go.

She felt strange. Torn. She didn't even ask him if he was available. She knew better. The fever had left her and she felt as if she could now think clearly. Collins Obaru. She had never met a man quite like him. He was so self assured. She shook her head. She was being naïve. What were the odds of a man like that being available? He was too perfect, too charming, too good to be true. She touched her lips. What had happened to her? Had she become so desperate she could no longer use her head to discern the suitability of a man? Since when did she go around kissing men she had just met? She groaned aloud and lay back in the owner's corner of the car. She was exhilarated and disgusted. She shook her head again, hoping to shake loose the doubts or the memories of how her body responded to his touch or both. Her phone vibrated. *I must be going crazy because I miss you already.* Collins had texted. She smiled inspite of herself. But she could hear the voice in her head. This is Lagos, and there are no smoother men in the world. And this one had a double education in Paris. She contemplated ignoring it, but even as she did, her fingers started to tap her phone. "I'll admit to feeling just as crazy, but I have one question, she typed: *Are you married?"* She hit the send button. She could almost hear him pause before a reply came. "Divorced". But promise me you won't write me off until I call you tonight?" he said. She frowned. Divorced, not necessarily a good thing, but it meant he was indeed available. Once again, she banished the thought and rolled down her window to purchase a glossy magazine. She flipped through the copy and then spoke to her driver "Okey, you know what, take me to the office instead." She knew working with images and figures would clear her head.

# City Life Magazine
## Gossip Page
## |"Guess who?"

There is a phenomenon that we at *City Life* need to bring to the attention of the general populace. We have noticed that it is a contagious and worrisome situation and because we are so concerned we have gathered and analyzed the necessary data that allows us to conclude that we have identified patient zero.

Our aristocrat husbands are morphing into something else, something that is not quite human. Take for instance, our patient zero. This man is often seen in society pages of various glossies, nationally and internationally. He is a man of note. In fact he was once a prize winning journalist and media personality with the pre-requisite bombshell of a wife. However his fortune has taken a nose-dive, though he tells people that he is able to keep his current jet setting lifestyle filled with Range Rovers and trips to Italy because he made some solid investments that paid off. Rumor has it that he has just one solid investment, his wife.

It seems patient zero has morphed into a cross between a cuckold and a pimp. You see this man pretends to be the alpha male who takes care of his family and his wife pretends to be the typical oliaku—eater of her husband's wealth—but we at *City Life* have gotten the real deal on the situation. His wife works! I know; we were aghast as well. More so, when we discover that this former beauty queen does her work on her back in various hotel rooms with various politicians and business men alike. In fact, we have it on good authority that the husband has actually been part of setting some of these runs up. They have three children. Well, let's retract that statement. There are three children living in their house. You know what they say, mummy's baby; daddy's maybe!

# Chapter 16

# Karen
# The rich also cry, but they carry their own tissue

Karen hated medical buildings. Something about doctors' offices made her feel uneasy, but since they had been trying for a baby, she had been forced to get over her qualms because she and Dele had seen several doctors in their quest to procreate. They were in the process of trying a second round of IVF with the hope of finally conceiving a child. Karen was trying for twins or triplets. She wanted the maximum result with the least amount of damage done to her body. She was sitting in this new doctor's office, and she kept crossing and uncrossing her legs to limit the exposure of her skin with the vinyl covering of the chair. She watched the doctor speak with her hands and she noticed that she badly needed a manicure. This doctor was not their usual one, because at her last appointment her gynecologist found some irregularities and had referred her to this new doctor who specialized in difficult cases. The doctor finally clasped her hands together and stopped talking. There was a long silence between them. She cleared her throat and repeated herself. Karen heard the doctor speaking, but she couldn't make sense of the words because there was so much noise. It was as if there was a train passing right through the room and the sound was deafening.

"Karen," the doctor spoke again, getting up and walking around her desk and sitting down next to her, "I know it is a lot of information to take in, but I'll be with you throughout and you will receive the very best care possible". She paused and put her hand on Karen's forearm, asking "Are you okay?" Karen finally turned to look at her and allowed herself to receive what she was saying.

The doctor continued, "I know this might have come as a shock to you, but I don't want you to lose hope, I have seen worse situations turn around. Medicine is continually advancing and new treatments come out for cancer every day." Karen understood what the doctor said, but it all seemed incomprehensible to her. Surely the doctor was talking about someone else, she thought. She couldn't have ovarian cancer. How could that be possible? She sat there straight backed, silently refuting what was being said because clearly there was a mistake. She was careful about what she ate, ran five or more miles a day and rarely indulged like so many of the women around her, who let themselves go. She had been so disciplined and now this woman in a white coat was telling her that she was going to die?

As the woman rattled on about conventional and alternative treatments, Karen zoned out, choosing to focus instead on the cover of the magazine that lay in her lap. It was an old issue of *Harper's Bazaar*; a magazine for America's socialites. The woman on the cover sat on an ornate sofa in her expansive living room.

"Karen...Karen!" The doctor roused her from her daydream. "Have you been listening?" Karen nodded her head. "Dr. Livingston, I want you to run the tests again please" Dr. Livingston nodded. "Of course, but I should tell you I already ran them twice and the results are still the same, and of course I will be happy to refer you for a second opinion, but I just want you to know that time is not on your side, you should really begin treatment immediately. Karen, again I am so sorry." The doctor leaned forward and looked at her "Karen, I know the prognosis for ovarian cancer at this stage is poor, but I am the kind of doctor who believes in miracles, and I and all my colleagues will do everything in our power to see that you live." For the first time in

Karen's adult life, she began to cry in front of someone else.

The tears fell like a miraculous rain after a drought, thick and heavy, forming stains of muddy black mascara on her blouse. Dr. Livingston passed her a box of tissues. "I am going to refer you to another doctor, who will be crucial in your treatment plan. Dr. Hedaye. She is an oncologist who uses a very effective hybrid of traditional and alternative therapies." Karen just blinked in response, regaining her composure somewhat. "She is a remarkable doctor, Karen. With her help I have seen many patients go from terminal to remission. Her work is unconventional but her results are very encouraging."

Karen just continued crying quietly. She wanted to stop, but the tears kept coming. She heard Dr. Livingston talk about the mind-body-soul connection and implore her to follow Dr. Hedaye's prescribed therapy no matter how strange it might seem, and she kept having flash backs to her mother's cold, clammy body and her father's face at the funeral. He had never shown her much affection when she was alive, but he wept like a baby at her gravesite and gave a moving eulogy to the woman whom he stopped sharing a bed with just a few years into their marriage. He called her the eternal love of his life on that dreary rainy day. Karen remembered being disgusted. She recalled how many times her mother would argue with him about his constant indiscretions. She had vivid recollections about nights when her mother would exchange liquor for tears as she sat up waiting for the man the world called her husband. She remembered moments when they both went out in matching aso ebi; her gele headtie matching his cap, and when they stood for pictures, he would place his arm around her in a protective and loving manner. Even as she sat in the doctor's office listening to what amounted to a discussion about her own mortality, she wondered if her father could have truly loved her mother; if his tears were genuine. Immediately, she visualized her own funeral, what would Dele say, would he also be moved to tears, did he even love her at all? She told herself that she didn't care but the tears brimming in her eyes seemed to betray her true hopes of a relationship that she never asked for.

As Dr. Livingston sat next to her, patting her hand, Karen began to collect herself. The tears finally ceased and she looked down at her blouse, which was now streaked with the light brown mix of tears and cafe au lait foundation. She retrieved her hand from Dr. Livingston, who said nothing, but watched her. Karen wiped her face, pulled out a scarf from her handbag, and draped it expertly across her shoulders, hiding the offending stains; she then pulled out her compact and reapplied her makeup.

When she was done, she looked at Dr. Livingston. "Thank you very much for your time and suggestions. If you feel seeing Dr. Hedaye is the best course of action, then let us begin immediately." She began rising from her chair. Dr. Livingston offered her some literature on a cancer support group. Karen waved it away. "I don't need support, I need treatment." The doctor nodded in understanding.

"Would you like me to schedule an appointment for you and your husband to answer any questions that he might have?" the doctor asked. She was sitting at her desk now, making notes in Karen's chart. Karen's eyes flashed wide open. "No!" Dr. Livingston smiled, but her eyes were determined. "Karen, you will need him to be part of your support team." Karen looked straight at Dr. Livingston. "I will say this just once, my husband is not and never has been part of my support team." She gathered her things and walked to the door. "Please have your office staff call me with the appointment date," she said, stopping to speak as she placed her diamond ringed fingers on the door handle. "And thank you."

She didn't look back as she opened the door and shut it quietly behind her. She walked with her head held high and her back straight out of the office. She kept walking until she found herself standing at the entrance to her hotel. It was perfect timing because her heels had begun to pinch her feet just as she walked into the lobby of the Waldorf Astoria hotel. She began to weaken as she rode the elevator up to her room. She opened the door to her room and it took all of her strength to remove her stained blouse and skirt, put on her nightclothes and get herself into bed. She had just started to drift into sleep when her phone buzzed for her attention. She looked at it, lifting her head slightly from the pillow. It was an uncharacteristic checking up email from Dele.

"Darling, how are you? How did the doctor's visit go? I will be in New York next week actually. Are you checked into the Waldorf? I've been trying to reach you for hours. For some reason, I find myself worried about you. Please let me know you are well. Currently in London, will see you in a week." Karen raised her eyebrows as she contemplated the unusual tone of the message; it was almost loving. She lifted herself up to type a response. "I am well. At Waldorf, usual suite. See you soon." Then she switched off her phone and lay back in the bed. She fluffed the pillows a bit and tried to get comfortable, but she couldn't find her sweet spot, no matter how many pillows she stacked up. Exasperated, she put on the television and tried to let the news anchors voice take her mind off the words the doctor had said, but it didn't work, she switched channels and turned to the shopping channel, she hoped the monotony of mediocre products being hawked would bore her enough for her mind to be lulled into a place of nonchalance. Then almost as if she had been bitten by something, she jumped out of bed and started taking off her clothes. She didn't want to feel anything on her skin; even her favorite silk pajamas were irritating her. She stripped naked and got back into the bed, turned the TV off then she pulled the covers over her and closed her eyes. The coolness of the sheets soothed her somewhat and she fell asleep within minutes without the aid of pharmaceuticals, and she dreamt. Dreams where she was falling and flying in intervals; fear and hope combined.

# Chapter 17

## Lola
# Is love is not stronger than pride?

Lola sat at her mirror and stared. She looked past the acne spots that were prominent on her clean and bare skin. She looked past her reflection and got lost. All her life she had wanted to be married; to be Mrs somebody. When John had chosen her, she was overjoyed. On the surface, she had what everyone wanted: a handsome, caring husband, two wonderful children, a comfortable and luxurious life. She remembered running into an old classmate at the supermarket a few days back. The woman had said to her, "I wish I could be you" as she remarked on how nice her handbag was. She smiled at the woman but in a moment of transparency, she took her hand and said, "No, you don't, believe me." There was a time when she felt as if she had a charmed life, but things had started to change as John acquired wealth. As his stature increased, he also became more arrogant and more difficult to talk to. He valued her opinion less and less, especially because she was just a housewife in his eyes. Funny thing was that she was *just* a housewife because he had insisted that she focus solely on raising the children. "I want to take care of you and my children." He had told her one night as he watched her rocking Kevin when he was still an infant. "I don't want my wife to have to work," he said. At the time it sounded romantic and she threw herself into being a mother. But before long, he was complaining that she was too mama-ish and got her a nanny so she could, in his words "get herself together".

Whenever she reminisced about her life, pre-marriage, she

barely recognized the woman in her memories. That woman dreamed of touching lives with her music. Now she settled for the occasional solo in church because John wasn't always comfortable with her singing. He even criticized her voice from time to time, saying that it sounded like she was a little off key. When she considered his "constructive" criticism, she wondered why she had ever believed a man who knew nothing about music. There were moments before she found out about his cheating when she had considered what life would be like without him. She sometimes felt like he had swallowed her up and she had lost herself completely. She fantasized about living alone like her sister in Chicago. She had a town home and raised her son alone after her husband left her for another woman. She used to pity her but now, her sister had created a successful events and media company and lived a beautiful life with her son who was in high school already. Meanwhile her former brother-in-law, who was so full of himself because he was a doctor, was just in the news because he was arrested for some kind of fraud and malpractice. She thought about confiding in her sister, but she knew she couldn't. She couldn't share this with anyone, it was just too shameful. She had always prided herself in being the perfect wife. She shuddered, as she decided that this would be her cross and her cross alone.

She kept looking at herself in the mirror. They had an event to attend but she had no desire to go. She was physically tired. Since she discovered his betrayal, she found herself unable to eat, and as such she was wasting away. Her collarbones were jutting out. In spite of her concern about her life, when she looked into the mirror, she smiled because she had lost so much weight; she was finally very slim, even looking almost waif-like, like a model. She preened for a minute, turning one way and then the other. Then she had a thought, that made her heart skip for a moment. Maybe it would all be alright, she mused. After all, she was now the right size and beautiful, surely John would forget all about the other woman now, she finished her thought. Surely he would see that she was too stunning to take for granted. She smiled as she imagined all the eyes that would admire her that evening. She loved her gown, a slightly more risqué version of a gown worn at the Oscars by one of the more glamorous movie stars. It was cut precariously low and would have looked obscene on a more endowed woman, but looked high fashion on her. She had paid a pretty penny for it, but the fact that it was one of a kind sealed the deal for her. She couldn't stand to look like anyone else. She had drifted away in a daydream and was smiling for the paparazzi when John intruded on her reverie.

"Sweetheart!" he said, looking at her with approval, "you look like a movie star!" and pulled her into his arms. Then he frowned, and held her at arm's length, looking at her up and down. "My God Lola, you are down to skin and bones!" He exclaimed after feeling the span of her waist. "Good Lord! No more dieting, please," he continued. "I noticed you haven't been eating and thank God you have lost weight, but this is getting ridiculous!" he ranted. "Slim is fine, but you are a step above refugee level, I beg start eating!" he said as he walked away into the bathroom.

She watched him walk away and turned back to the mirror, but it was too late. The glamazon was gone, in her stead stood an ugly, over done, sickly looking woman with no sex appeal. Just like that, with a handful of John's words, her confidence evaporated. She frowned and was rewarded with the reminder that her forehead was already forming wrinkles and she couldn't help but squeal in frustration causing John to shout out from the bathroom asking if she was okay.

"No!" she wanted to holler. "No! I am not okay. I am sick and tired of trying to contort myself into some acceptable image for you and everyone else. No! I am here watching my skin age in per second increments and topping it all off with the knowledge that my precious husband has a mistress. I am definitely not okay!" She listened for an answer even though she knew one was not forthcoming since she had said the entire thing inside her head. Damn John Amadi, she thought for the thousandth time that week. Damn him to hell. She had planned to confront him about a thousand times, but she couldn't bring herself to do it.

"Lola! We are going to be late! Aren't you done getting ready? I'm going to the car!" John said, walking out of the bathroom and buckling his belt. The toilet was still flushing in the background and Lola noticed that he hadn't washed his hands. She was suddenly filled with disgust and then the words swelled in her mouth, forcing her mouth open. "John, I know about Natalie!"

He stood still with his back to her. For a few seconds, he didn't move and neither did she.

"What did you say?" He asked, turning around slowly.

"I said, I know about you and your whore!" Lola said, gaining confidence from his obvious discomfiture. John just stared at her.

It was as if a dam broke and every hidden hateful thing she held in her heart broke forth and tumbled out of her lips. She watched him pale as she called him, a despicable excuse for a husband. She told him that he disgusted her. She told him how his spare tire and sagging equipment filled with her such revulsion that she sometimes threw up. It was then that he crossed the room in three quick steps and hit her so hard, that she fell to the ground.

At first she couldn't believe he had hit her. She was shocked into silence, but only for a minute because she became so enraged that she got up quickly and got back in his face. And this time she took her time. She kept saying things she knew would wound him because she wanted him to hurt, she wanted him to feel the contempt she had been carrying around for months.

"Shut up!" he roared in response, "just shut up!" And he hit her again. She reeled back, but she didn't fall and she didn't shut up. She couldn't. She couldn't stop screaming obscenities at him. She could no longer control the anger that had been bubbling up inside of her. Anger that was currently spilling onto her life and burning through her marriage like hot lava.

He began to pace the room as her words filled the air. She was standing on the other side of the room now, using her voice as a weapon. He started towards her and she shrunk back when she saw his face, in that moment, she feared for her life. He charged at her, but stopped short and then he backed away from her and started punching the wardrobe so hard that he put a hole in the door and bloodied his fist. He looked over at her as if he had something terrible he wanted to do, but then he stopped and walked out of the room. Lola sank into a chair in relief. She thought about his face and she had no words to describe his expression. Just then she heard the door slam as an exclamation point.

She sank from the chair, down on to the floor; feeling spent. She listened to the gate creak open and heard his engine revving as he drove out. It was only then that she picked herself off the floor. She went to the bathroom and took a long shower, her tears mingling with the cool water from the faucet. When she finished, she got into her pajamas and walked over to the boys' bedroom, where the nanny looked at her with large, concerned eyes. Lola wondered how much she had heard. Nothing was ever hidden in this house. Despite the concrete walls, sometimes sound carried as if they were made of paper. She ignored the nanny's unspoken questions and told her to take care of the boys and put them in bed because she wasn't feeling well. She gave them both a quick kiss and walked back to her bedroom. She put the air conditioner on the highest setting, then got into her bed, pulled up the covers and lay there with her eyes open. She thought perhaps that she should pray, but she was too agitated. Finally, she fell asleep and slept so deeply that she didn't realize that John's car didn't return to the compound that night.

# Chapter 18

# Chika
## Wherever you go, there you are

Chika looked at herself in the mirror and she had to admit that Bibi the new makeup artist at the studio had hands of magic. Chika knew that she had been blessed with a pretty face, but Bibi had made her look simply stunning. She blinked, thinking that she barely recognized herself. She looked like a model in a magazine. *You don't just look different, you are different,* her inner voice chimed in, chastising her.

She had been acting out of character for the last few weeks. She hadn't even been to church in as much time. Ify, the pastor's wife had left her more than a few messages and she hadn't returned any of them. She had no explanations that would be acceptable. She couldn't tell her Pastor that she felt overwhelmed; couldn't admit to her that at the moment she was so caught up in her life that church activities felt like a burden. She couldn't say that she felt just a little bit lost and carried away.

It wasn't as if she had stopped believing, she still read her Bible from time to time and enjoyed good preaching. At first, when she started missing services, she would always send her assistant to get the CDs, but these days she rarely made time to listen to them. Instead she had thrown herself into work and all that came with it. The media frenzy to promote the new show was exhausting. She had been interviewed by all the major magazines and a few morning talk shows, but even though making the rounds was tiring, it seemed well worth it, early reviews of her show, *A New You,* were excellent. The show was powerful and Chika had to admit that she was just as touched by the segments as her audience, and even though she was in the position of teacher, she often left the stage feeling as if she had been the student. There were so many people going through difficult things.

She was getting ready to tape a new episode with a woman whose husband had divorced her because she had a third miscarriage. Chika sighed in anticipation of the woman's agony and made a mental note to ask if she had waterproof mascara on because segments like this always made her cry. Why were some men such beasts? Why couldn't all men be decent? She smiled and asked herself the real question on her mind: why couldn't they be like Collins?

She spent most of her spare time with him. Each encounter was more exciting than the last, and though she still had that slight nagging feeling of unease, it was displaced by the heady feeling of intoxication she felt when he was near her. She found herself more attracted to him than she thought possible. He was so romantic and exceptionally sweet, and she wondered if it was just fear that made her feel that things were just a little too perfect. He always knew what to say. He wrote her emails that made her legs weak and whispered things that made her feel warm in places she dared not mention. He had her from that first lunch. Their affair had redefined the term, whirlwind romance. She couldn't believe that she had fallen for him so quickly and though she had some concern about his divorce, she chose to ignore them because his lure was so strong.

Chika had no doubt that he had been with many women; just watching him she could tell that he was extremely experienced, but she believed that he was a reformed player perhaps, after all he was now in his late forties, divorced and probably wanting to settle down. During their conversations he always surprised her, showing himself to be vulnerable and sensitive even while maintaining his alpha male personality. He talked to her about the breakdown of his marriage and even his regrets about his actions.

He admitted that he had been unfaithful, citing the irresponsible and selfish nature of youth as a cause and he told her that the truth was that somewhere deep down, he still loved his ex, though he was no longer in love with her. Chika balked a little at that, but she rationalized that since they had children together after all, how could she expect him not to have some measure of love for his ex-wife. He had long since moved on though, he reassured her, saying that his ex had become a bitter, angry woman and while he recognized that he was complicit in her transformation, he could not allow his future to be completely destroyed by her inability to accept him as a changed person and to look forward with him and not at the past. He was more remarkable that she had imagined. Here was a man willing to take responsibility, she thought, yet he was not going to get mired down by someone else's refusal to see how he had grown. Chika resolved right then to give him the love he had been missing. He came over on most nights after work and they just relaxed and watched movies, or listened to music like teenagers, and the last weekend, he had surprised her with a quick weekend trip to Obudu Cattle Ranch, where they stayed in the same room.

The weekend had been tough because Chika was trying hard to stay true to her beliefs and not be intimate with him. Chika had shared her stance on sex with Collins on one of their very early dates. He said nothing, just smiled, but he still kept asking her out. So Chika assumed he accepted her rules, but like every man, she expected that he would still try. So she was not surprised when on that trip, when the manager told her that he had no other room except the king suite. Chika strengthened her resolve and though they slept in the same bed and they made out a bit, she held fast to her rule through grace and prayer. If the weekend had lasted longer than Sunday, she was unsure that she would have continued to hold out on him because now, when he touched her, she trembled.

She looked over at the roses on her desk. She had made a

remark about red roses being so prosaic a few weeks back, teasing him when he sent her the first bouquet. He had laughed, saying that he had never been referred to as dull before, then he gave a stern look and told her he hadn't been tested on his vocabulary since he was in secondary school. She cringed because it had been a test, but she hadn't meant to be so obvious. She liked a man who was intelligent and a good vocabulary did it for her every time.

He claimed to be irritated by her test, but still sent her roses every couple of days. He made sure they were anything but red. The first were a wonderful shade of orange, then some sort of hybrid, and the next was the deepest, most vibrant fuchsia, and then they were these lush, full yellow. Each one came with a card that said something to mock her vocabulary test, "My darling, even these cannot compete with your prodigious beauty!" She laughed again as she reached towards the bouquet currently sitting on her table, maybe today she would wear a bloom in her hair.

Even as she plucked the flower and placed it into her hair, her inner voice spoke up again: could Collins be the one? The one made just for her? But then again, was she really being herself? Who had she become? Who was she really? This glamour puss who rarely made it to church? Who was she and what was she really doing? The voice in her head warned her citing the verse "charm is deceitful". She shook her head to get rid of the thought and the bloom fell out of her hair on to the floor. She was about to bend down to get it when she was interrupted by Gbenga, who gently rushed her onto the stage. As he guided her, he put his arms around her, and even though she felt no particular attraction to him, the feeling of being safe, reminded her why she wanted a Nigerian man, something about the way they took control was sexy to her. Gbenga's arms were strong and she knew if she fell, he would catch her. Collins arms were stronger still, maybe he was the one. The audience started clapping immediately and she had no more time to ponder on her love life. The show had started and at that moment, it was simply lights, camera, action!

"Hello Nigeria!" she said, turning on the charm that made her so appealing. She looked right into the camera and cooed, "It's a new day, a new life and a new you!" The audience started to clap and she dialed up her smile to full wattage.

"Good evening, friends! What a wonderful day it is today! Welcome to my show, *A New You!*" she said, waving to the audience and the camera at the same time. "Like any day, it comes with its challenges, but this I know for sure, no matter what the day will end and the morning will come again and every day brings with itself, new mercies, new life, new wisdom and a new you!" she preached and the audience started to cheer.

"Today we talk to Ama, who was abandoned by her husband after suffering another devastating miscarriage" She paused to leave room for the expected clucks of sympathy from the audience, and she was not disappointed. She paused again for maximum effect and then continued, dropping her voice by an octave and letting it rise back up as she finished the sentence. "Today she has come here feeling broken, feeling rejected, but together we are going to show her that she is alive, that today is a new day and she is going to discover her new self! Are you with me?"

She was a seasoned speaker and knew how to get the desired response from her audience. Chika started pumping her fist into the air and the audience stood up and cheered, which caused her to smile even wider. "Well then, come on and let's start the show!

# Chapter 19

# Karen
# Breathing

Karen sat up in her bed and sighed. She leaned back against the plush hotel pillows and exhaled again. She didn't feel like getting out of bed, but it was already 9am and she felt like she was wasting the day. She looked over at her bedside table; her phone was flashing. Twelve missed calls. Ten were from Dele. She put the phone down and picked up the journal that was lying next to it. In her preliminary consult, Dr. Hedaye had asked her to journal her emotions. She rolled her eyes just thinking about it. *American psychobabble!* she thought. However she picked up the green leather bound journal and put her pen on the paper.

"I feel like shit!" She wanted to write more, but she couldn't. She searched for the words to describe the emotional chemotherapy she was going through. She couldn't describe the pain she felt at the moment as she tried to relive every humiliation and every betrayal in her years of marriage. It felt like the faucet has been opened, the knob broken off and there was no way to stop the gushing water of agony that was washing over her. She lay back in bed and asked the emptiness around her why this was happening. What did she do wrong? She wanted to know. She ignored Dele and his antics. She learned how to deal with the realities of her life, just like countless other women around her. Sure it had its difficulties, but whose didn't. The fact that her husband was a womanizer didn't bother her, so why should that cause a tumor to build up within her? After all, was she the first or the only one to have a husband who couldn't control himself?

She looked across the room and saw a partial reflection of her face in the mirror. She screamed out loud, "Why!" Why did her body betray her? Why did it turn against her? Was the betrayal of her husband and her father before him not enough? She lay back against the pillows again, feeling drained and spent, but still restless. She opened the drawer next to the bed, her hands fidgety from her emotional state and saw the Bible there. She hissed and shut it. There was no God. Simple. Because even if God was man, he would dispense justice in a better manner. Dele who lived by a code of selfishness, was healthy as a horse, while she lay here dying. What wrong had she done to deserve this punishment? All she had done was survive the life that she had been born into. She didn't choose it, it chose her.

She closed her eyes and tried to turn the direction of her thoughts. It didn't work. She lay there thinking about her death and wondered if Dele would mourn her. She realized Dele would simply bury her and be on to the next, while her life, barely half lived would be over. She felt a tear drop onto her cheek and again she affirmed silently, that there was definitely no God. Images of the life she had lived flashed through her head. People envied her, for her gold and diamonds, but they had no idea how hard and cold her life could be. She went months without ever being hugged as a child; she had learned early how to be strong by watching the lives of the women in her world.

\*\*\*\*\*\*\*\*\*

Karen was already awake when Dele knocked on her hotel room door the next morning. She let him in and he walked into the room carrying coffee and pastries. He smiled widely and gave Karen a long hug. Karen looked at him strangely when she pulled away.

"What's going on Dele?" she asked.

"What do you mean?" he said, trying to pull her back into his embrace. She pushed his hands away.

"Since when were you this touchy feely with me? With you it's normally a kiss on the cheek and text messages. Besides I thought you would end up being too busy to leave London right now, and the IVF clinic didn't need you for this procedure, so why are you here?" Dele smiled sadly and Karen knew immediately. Dr. Livingston had told him. So much for doctor patient confidentiality, she thought. "You know, don't you?"

Dele sat down. He had been standing up, nervous and fidgeting with the breakfast in his hands. He placed his breakfast offering on the dining table.

"Yes. I know," he admitted. "Dr. Livingston felt it was necessary."

He looked at her. "But why didn't you want me to know? Didn't you know I would come immediately?"

He continued speaking and Karen felt as if she was having an out of body experience already. She listened to him tell her that he was so sorry and that he was going to fight the cancer with her, but when he said that he couldn't lose her, Karen shook her head wondering if this was indeed the same man she had been married to for all these years. He kept talking and Karen was confused by his reaction.

"Dele, why are you acting like this is a blow to you. I mean, we have never been close or loving, so why the great show of concern? I am sick, so what?" Karen said, pulling her hotel robe closer. "Are you feeling guilty? I don't have AIDS, I have ovarian cancer. You didn't give this to me, so let yourself off the hook and let's just keep things real." Karen was exasperated.

Dele stood up again and threw his hands up in the air. "My goodness, a man can't win with you! I don't feel guilty Karen. I came here because I care about you. You are my wife. You have cancer and I want to take care of you," he said looking at her.

Karen started to laugh. "Give me a break! You want to take care of me now because I have cancerous cells inside of me? Is that what I needed to do all along to make you be a husband to me? You didn't think I needed taking care of while you ran around with everything in a skirt. Now that I might be dying, you want to play the honorable husband role? Forget it. I don't need you or your pity," she said, her voice low. Crossing her legs, she sat down and leaned back into a silver velvet covered slipper chair by the bed.

Dele groaned. "Karen, why do you make everything so difficult? It's not like that. I don't pity you. I am your husband after all and I really want to be here for you," he said. "Plus Dr. Livingston felt my support would be vital in helping you fight this thing."

Karen raised an eyebrow. "When you spoke to Dr. Livingston, did you tell her that we haven't slept together literally and figuratively in years? Did you tell her how many women you have had during our marriage? Did you tell her that you and I are in a marriage of convenience?"

Dele was taken aback at the force of her words. "Is that what you think our marriage is? A marriage of convenience?" he asked.

Karen stared at him in disbelief. What was wrong with this man? She thought. Is he suffering from some form of dementia? Is this not the same man who last year, bought a house for another woman? Karen put her hand to her temple because she suddenly felt as if she had a headache. Dele continued, "Karen, I am just concerned for you. Regardless of whatever you might think of me, or our failures as a couple, you are still my wife. Isn't it normal that I would be concerned?" he said, sitting down again and fiddling with his monogrammed cufflinks.

Karen was unfazed. "Fine, thanks for your concern, now kindly get out. I would rather deal with this on my own. Like I said, I don't need you."

Dele stood not moving. "Karen, I know this isn't easy, I know how you must be feeling..."

"You have no idea how I am feeling. No idea at all."

"Well, I just mean that I care about you. I want to help you. Let me help you," Dele pleaded.

"Look, I really don't have the energy to argue with you. I am tired. Please leave," Karen said. She stood up from the chair and walked over to the bed to lie down.

"Fine. I'll leave. But I am not leaving New York. I want you to know that I am here when you do need me, Karen. I am here," Dele said.

"Whatever," Karen mumbled as she pulled the covers over her head. She lifted her head up only after she heard the hotel room door close.

She sat up against the pillows and allowed her tears to flow. So now she had been reduced to an object of pity? Dele may have never really been the husband of her dreams, but at least he never looked at her the way he did today. He looked at her like she was already dying. She touched her hair and tried to imagine how she would look bald and sick? Was that what he saw? A disgusting sick person? She couldn't stand it. She wouldn't let anyone see her that way. She would let Dr. Livingston know that she had no right to share her medical information with her husband. She would let her know that she would report her to the medical board if it happened again.

She laid her head back onto the pillows and looked at the crown moldings on the ceiling. She liked this hotel. It reflected her exquisite taste. She began to reminisce about the last party she had thrown that was talked about for months after. The phone rang, interrupting her reverie. She answered. It was Dr. Livingston's assistant.

"Mrs Thompson? This is Ashanti. I would like to inform you about your next appointment with Dr. Hedaye tomorrow morning at 9am. Will that be okay with you?"

Karen told her it would be and got off the phone. She lay in bed for a few more minutes and then she got up. She went to the mirror, inspected her face and fluffed out her hair. "Well, I am not dead yet!" With that she called and asked the concierge to make an appointment with the personal shopping department at Bergdorf's. Cancer or not, she was in New York, one of the fashion capitals of the world and today, she was going to indulge in some retail therapy.

# Chapter 20

## Lola
## Hungry he-goats never get full

The time on the clock flashed at her as if accusing her, *It's 5am, do you know where your husband is?* Lola sat up torn between indignation and fear. Now this was taking it too far. She had called his phones but they were all switched off. She tried to sleep but couldn't. As soon as she drifted off, within minutes her anxiety shook her awake. This was another level.

She had not expected John to react in the way that he did. He had left the house and returned the morning after. At first he denied everything. Then when it became clear that she not only heard the phone conversations, she had also read the damning text messages. John sunk into a chair and confessed. He said he had lost his head. He told her he had no intention of taking it further, in fact he had tried to break it off several times. She meant nothing to him. It was just that she had gotten under his skin somehow.

Lola listened quietly as he professed his love over and over to her. She watched him as he knelt before her and asked for her forgiveness. She knew she was not going to leave him, but she also knew that the part of her that loved him without reservation was now dead. Their relationship would never be the same, but she went through the motions. She allowed her eyes to fill with tears. She asked the questions, she acted out all the drama that she had watched others play out, never knowing that one day, she too would audition for the same role. It seemed to work because he swore to end it with her and even called the other woman in her presence and broke it off.

Lola listened intently as Natalie vacillated between shock and anger. When John, told her that he was ending it because he loved his wife, Natalie screamed, "You love your wife! Now you love her? When you were jumping on me like a hungry animal, you didn't know you had a wife? You bastard! You think you can just use me and then end things when you want? I will deal with you. You and your idiot wife."

Lola stared at John in disgust. He tried to save face by getting sterner with her, but she clearly had the upper hand as her tongue dripped pure venom. "What happened? Your wife found out? So what? Is she the first one? That's why you want to end it? I thought you were a man, I didn't know you were a woman! Useless cretin!"

John hung up. Lola sat in her chair, not moving, not speaking. She couldn't understand it. Her John, the man she loved so much and held in such high regard. This was how low he had chosen to fall? What secrets could that woman's body hold that would have been worth this disgrace? He got up. "Are you satisfied now!" he shouted at her.

Lola stared at him. Why was he mad at her? Was she the one that broke their vows? Was she the one that just belittled him? He was the one that chose to lie down with this mad woman and now he wanted to shout at her. She spoke softly, but her words were heavy and cold as steel. "No, I am not satisfied. Why would I be satisfied? I married you when you had nothing. I helped you build yourself up. I loved you. Only for you to allow this woman who can't even hold a candle to me to pull you down. No, my dear, I am not satisfied at all," Lola said and walked out of the room leaving him to face the man that he had become.

Lola sat in the living room and grabbed one of the sofa pillows to hold onto for comfort. She stroked the soft fabric. How had their life come to this? She pondered. She remembered the first time they met, it was at a wedding of a mutual friend. They sat on the same table. He sat opposite her and they shared a laugh when the pompous man next to her, who had been trying to get her number, spilled red wine on his shirt. Not long after that, he asked her to dance and they talked everyday since.

She remembered the day he told her he loved her. He lived in a studio apartment in Newark and she shared a two bedroom in Brooklyn, so they often spent time at his place. She had just made them dinner. They were sitting on the floor because they had no dining table and she was leaning into his chest. He kissed her. "I love you Lola."

It was simple and clean. And it was everything.

When the opportunity came to move to Lagos. She didn't hesitate. They had just gotten married and she was teaching music at a local middle school. Even though moving to Lagos meant moving away from her producer friends and the singing back up gigs she did on the side, she didn't care. She wanted to be a good wife, so she resolved to follow her husband, wherever, however. She remembered the first moment she was called a wife. The day they walked down the aisle. She had never been happier. Here she was, still a wife. Alone. Angry. Anxious. And here they were. A statistic like so many others. Lola sighed and accepted that her husband wasn't the man she thought he was. It had been weeks since that first confrontation and things were just beginning to go back to what seemed like normal.

They were working on their marriage. He had promised to stop seeing the woman, but lately Lola suspected he hadn't. After the confrontation, they had agreed to begin going to counseling at the church, but he had canceled the last few appointments and had even stopped going to church all together. She knew if he wanted to continue his affair, his partner in crime would be glad to. There were so many women like her in Lagos who didn't care if they were a man's anything on the side. They were like broken down plastic dolls, desperate to be played with. It didn't matter who and it didn't matter for how long. She knew that the Natalie woman would be content to subsist on whatever scraps of affection, time and money, she could get. But if he had gone back, Lola wondered what her next step would be? How would she handle it? She needed to push him, because she couldn't allow this to continue indefinitely, she thought, but the wrong sort of force would push him right into the other woman's arms. A friend of hers went through something similar and she demanded that her husband stop seeing his mistress and adhere to her new rules. Unfortunately her ultimatum backfired when he pushed back and she had nothing to anchor her. He eventually became so bold that he even starting entertaining his mistresses in public places. She knew that when men got to the point that they stopped hiding their indiscretions, then the affair was more than just physical, it usually meant they had become so emotionally involved with a woman or that they had become so resentful of their wives that they either couldn't control their feelings or no longer cared what their wives thought. She sat there thinking. John came through and left the house, mumbling something about having to attend a meeting. She said nothing and continued to sit quietly and think, until the day turned into evening and the evening into night.

She wished she knew how to pray. Sweat drenching prayers like the wives of the womanizers in the movies she often watched on African Magic channel on cable. She looked through her phone, wondering who could she call. She resolved to get a pastor she could keep on speed dial. Finally she got up and went to the bedroom and resolved to go to sleep. Just as she forced her eyes to close, she heard the door open. She listened as John tiptoed into the room, trying not to wake her. He took off his shirt which she was sure would be scented with another woman's perfume and quietly removed his shoes. When he unbuckled his belt, it clattered to the floor and she took the opportunity to question him.

"Are you just coming in?" He was startled. "You woke me up!" she said, sitting up and switching on the lights. He looked sheepish and guilty.

"So sorry sweetheart, had a late meeting that ran on and on."

Her raised eyebrows hinted at her thoughts, *was this joker for real?* Nigerian men and their meetings. She hissed in spite of herself. The way they talked about their "meetings" you would think they were more powerful than the president of the United States, the UK prime minister and the leaders of the Arab world combined.

"What kind of meeting lasts until 2am and even then, couldn't you even call me? John, you know the counselor said we need to work on rebuilding trust," she said pouting in frustration.

She watched as her husband took off his undershirt and dropped it on the floor as if nothing had happened. "Lola, give me a break. You know I've been trying to close this deal with Alhaji Musa for a few months now. It's finally done! I had to wait for him to be done with some other people first so my time wasn't my own."

He paused and Lola knew he was waiting for her to say everything was ok, but she didn't believe him and so she remained silent. He tried again, "I was with Gota, sweetie. If you don't believe me, you can call him." His continued insistence at his innocence, only made him appear more guilty.

"Whatever, John!" Lola said and turned away from him, so he would not see her pained expression.

"Lola, come on," he said as he stripped off his boxers and got into bed. "I am sorry, okay?" Lola ignored him. As far as she was concerned, he could put hot pepper sauce on his apologies and choke on them. He put his hand on her shoulder and continued using soothing words, but his words were like glass shattering against a wall. Lola was so irritated that even her silence was condemning. He moved and kissed her neck and she stiffened in disbelief. He went further by reaching for her waist. She slapped his hand away, turned and glared at him. Her stare must have been filled with contempt because he pulled back from her.

She was enraged. The nerve of him. Just who did he think he was. Did he think that he was so wonderful that she would forgive him, just because he touched her. Arrogant buffoon. She hissed and John moved even further away, pulling away some of the covers from her. She snatched them back fiercely. He turned and looked at her in disbelief.

"Exactly, what is your problem Lola? Look I told you where I was. I am exhausted. If I can't sleep here, maybe I should have slept outside!" His voice was low, but the threat came through loud and clear. Lola turned away from him; she was filled with self pity. What sort of world was this that a man could cheat and then turn around and be the indignant one? Just because he had the money and the social standing? How had she allowed this to happen? She hugged her pillow and counted various ways of exacting revenge until she fell asleep.

# Chapter 21

# Chika
# Make new friends, but keep the old

When Chika opened the door, she was surprised to see her Pastor's wife standing there. She wasn't expecting her to show up at her house unannounced. She felt like a naughty child caught by the principal. "Ah! Pastor Ify! How are you? What brings you here?" she sputtered, rushing to open the large padlock, that kept the wrought iron burglary gate secure. The woman clad in a brightly patterned ankara chiffon boubou, smiled warmly at her, waving away Chika's discomfort.

"Chika, I have told you over and over again to call me Ify!"

When the iron barrier had been removed, Chika welcomed her into her apartment and Pastor Ify, pulled Chika into her arms for a span of time, holding her close for longer than a mere greeting. Then she put her hands around Chika's shoulders and while still holding her, pushed her back a bit so she could look more closely at her. Chika felt uncomfortable as Pastor Ify stared into her eyes.

"Chika! How are you, my dear? Longest time." Pastor Ify spoke with a lilting accent that usually made Chika feel peaceful and inspired. Today, she just looked away and fidgeted as her guilt rushed to her face.

"Yes, Pastor. I know I have been missing services, but I have been just too busy with work," she said, motioning towards the sofa and inviting her to sit. Pastor Ify watched her, not saying a word, taking the offered place on the sofa, and arranged her Boubou in cloud-like gatherings around her.

"I understand. It can be overwhelming, moving to a new city with a new job," Pastor Ify said, nodding her head and clucking in between syllables. "But all the same, it is important not to get so pulled away that one gets lost." Chika nodded her head in acquiescence, hoping that her face wouldn't betray her current ambivalent state.

"Can I offer you something to drink or eat? I have some chin-chin, would you care for some?" Chika said, standing up.

"No, thank you my dear, nothing for right now" Pastor Ify refused her offer of Chika's favorite Nigerian delicacy, sweet crunchy pieces of fried cookies. Chika slapped her head as she realized why. She had forgotten that the whole church was supposed to be fasting this month. She grunted in disgust at herself. "Sorry, I forgot about the fast." Then she sat down and sank into the cushions, grabbing one to hold on to.

"I can't imagine what you must think of me," Chika said sounding as pathetic as she felt. Pastor Ify, rose from her seat and sat on the sofa next to her, and then tenderly took her hand. "Chika, it's alright. True Christianity is not about setting down rules and flogging people when they fail to obey them, it is about love and redemption. That is after all the example Christ has set for us. I didn't come to see you to chastise you; I came to see you because I was concerned about you. I just wanted to be sure you were alright and also to remind you that you have people who love you."

Chika felt so overwhelmed, she wanted to cry. Pastor Ify was one of the main reasons she had joined that church when she moved to Nigeria. She had met her at a women's conference where she had been invited to speak after launching her book, *A Love Song to Jesus*. It was Chika's second book and she was so on fire that day when she addressed the audience that Pastor Ify came up to her later and told her that she wanted her to come and speak at her church. After that, they formed a friendship and when she moved, it was a given that she would attend Living Waters, the church Pastor Ify and her husband led as co-pastors.

Ever since then, Pastor Ify had been like a mother to her, exuding the grace and elegance that Chika herself longed for, and she was a wonderful role model for any Christian woman because she operated out of love. As Chika remembered all this, she felt even more ashamed. She didn't need the Holy Spirit to tell her that she had become lukewarm about her faith and her conviction was just as weak.

Since the weekend she and Collins had spent away, things had become increasingly physical between them and it was getting even more difficult to hold out. It was like the song said, Collins gave her fever. He knew that whenever he touched her that her desire for him would grow and her defenses would weaken and so he pushed the boundaries with each encounter. The other night they were supposed to be watching a movie but before she knew it, she was in just her panties, her bra was off and Collins was flicking his tongue over her nipples so expertly that she cried out in pleasure. If not for the fact that the power went out, she would not have been able to stop herself, or him. As she remembered his caresses, she felt herself getting hot and shifted a little in her seat and remembered where she was. She was so embarrassed about her thoughts in front of Pastor Ify that she stood up and announced that she would have to abruptly end the visit.

"Err, Pastor Ify, I am so sorry, but I have another appointment I have to rush to. Can I come and see you tomorrow?"

Pastor Ify narrowed her eyes and adjusted the neckline of her chiffon Boubou. She uncrossed her legs and then smiled. "Chika, it is obvious to me that something is going on with you and I am really concerned, but I can't force you to confide in me, so I'll be praying for you. Please remember that I am also your friend," she said as she rose up from her seat, looking Chika in the eye.

Chika felt so exposed, as if her whole life was on display and deep inside, she felt slightly afraid. "Don't worry Pastor, I will be at church this Wednesday for Bible study," she said, committing right there and then to be more diligent about attending service.

Pastor Ify smiled and took her hands. "I would love to see you there!" Then she gathered her things and left. As Chika closed the door, she felt like a weight had been lifted.

# Chapter 22

# Karen
## Once upon a time

Karen sat in Dr. Hedaye's office reading an article about the benefits of a vegetarian lifestyle. She was contemplating changing her eating habits when she noticed Dele come in. For some reason, she was struck by how handsome he looked. He was dressed in a simple T-shirt and jeans with leather slippers. It had been a long while since she had noticed him this way. For years now, they had been like ships passing in the night; occasionally running into each other as they lived their separate lives. She felt a pang of sadness. Dele looked up just then and smiled and it occurred to Karen that he was there out of pity. The thought that he probably didn't feel anything for her made her sad. She dwelt in the pain for a moment, what was it about her that made her unloveable? She took a deep breath and forced back her tears. He wasn't worth them. By the time he sat down next to her, all her soft feelings had disappeared and her speech had hardened.

"Why are you here?" she said in a clipped tone.

He leaned back in his chair. "Dr. Hedaye asked me to come."

Karen hissed. "Did you tell her you were my husband in name only?" she said rolling her eyes.

"Actually I did," he said, "and she said that was all the more reason to come. She felt this was important for the healing process to begin. So I am here."

Karen started to say something nasty to him, but he put up his hand before she could get it out. "Karen, just stop it. I understand this is difficult for you. But it's not a walk in the park for me either.

I cancelled some very important meetings, to be here for you. Accept it or not. I am your husband and yes, I agree, we have had a shitty marriage, but I am here and I am not going anywhere. So just save your vitriol. Don't want it. Don't need it," and with that he started reading a magazine about running.

Karen rolled her eyes and sunk deeper into her chair, flipping the pages of her magazine. She acted as if she was engrossed in an article, but she couldn't focus on the words. She kept sneaking glances at Dele, who was sitting comfortably in the chair next to her engaged in his reading. She couldn't understand him. For the years they had been married, he had always acted as if theirs was a marriage of inconvenient convenience, as if she were a necessary irritant. Karen thought back to one of their early dates, when she was still open to the possibility of the marriage being a union of love and partnership. She remembered how excited she was getting dressed for him. She thought he was so smart and she was impressed by his success and savvy. When they spoke on the telephone, they seemed to get along well enough. They had similar backgrounds and had similar tastes and ideals. So she was excited. She was not an easy girl when it came to relationships; she rarely found men attractive, and then only men of a particular pedigree. At the time her grand aunt called her to introduce Dele, she was about to finish a Masters in International Relations and had never had a serious relationship, so despite her misgivings about matchmaking, she found herself rather anticipating the meeting.

Their first date was in a fancy French restaurant. Dele asked her what she would like. He was a perfect gentleman and they laughed and joked throughout dinner. He told her she was very elegant. She told him, he was quite debonair, and Karen became hopeful for their future. Before the end of the evening, he asked her if she knew that their families had thrown them together and had already determined that they should marry. She laughed saying, it didn't matter. He laughed too, and said, he agreed with them. He said his father had sat him down and told him all about her and why she would be a good match for him. He said that now that he had met her, he was sure she would be a perfect match for him, and that he would be willing to wait for as long as it took her to be sure, but that as far as he was concerned, she was the one for him.

For two months, she felt all giddy inside when she thought of him. She allowed herself to start falling in love with him. He was a bit more aloof than she had hoped, but his actions and his words were always what they should have been for a potential husband, if not quite those of a lover. On their third month anniversary, he invited her to his father's birthday party in London. Karen's grand aunt was in attendance. Dele gave a toast to his father saying that he was his hero and he considered it an honor to be called his son. Karen was so enthralled by Dele that she didn't stop to wonder what it meant to idolize a man who was a known philanderer and was rumored to have fathered over five children outside his marriage with various women. That concern was far from her mind when she accepted the glittering four carat princess cut platinum diamond ring that Dele offered her that night when he asked her to marry him in front of all his family and friends. When he put it on her finger, she smiled and kissed him passionately. Everyone cheered and for the first time in her life, she felt like she was living a fairytale.

She spent the next few months in New York with him and that was when her bling started to lose some of its sparkle. First, it was the incessant phone calls. Sometimes Dele would answer and tell whoever was on the other line that he would call them back later. At first, Karen thought they were business calls and felt special because he prioritized her, but a few times it became obvious they were calls from women because from his responses it was clear they wouldn't accept his refusal to converse with them. One day, she picked up his phone because it was ringing and when she answered, a woman hissed and hung up on her. Then a text came in almost immediately. It read *"Baby! Who is that bitch answering your phone? Sweetheart, you know I am waiting for you tonight? Guess what, I'll be wearing that dress you like, and I won't be wearing any panties"*. Karen dropped the phone in disgust. When Dele walked back into the room, she confronted him.

He sat down and was calm and watched her quietly, as if she wasn't shouting at him, sipping from the beer he was holding. "Can I have my phone now?" he said as if she had not just questioned their whole relationship. She threw it at the sofa beside him. He picked it up and said, "I am going out," getting up and putting his phone into his front pocket. "Don't wait up."

Karen stood there aghast. She called her auntie and cried and cried and then she announced she was breaking up with him. Her auntie informed her that she would do no such thing. Infidelity was par for the course with men like Dele. Successful men all had their wahala, so she should just grow up. Her aunt told her simply to stop loving him and save her love for her children. Men were a means to an end. This was the way of Nigerian aristocrats. She listened to her auntie and after a while, decided she was right. She had heard too many stories to be romantic about marriage. She would take her heart out of the matter and move on, but she resolved to make him beg first. She couldn't just accept it as if it was nothing. She left his house that day, expecting him to chase after her, but he didn't call her or reach out to her for three months. Every morning when she woke up and realized that he didn't call, she felt as if she was forced to sit still in a tub of ice water. The pain was that significant. During that time, various family members reached out to her, pleading with her not to break the engagement.

Finally, he came to London and showed up on her door step. He looked none the worse for wear. He asked if he could come in. She allowed him. She offered him tea, he accepted and they sipped quietly. Then he cleared his throat. "Karen, I apologize for allowing you to feel disrespected. You didn't deserve that and it will never happen again." He then told her about a house he was buying in Atlanta for them. He wanted her to come and see it. He started to soften as he painted a picture of the life he saw for them. He said a few more things about how she was the only woman in his life worth giving his name to. He told her how much he had missed her. As he spoke the words, Karen just looked at him. It wasn't a question of whether or not she believed him; it was just that she found herself indifferent. She didn't know whether he just wanted to do his duty or if he truly wanted a relationship and she didn't care to find out. She had already made up her mind to become Mrs Dele Thompson but she had also locked that door of affection that he was trying to open.

When she got to Atlanta, she could tell that the realtor had been sleeping with him. Her name was Titi. She was attractive in an obvious sort of way, clearly she traded on her sex appeal. At first, she referred to Dele as darling, but covered it up quickly. Dele meanwhile, covered her hand with his and kept saying, "My fiancé," in a way that made the woman cringe. When he left the room, the Titi girl gave her a look of contempt. It was then that Karen decided to speak to her, to pour some ice water on her hot to trot self. So she told her that Dele would never marry her sort and that to him, she was nothing more than a passing dalliance. The Titi woman seemed unmoved, so at the end of a speech, Karen decided to say more. She thanked her. She thanked her for her service because as far as she was concerned, it was a service. She informed Titi that women like her didn't do anything they didn't want to, so she thanked Titi for filling the gap, for regularly getting on her knees in front of her husband and doing what she had no intention of demeaning herself to do. She thanked her and offered to compensate her further if Dele had not given her enough. It was after she said that that Titi's eyes darkened and her face paled. From the way she looked, Karen could see the sharp, icy, tingles of pain coursing through her. It was only then that Karen was satisfied. By the time Dele had come back, Karen felt completely in control and Titi looked a mess.

Even though she looked as if she was reading the magazine, her face must have exposed her thoughts because she could feel Dele's eyes on her. He was probably wondering what she was thinking. She stared straight ahead. Let him have his whores if he wanted to. She no longer cared, because ice water started flowing in her veins a long time ago.

"Mr. and Mrs. Thompson" the receptionist called. "The doctor will see you now". Karen took a deep breath and thought, "And so it begins" as the receptionist ushered them into the doctor's office.

Karen sat next to Dele on the modern but comfortable sofa in Dr. Hedaye's office. It didn't look like a doctor's office. It looked more like someone's living room. There was no desk, just a cluster of comfortable chairs and sofa and there was beautiful art on the walls. One painting in particular caught Karen's eye, it was a waterfall and the artist's rendering was so vivid that Karen could almost feel the rush of the waves.

"It's an amazing piece isn't it?" Dr. Hedaye said when she walked into the room. The sound of her voice was like swiss chocolate on the tongue.

She shook Dele's hand first. "Hello, I am Dr. Hedaye, you must be Dele." She pronounced it perfectly. Dele smiled. "Yes. You pronounced my name so well. Most Americans use a different inflection." Dr. Hedaye smiled. "I am not your typical American; my father is from Senegal and my mother is Ethiopian. I, however was born in Brooklyn."

Her description of her heritage explained her stunning looks. Devoid of makeup, she was beautiful with her high cheekbones and large slanted eyes. Karen watched Dele lighting up as he listened to her and rolled her eyes. "Of course," she thought. "Not even my doctor is sacred."

Dr. Hedaye turned to her. "Hello Karen. Last time we met, I could see that you are a remarkably strong woman. Today, I can also see that you have an incredible sense of style. At the risk of sounding unprofessional, you simply must disclose where you got those shoes." Karen smiled. Clearly Dr. Hedaye was skilled in the art of making people feel at ease.

"I am so glad you both are here," she continued, taking her seat in graceful manner. It almost seemed like she melted into it. She had an ethereal quality to her which was quite hypnotic. "I want you to know that some of the work we are going to do might seem unconventional, but I want you to trust the process. I practice both traditional and holistic medicine. So while I am going to put you on a chemotherapy regimen, I believe that cancers are part of the bodies defense mechanism turned against itself sometimes in response to intangible threats to our hearts and soul, and so we are also going to meet here and do work on the spirit and emotional center, and that will in turn allow the body to begin to shut down its heightened response."

Karen had heard it before in her previous meetings with Dr. Hedaye and she was still not a believer, in fact to her, everything the pretty doctor said sounded like mumbo jumbo. Chemotherapy, that she understood, surgery and radiation she would have understood as well, but this spiritual therapy bit, she didn't think she needed it. However when Dr. Hedaye smiled at her, she calmed herself and resolved to give these sessions a chance.

Dr. Hedaye turned to Dele and said, "Let's get right into it." Dele leaned forward. "Tell me what you love most about your wife?" Dele looked taken aback. He wasn't expecting that question. Karen felt an unexpected pang inside of her, hoping that he would have at least one positive thing to say. She stared him down with anger in her eyes. He avoided her gaze and was silent for a moment. Finally Karen watched his lips begin to move.

"I love her stoicism and strength." Dr. Hedaye leaned forward, her eyes inviting him to say more. "She is always steady, like the rock of Gilbratar. Nothing moves her. Nothing gets her frazzled. In all our years of marriage, I have never seen her cry or lose control."

Karen found his statement unsettling. You would have thought he was describing one of those English beefeaters not his wife. Then his tone changed. "It is also the thing I most hate about her. I feel I can never reach her. She is so shut down to me emotionally. Actually, I often feel emotionally stranded." Dr. Hedaye looked at him with sympathy.

Karen became enraged and she hissed. "Surely you must be joking!" she exclaimed. "Emotionally stranded? What a crock!" she spat out. "Have you been emotionally available? Tell me, how have you tried to reach me? Through your incessant cheating? Or are you trying to tell me you believe that the love of your wife can be found in the vagina of another woman?"

Dr. Hedaye appeared unfazed by Karen's outburst, and when she apologized for losing her cool, she asked her not to apologize and encouraged her to release her emotions. She told them that this was a safe space, and that in order for the therapy to work, they had to be open and honest, no matter how ugly things may seem.

Dele didn't look pleased about Karen's outburst. He kept shifting in his seat. "Yes, yes, I know, paint me black. Dele the philanderer. Dele the womanizer. In fact call me the devil himself," Dele whined. "Fine, I agree, I have been an asshole at times, but I tried to change many times, and you wouldn't let me!"

Karen rolled her eyes again. "Oh please, grow up. What are you? Two years old? You made your choices, now own them!"

Dele jumped to his feet. "I am sick of this. Who wouldn't be with other women? Have you looked at yourself? You are judging me when you are so cold and aloof! I have had to seek solace outside. What am I supposed to do? When my wife can't be a soft space for me?" he shouted. Dr. Hedaye leaned back and watched them argue.

For years, Karen and Dele had maintained cool and polite communications, but she never told him how much his philandering hurt her. She never spoke to him about it and was determined never to let him see her pain. She locked it away in a place so that it couldn't push through her every day demeanor. She was amazed at the things he was saying. He kept going, calling her an ice princess, a cold and judgmental bitch. He told her that when he thought about being with her intimately, he couldn't get it up because she was so frigid. Karen shrank back into the chair, but her heart was racing. She couldn't even process all the emotions swirling around in her mind. She didn't know her husband felt so much contempt for her. She always felt at the very least he respected her and held her in high esteem. She was quiet while she waited for Dr. Hedaye to speak. Maybe the doctor could explain to him how something inside of her died the first time he betrayed her. Maybe then her husband could understand that he was asking for the impossible. He wanted her to be a soft space for him, when all he had done was cause her pain. Dr. Hedaye remained silent. She wrote in her notes from time to time, and her face remained passive as she looked at the both of them.

By the time Karen decided to speak, Dele was calm and his heavy breathing had returned to normal. "Do you think I am made of stone?" she asked Dele in a quiet voice, turning to him as she spoke. He looked away. "Really? Do you?" her voice steady and calm. Karen felt proud of her ability to keep her composure, she would not allow this man to reduce her to hysterics. "You speak about solace and soft spaces. When have you provided that for me? Perhaps you have interchanged it with silk and cashmere?" Dele looked at her then, but his expression was inscrutable.

"Haven't I always given you everything you wanted?" His voice was deep and thick.

"You don't even know me, so how can you know what I want?" she asked. "Let's not put on an act for Dr. Hedaye please. You told me in more ways than one from the beginning that you viewed our marriage as an arrangement. A transaction. Simple. Full stop. And so I played that role of an aristocratic wife. I was class personified, cultured, intellectual. Pray tell me, how many deals did I close for you over dinner?" Karen frowned as she made this inquiry. "So don't act like the wounded tiger, please. I simply can't stomach it."

Dele shook his head and looked to Dr. Hedaye as if for help. "You see, what I mean. She's a bloody ice princess." Dr. Hedaye simply continued scribbling in her notes.

"I beg your pardon!" Karen interjected. Please don't use that sort of language on me, and kindly address me as I am still in the room" Karen said as she crossed her legs and flicked off a nonexistent piece of lint from her dress.

Finally, Dr. Hedaye spoke. "Karen, how does Dele's philandering make you feel?" she asked.

Dele sputtered and interrupted. "She is the reason I do it!"

Dr. Hedaye smiled at Dele. "I asked Karen how she feels about your behavior. And you and I both know that she is not why you do anything. If you want to discuss the root cause of your sexual addiction, rest assured, we can at a later date."

Karen smiled. "Oh, I don't much care."

Dr. Hedaye said, "Is that right?"

"Oh yes," said Karen. "I mean, what can I do, kill myself? Plus, it's fairly common in Nigeria, I'm afraid."

Dr. Hedaye nodded. "I am familiar with Nigerian culture. However the fact that it may be somewhat widespread, doesn't mean it is not degrading, demoralizing and hurtful."

Karen shook her head. "I don't feel degraded at all. Those are his choices not mine." Dr. Hedaye fell silent again.

"I mean, the fact that he needs to stick his penis into every available hole has nothing to do with me," Karen spoke, but inside of her there was a scream beginning. "Really, who cares? Love is just an illusion anyway. I didn't have any expectations, so I was never let down." She raised her voice a little because she couldn't hear that well, because the screaming was getting louder. "But I want the record to show that I am not cold. I was not always so aloof. I withdrew because that was the sort of marriage you wanted," Karen said, her voice getting even louder as she turned to address Dele directly again.

"You encased me in ice. You. The night before we got married, where were you? On our honeymoon, weren't you having phone sex with some girl in the bathroom. And you wondered why I couldn't bear to have you touch me that night. You men! You think we women have no hearts? Well, I wasn't going to allow you to break mine. That is what you wanted, I expect, someone to cry and scream and beg you to stop. You want drama, so you can feel needed? Screw you! You got what you asked for, a queen. So deal with the protocol," Karen said and then she got up and walked to the window.

She couldn't see the view from the window because her vision was becoming cloudy. "I cried once. Just once. I watched a wedding video of a former classmate and they looked so in love. I realized then, that I had made a bad choice and I was ruined. I cried then. But I only allowed myself a few minutes. Life must go on, abi?" She spoke into the glass as she stared out at the park below. She could see the view now. There was a woman jogging with her dog and another pushing a red stroller. Two lovers held hands and stopped for a kiss. Suddenly Karen realized that she was crying. She turned around in a rage.

The tears had come fast and hard, and she could taste the saltiness. "You bastard! Is this what you needed to see? You wanted to see me reduced? You wanted to know you could hurt me? Well, here you go. Consider it an early Christmas present." She walked over to the sofa, grabbed her purse and retrieved a handkerchief from it and dabbed at her face.

Dr. Hedaye stood up. "Wonderful! We have made incredible progress today. I am very hopeful about what is to come. Please make sure you both come for the next appointment. In the meantime, I want you to journal. There will be a lot of emotions that come up from this excavation and I want you to allow them to come. Journaling will help you process them. Don't resist them, just allow them to come out and then release them," Dr. Hedaye said, as she hugged them both and ushered them out of her office.

Karen pulled at her trench coat, clutching her handbag as she walked out of the office and giving Dr. Hedaye a tight smile. She wanted to say thank you, but she couldn't trust her voice not to betray her. Dele said it for both of them. Once they got into the passageway that led from the office back to the waiting area, Dele grabbed her hand and asked if they could talk. She drew her hand back and shook her head. She still couldn't speak and what was more, she didn't want to speak to him. For all the years that they had been married, she had maintained her composure. Now in one hour long session with a therapist masquerading as a cancer doctor, all that had unraveled and now Dele knew how much she hurt. Well, she couldn't do anything about that now, but she wasn't going to give him any more ammunition. She walked fast and left him standing on the pavement as she hailed a cab and directed the driver to take her to Fifth Avenue.

# Chapter 23

# Lola
## The long road home

Lola sat down at the table, where dinner was getting cold again. In the last couple of weeks, John had gone from bad to worse. He was even more secretive, constantly taking meetings and now he had added even more business trips to Abuja. She knew some of it was business, but she also knew he was still seeing that godforsaken Natalie. She found out who the woman was. She worked at a bank that John did business with. She couldn't understand the attraction because the woman was nothing to look at; Lola could trump her in any beauty contest, even if she scarred her face and gained fifty pounds.

She confronted John about her again, and he told her that he was not going to talk about it anymore. He told her to believe what she wanted because he had no intention of competing with her imagination, and if she couldn't handle herself, that she should just leave his house. Lola was beside herself as she remembered his words and felt the same panicky, painful emotions rise up inside of her. He was acting as if she didn't matter at all to him. As if all their years together no longer mattered. As if she was disposable. Lola had been so baffled that she had confided in Mimi. Mimi stated it had to be some sort of love potion or spell. When Lola started to shake her head, Mimi cautioned her saying, "Keep shaking your head o! Next thing you know, that rat-faced girl will just move you out of your own house!" With that Mimi finally had Lola's attention.

When Mimi said she was going to help her. She whispered

that she had used a love potion on her own husband, and Lola nearly fell out of her chair. Mimi was not the sort of woman that Lola expected to say that. She thought love potions and all that jazz were the things that Nollywood movies were made of. She had never seen the inside of a shrine, so how could one of her best friends talk about using something so crazy on her husband?

"What are you saying, Mimi!" she retorted loudly. "You are lying!"

Mimi nodded her head. "I did! It's not like I'm proud of it, but a girl's got to do what a girl's got to do!" Mimi cocked her head in defiance. "After all, hasn't my husband settled down now? Before he was chasing girls round the clock, now he comes home after work and chills. Please as far as I am concerned, I did him a favor. His blood pressure is down, he has less stress. Shoot, the man will live long because of me."

Lola listened in disbelief. "I can't believe this!" she stuttered. "You are telling me you dabble in the diabolical?" Ha! She thought, and this girl went to a church every Sunday.

"What! What did you want me to do? If you like, stay there asking foolish questions, the question you should be asking is who is your baba and what can he do for me?" Mimi said, standing her ground.

Lola stood up, "Actually the question I need to ask is why am I here listening to this nonsense" she said gathering her things and turning to leave. Mimi tried to stop her. "Lola, wait! Calm down! This one no be *ajebutter* matter o!" But Lola started walking and didn't look back.

Something had clicked inside of her. She found herself getting angrier and angrier. Why was she acting as if John was the end all be all. When had she given up all of her power and strength? If they were still in America would she stand for this foolishness? So what if this was Nigeria, where men cheated with impunity; a country that lifted men so high on a pedestal that some men believed that their own shit no longer stunk.

She still couldn't believe Mimi, love potion! Juju ke! She thought hissing. She was tired of everyone always ascribing the bad behavior of men to juju. It was as if everyone conspired to make excuses for men. If a man leaves his wife and kids for some random woman, then it was that the strange woman that fed him juju, but if a woman left her husband then she was a loose woman and not to be trusted again. If a man beat up his wife and kicked her out of the home, then she was encouraged to pray for him to return to his senses and pray against juju; meanwhile if she so much as spoke a rude word to him in public, then she was branded a useless wife. It was always the men who were being "enchanted" by juju, and never the women. It was as if there was a belief that men were good and women, bad. The double standard was so thick and often perpetuated by women. Even as Lola identified it, she knew she was also subject to it. As she thought about things, she became even more depressed.

On the ride home, a boy knocked on the window selling chin chin and plantain chips. Lola rolled down the window and bought four packets of each. The driver looked at her through the rear view mirror. "What are you looking at, Sule?" she snapped.

"Nothing madam. nothing ma," he said quickly, focusing the road. Lola opened the first packet of chips. She bit into the sweet and crunchy chip, but it gave her no satisfaction. Then she opened a packet of chin chin, sweet and doughy. It too, couldn't do the trick. She closed her eyes. Life sucks, she thought and opened her eyes. Life really did suck right now, but these packets of sugar and fat wouldn't make it suck less. She lowered the window again and threw the packets out. Some children picked them up and went to the side of road to feast on them. Lola watched them eat. They probably hadn't eaten all day. That incident gave her perspective. This was not the end of the world. So her husband was cheating. She figured that had two options: stay and accept it or leave and take a different path. "In time," she spoke out loud because she knew that very soon, she would figure out what to do. Another vendor pushed his wares against the glass of her window. He was selling magazines and she looked at the glossy cover, it was Chika on the cover. She bought the copy and started to flip to the cover story, but something else caught her eye; an article titled, "It's all about YOU". She read about how she had the power to change her life, even if she couldn't change her circumstances. The author was an American based life coach who gave three questions for readers to ask themselves. The first was whether or not they were happy? The second was whether they were doing what they believed to be their life's work and the third was what they could do to change their lives. She answered the first question easily. She was definitely not happy. The second question made her think. Was she doing her life's work? She leaned back against the plush leather seats in the car and all of a sudden became conscious of the air conditioner's cool air blowing in contrast to the thick heat. And she finally answered the question. No. She was not doing her life's work. She was not doing anything. When she was younger, she used to write songs and she always fantasized about being a singer and songwriter.

She had the voice, but nowadays she never really used it. She sang in the choir at church, but only sometimes. Two months ago, she sang a song she had written during service. She had penned it during her second pregnancy, when things had been so difficult the doctor had placed her on bed rest. She called it "No matter what". At the end of the service that day, many people came up to her to tell her how the song had touched them. Why didn't she ever do anything with her talent? Why did she limit herself to just being a wife? The article had pointed out that not being engaged in your life's work was one of the root causes of deep unhappiness and that just like people can have physical referred pain; people can have emotional referred pain, and so they focus on their relationships, finances or other aspects of their lives and think that if those things were sorted then they would be happy. The author even went further to say that people who were engaged in living purposefully could be happy regardless of any situation they found themselves in.

She thought about that theory. She wasn't sure if it was all true because she felt that a cheating spouse would still cause her pain even if she was "fully engaged", however, she did think that the author was right in the sense that it might make her happier in a way. At this point in the article, the author urged her readers to take their focus off other people. If they felt they needed other people to change their behavior in order to be happy then they needed to shift their focus to the person in the mirror because as the author theorized, each person was responsible for their own happiness. Finally, Lola answered the last question, "What could she do to change things?" Lola looked out at the sea of cars in front of her and the hawkers aggressively trying to get their attention. "The whole world is hustling!" she exclaimed. "I am going to go for mine!"

Sule nodded his head slightly and smiled, but kept his head facing forward.

Lola picked up the phone and called her friend Larry Williams. Larry was really Lara but for some reason, everyone called her Larry. Larry was one of the cities power brokers. She was a PR sensation and early on when they met, Larry had urged her to let her manage her singing. "Sweetie, I can help you get where you want to go!" she had said, but at the time Lola wasn't sure she wanted to go anywhere. This time, she knew exactly what she wanted.

"Hey babes!" Larry said when she answered. "Long time no hear? How far?" Larry continued in her quick and jovial way.

"Larry, I need your help. I want to sing!" Lola said, forcing the words out quickly before she changed her mind. Larry was quiet for just a second longer than usual. "Is that right?" she asked in her characteristic American twang, Larry had just relocated back to Lagos a few years earlier and was already dominating the scene. Lola continued to assert her desire to pursue her passion when Larry interrupted her by laughing. Lola's heart sunk; perhaps she had waited too long. She leaned back into the leather seat with her phone up to her ear; she prepared herself for the rejection when Larry said, "Well, my darling, I have just the thing for you, you are about to get somewhere and be somebody! Yes sir, now we are cooking with gas!" Lola laughed with her and she knew as she let Larry's voice continue to tickle her, that her life was truly about to change.

# Chapter 24

## Chika
## I need the lover of my soul

Chika was getting ready for church. She had resolved to start attending again. That morning she had prayed and spent some quiet time reflecting and reading her Bible. She resolved to slow things down with Collins and refocus her energies on her spiritual growth. It had taken some time to get her mind quiet after she thought about Collins. Her mind buzzed with questions like: Why slow things down? What if he is the one? Even queries like what's the big deal about being intimate with him, after all you love each other. It was at that point that she prayed for direction and guidance and supernatural strength. Yet even as she prayed, part of her still yearned for his touch. Even as she spoke the words, she could still remember the feel of his mouth on hers, how he sucked on her tongue. She shuddered and asked for wisdom but she also asked to be with him. It was an unspoken request, but she knew God who held the heart of kings in his hands could see her deepest desires. She felt both shame and joy at that thought. She shook it off and put her lipgloss on, brushed her hair one last time and adjusted her blouse. She needed to be in church as soon as possible, she thought.

As she put her Bible in her handbag and called for the driver, her phone tinkled with the melody she had programmed just for Collins. She was tempted to answer, but she didn't trust herself, so she texted in response. "Can't talk now, busy," and sent a kiss emoticon to soften the message. He responded immediately, "I need to see you baby. I haven't been able to concentrate all day, can I come over?" he asked. Chika felt shivers running through her, "Father help me!" she thought. She remembered their last encounter; he had made her dinner at his house, a chicken stir fry that was bland, but the kisses he gave her afterwards more than spiced up the evening, again she barely kept her promise to be abstinent.

"Can't sweetie, have a prior engagement," she typed back. Even as she pressed send she wondered why she didn't tell him she was going to church for Bible study. "Where is your conviction, O woman of faith?" her conscience accused her, but she silenced it. He called again and this time she picked up and as soon as she heard his velvety voice, she sat down and kicked off her shoes. "Darling, please cancel it. Please. I am actually at the beginning of your street and will be there in moments. I am desperate to see you and I want to discuss something very important with you." It was 6pm; perhaps, she could see him briefly and still make it for the 7pm midweek service. Even as she rationalized her decision to wait for him, she knew she was lying to herself. She was still beside herself when the house help announced his presence in the living room. She had gone to her bedroom to change. As her housemaid finished speaking, she fluffed out her hair, reapplied her lip gloss and then she went out to meet him.

He enveloped her in his arms and she allowed her face to be buried in his chest. He had a broad chest and thick muscular arms and thighs. He pulled her closer and then lifted her face to his. She couldn't read his expression until he covered her mouth with his and probed with his tongue. His hands roamed over the curve of her hips and more as he kissed her. She began to melt into him, becoming more liquid as he held her close. His voice had deepened by the time he released her lips and told her that he wanted her in his life forever. When he told her that he realized that he had been waiting for her from the moment he was born, the words were so thick; he had to breathe in between them. "I want you to be mine and I want you to know I am yours; and only yours." Chika gasped. "Chika, you are everything I have ever wanted in a woman. I know you have reservations about being intimate with me and I can respect that. In fact it is part of what I love about you, but I want you to know that you are safe with me. In my heart, you are already my wife. Spiritually we are already connected, surely you can feel it." He began to kiss her neck and within seconds had undone her bra.

Chika allowed him to pull her to her bedroom. She felt weak against the tide. He undressed her, kissing and caressing every part of her body, whispering words of love and painting a picture of forever as he imprinted her body with his marks. Chika allowed herself to fall into his image of togetherness, even as her spirit raised objections that she forced herself to quell. He loved her and she loved him. In truth was that not all that mattered? She ran her hands over the span of his now undressed body and pushed past her hesitation. Her body was sure even if her spirit was not because it responded of its own volition, warming and arching to receive him. Soon, they were completely together, Collins made sounds of appreciation as if being fed after a long period of hunger. She welcomed him like a woman desperate to feed him.

Later, they lay in each other's arms and even though there was an afterglow, all the doubts came rushing in so such force that Chika didn't have the strength to fight them. She began to feel ashamed and started to pull away. He appeared to be sleeping, but as soon as she moved, he pulled her closer to him. He didn't open his eyes but he whispered, "It's alright, my darling. I promise. It's alright." Though his words were assuring and she stayed in the warmth of his arms, she couldn't fall asleep, she found herself wondering if indeed this compromise would be something she would come to regret.

# City Life Magazine
# Gossip Page
# Guess Who?

There is a Chief who recently married his latest wife and he is in his seventies. His first wife initially bore him six kids, but it seems it wasn't nearly enough. With his various wives and concubines, our Chief has sired over twenty children. Well done, sir! Now what do we make of the fact that he cannot remember all their names. People have said that he calls the younger ones, "Hey You!" His latest wife had one son last year and kept it moving, losing the baby weight in record time. Rumor has it, that he still wants more kids from her, but she has tied her tubes, choosing not to ruin her figure. And what a figure it is. She is only in her twenties after all and according to gist, she had won him over by jogging every day on his path to work. You see Chief is a creature of habit and leaves his house at 6am every morning to ensure that he is in his office before 8am. His work ethic was what made him a multimillionaire before age fifty. His desire for women was just as serious, as he no dey take eye see woman. Apparently his last wife is just as ambitious because she would jog on his path in shorts and a tight tank top with no bra with her nipples reporting. It took only one week of that for

Chief to make her his business and the rest is history. Well it seems the randy Chief is not yet done because he has been frequenting Ikoyi Tennis Club, and apparently another potential pro has been dazzling him. Let's keep watching for another wedding.

# Chapter 25

# Karen
# Green lights

Karen opened her hotel door and was startled to find Dele standing there with his hands in his pockets. She became tense. "Dele, please I can't deal with this today. We are not meeting Dr. Hedaye today. So there is no need for us to see each other."

It was true that she was not seeing Dr. Hedaye, but what she didn't tell Dele was that she had gone in for further testing and Dr. Livingston had recommended that she start an additional radiation treatment right away. She had spent the morning on the phone with her aunts and she had tried to call Chika, but couldn't reach her. For the first time in her life, she was really scared.

"Karen, please. I just need a minute."

Karen shook her head. How long have you been standing out here, why didn't you knock?" she asked.

"It doesn't matter how long I've been out here. Can we please go in for a minute?" he said.

Karen shook her head. "I have an appointment and I am already late," she said trying to push past him.

"Karen, I am so sorry," he blurted out quickly.

Karen was stunned and she was grateful that she was facing away from him, so he wouldn't see her expression.

"Karen, did you hear what I said. I said I am sorry. I know you may not be able to forgive me, but I need you to know that I finally understand how my actions have hurt you. I was selfish and I didn't think about you at all. You deserved better."

As he talked, Karen couldn't help herself. She started to cry.

He said everything she had always dreamed he would in those dreams that she was afraid to admit that she had. When he put his hands on her shoulders and turned her to face him, he saw her tears and pulled her close. In all their years of marriage, it was the first time that Karen had felt safe with him.

"I know you want to fight this alone and I know you are strong enough to win on your own, but please let me be there for you. Can I?" he asked.

Karen still couldn't speak. He lifted her face and she saw tears in his own eyes, he looked at her and kissed her cheeks. It was a tender gesture. Karen had never received a gesture like that. Not even from her father, who was always a little disconnected from them. Dele kissed her cheeks, then her mouth. "I'm so sorry Karen, I'll make it up to you. I'll spend the rest of my life, making it up to you."

She said nothing; she was at a loss for words.

The elevator bell went off and Karen felt like she was waking from a deep sleep. She looked at Dele. He was still standing there, looking more vulnerable than she had ever seen him. They stared at each other for what felt like a long time. "The cancer is getting worse. I have to start radiation today."

Dele's expression went from hope to fear that instant. "Is that where you are headed?" he asked. Karen nodded in reply.

"May I go with you?" he asked.

"Yes," Karen replied after several minutes. "I would like that very much."

He held her hand and led her in the direction of the elevator. He kept holding it as they walked through the lobby. The hotel doorman called them a cab and they sped off in the direction of the hospital. He didn't say another word and neither did she, but she was grateful for his presence. Grateful for the weight of his hand covering hers, especially as the nurse began to prepare her for treatment. Dele just sat there holding her hand. It was exactly what she needed.

# Chapter 26

# Lola
# One step forward, two steps back

Things had been moving fast for Lola since she and Larry met. She felt like the opportunity had just been waiting for her. Larry introduced her to Boyo Ejike. He was a well known contemporary playwright and he had recently started venturing into movies. His first offering was accepted into the famed Cannes film festival. He also did musical theatre and he was looking for a new leading lady.

When she met and sang for him, he said simply, "My dear, you are already a star." He was putting together a production that was going to be the biggest African production on Broadway. He asked her if she would be free to travel. When she said yes, he raised his eyebrow, "Are you sure, you don't have to check with your husband? I don't usually like to work with married actresses because their husbands tend to cause drama." Lola smiled and said, "No worries, there will be no drama." If John wanted to sleep around and have a separate life, then he dare not begrudge her this, plus she had no intention of discussing it with him; he could read about it in the newspapers like everyone else. After all the years of marriage when she gave him everything. Even when people doubted Nigerian men, she always stood up for him. Always believed in him. Always loved him. She put all her dreams on hold for him, just so she could be the wife he needed. In all their time together, she had never even lied to him. In just a few short months, he had thrown all that loyalty and love away like it was used toilet paper. With no remorse or regard for her. There would be no problems at all.

"Great then! We'll start immediately. I am doing a contemporary Nigerian romance story. And you will be my lead. I love women like you, beautiful, sexy and ready to live life!

Boyo was an effusive man. He spoke with such passion about his work and his personality was overwhelming, yet he had a way of making everyone around him feel special. Lola sat with him for hours and she didn't even realize it. They ran through the story concept and Lola started to get excited. The story was great and she could relate to the central character who was on a journey to find herself. It was also very funny and smart and even had contemporary music. She was looking forward to playing the role. Boyo put his hand on her knee and Lola watched as his fat fingers began to strum her bare flesh like a guitar. He looked lost in thought. Lola was uncomfortable, but she didn't want to interrupt his creative process. "I got it" he shouted, taking his hand off her knee and clapping both of his hands together. "Ah! Lola, this is going to be big! You are going to be a star!"

Lola couldn't help but clap her hands together with glee! She felt giddy, almost like a child who was just offered a large piece of chocolate. She could barely wait to experience life as a star, when people would know her as Lola, not just Mrs Amadi.

"I'm so ready to get started! When do we start rehearsals?" she asked, eager to stand in her spotlight.

"All in good time" Boyo responded, smiling and looking at her intently. His hand had returned to her leg and now he was putting gentle pressure on her knee.

"Well, I'm not afraid of hard work, so don't be afraid to push me," she said, ignoring the slimy feeling that was rising up her back.

"Oh, you might regret saying that! Pushy is my middle name!" Boyo said, laughing at his own joke and his hand sliding ever so slightly up her thigh, his fingers stroking her skin.

She felt as if she were standing in quicksand and at the same time, slime was dripping down her neck, but she remained quiet, wondering if what he said was true, could he make her a star? She silenced her inner warning signals and focused on the possible sound of a standing ovation. She needed this to happen. She needed her life to change. She would do anything to create the life she desired. What did that article say again? That she had the authority and responsibility to choose and create the life she wanted, right! She gave up so much to play the role of the good little wife and look at how far that got her. In spite of her trying to be the best wife possible, John was still cheating on her with some nonentity.

Just the thought of John added to her already disgusted sensibilities. Her thoughts and the disturbing sensation of Boyo stroking her leg, made her feel as if she was suffocating. "Oh my! I think I am feeling a little lightheaded," she said, as she tried to fan herself with her fingers. Boyo stared at her. "You are such an interesting creature... Relax, my dear, this is only the beginning."

Lola smiled and looked at her watch. It was getting late and she hadn't seen her children that day. "Boyo, this has been excellent, but I really have to get going, I look forward to hearing from you soon." She said standing up and extending a hand. He took her hand and pulled her close into a hug. "I hug o!" he said laughing. Then he said, I'd like to tell you a secret and before she could protest he whispered into her ear, "It's going to be delicious, working with you." He emphasized the delicious and punctuated the whole statement by darting his tongue back and forth into her ear. Lola was nauseated and struggled to keep her face blank.

"Well, okay then," she said, "good bye" and she walked quickly out of the office and didn't stop until she reached her car where she sank back into the seat, removed her moist wipes from her bag and began to wipe her ear, then her neck and her arms and legs and every piece of bare flesh she could find. As she tried to scrub away the memory of his fat fingers on her skin, she watched the diva image of herself like her idol Diana Ross disappear because she knew then that she could never work with Boyo Ejike.

Why was Nigeria like this! And just like that she became depressed again.

# Chapter 27

# Chika
# Walking tall in stilettos

Chika leaned back in her chair. They were having a program meeting and she couldn't keep her mind from wandering. She kept thinking about Collins and the path she was heading down with him. Even though he was a wonderful man and they got along great, she felt uneasy about things. As a Christian, she knew the verse about being unequally yoked, and she used to quote it often when she spoke at seminars with young women. As the thought, she felt a flush of shame spread through her body. She had become a hypocrite, preaching one thing and yet doing another. What would people say if they knew that she was sleeping with a man and even living with him? Since moving to Lagos, she had pretty much lost touch with most of her old friends from her church. It was somewhat deliberate after Collins because between Skype, instant messaging, Facebook and all, she really had no excuse.

Even Pastor Ify, who was in Lagos with her, seemed to be a bit frustrated with her lack of consistency in church attendance and total lack of communication. Chika thought about the last text message she received from her, "Chika, I have very serious concerns about you these days. I feel in my spirit that you are in a precarious place and coming to a crossroads. Please meditate on God's word today. Be careful beloved. Some things are a slippery slope and you are such a bright star in the kingdom."

The day she received that text, she went into her bedroom and cried. She felt so bad, so compromised. She had resolved that night to change the way she interacted with Collins. She decided that she would maintain her own standards and stand up for what she knew was right. She had arranged to speak with him that evening when they met at Red Peppers, her favorite restaurant. She told him how she felt and her concerns about sleeping with him. She shared the fact that she had promised herself and God that she would not have sex before marriage and yet she broke that vow. She felt good when she told him that she honestly loved him; however, she would understand if he refused to stay with her because of her decision to abstain.

She spoke with conviction, but inside she was afraid to lose him. She was worried that he would say no and get up and leave. She was already wavering even before he spoke, but she remained quiet waiting for his response. When he spoke, he said he understood, and he even respected her more because she had values. He kissed her hand and told her that he wasn't going anywhere because he had never met a woman as amazing as she was. She breathed a sigh of relief that night because she couldn't bear to lose him. He seemed so at peace with the decision that she relaxed that evening. And when he suggested that they ride together to her place to chill, she said yes. They talked and talked and even lay down in bed together. He held his hands up saying, "No hanky panky! Scout's honor!" Crossing his chest as he laughed. Chika laughed too and they lay in each other's arms telling each other about their hopes for the future. Before she drifted off, he asked her if she wanted to have children. She could barely respond before the waves of sleep pulled her under. As she said yes, softly, he kissed her forehead and whispered, "To me, you are already my wife."

The next morning they had breakfast, shared a lovely kiss and went off to handle their respective schedules and for a few days everything seemed better. He even agreed to accompany her to church sometime in the future. But there was this one night when he came into her apartment. She was already in her nightgown and seated at her vanity dresser, cleaning her face for the night. He walked into the bedroom and kissed her neck and rubbed her shoulders. Soon, he pulled her up from her stool in front of the mirror and kissed her on the mouth and his mouth was so hot, she felt as if she could taste his hunger. She didn't resist; couldn't resist. Soon, their clothes lay bunched up at the foot of the bed. All principles were forgotten as they explored each other's bodies. It was only after, when Chika became aware of the sweat on her body and the coolness of the night air against her naked skin that she allowed herself to focus on her emotions.

That night she looked at Collins snoring lightly. Naked, with his arm still holding her as she slept, she knew that she was not ready to let him go. As she thought back what they had done that night, she justified her actions. After all she wasn't eighteen, she wasn't even twenty-five; she was a full blooded grown woman. Bottomline, people did worse, and really what was the difference between what she and Collins had and marriage anyway. Some married couples didn't love each other as much as she and he did. Like he said, they were married in spirit already. Still for days after she struggled with her conscience, so much so that she was often distracted at work. She needed to be consistent and stop waffling one way or the other, she concluded.

"Chika!" Her program director interrupted her thoughts. "Have you been listening?" Chika had to admit that she had not. "So sorry, I have a lot on my mind, where were we?" Nkechi shook her head. "Girl, get it together!" she said in her American drawl. She had moved back to Lagos from Los Angeles and had just taken over the job. She was looking to bring more life to the show. "I would like to do a series on relationships. We could do a show with mistresses, answer questions like why do they do what they do?" Nkechi chattered excitedly. The administrative assistant just stared at her instead of taking notes. Chika knew it was because she was having trouble following what Nkechi was saying, and she spoke so quickly that she had to remind Nkechi to slow down, so the poor girl could take notes. Nkechi nodded, but didn't change her pace. She was talking with passion. "I just think it will be so insightful, to actually hear from the other women, don't you?" Nkechi said, finally slowing down to take a few breaths between her words. Chika shrugged, "I mean, what's to know. They are women with no integrity. Why would you consent to be a source of pain for another woman? Why would you think so little of yourself that you would accept the scraps of another woman?" Chika said speaking with equal amounts of zeal.

Nkechi started to gesticulate wildly. "Exactly the kind of questions that I want us to ask and have them answer! And you should be as passionate as you are now, perfect!" she said.

Chika agreed with Nkechi. "I guess it would be an interesting show."

"Of course it would," Nkechi said, chattering again. "And I also have a few wives who live abroad while their husbands live in Nigeria, but that could come on another show. I mean what's up with that! Let's delve into the whys and the hows, I mean how do they make it work? Phone sex? Skype sex? No sex?"

At this point, Chioma the assistant just put her pen down and just stared, her eyes now wide as saucers. Chika switched gears, "My friend, will you keep taking notes!" she said in a sharp tone.

Chioma put her head down and began to scribble furiously. Chika thought about it and then proclaimed, "Absolutely, that would be a great show. It is something to understand, this new phenomena of husbands and wives living on different continents. It has become quite common, right?"

Nkechi rubbed her hands together and said, "Ooh...these shows are going to be good!" Chika could only nod in agreement.

# Chapter 28

# Karen
# Stronger

Karen woke up from a deep sleep, but she was too weak to move. She had been vomiting for hours. Dele helped her each time. The last time, she couldn't make it to the bathroom and vomited all over herself. She cried because she was mortified and in so much discomfort. Dele picked her up and carried her to the bathroom. He took off her clothes and lowered her into the bathtub and bathed her. Karen just cried and mouthed thank you. After, he dressed her in her favorite silk pajamas. She thought he never noticed.

He smiled. "I always knew, Karen. Always." He leaned back in the bed and let her rest her head on his chest. He kissed her forehead, just before she fell asleep.

She turned hoping to see him, but her head was against the pillow and he wasn't next to her. She struggled to sit up. Her mouth was dry, she needed water. She looked up at the door because she heard the sound of the lock opening and when she saw Dele, she smiled. He was carrying a change of clothes and ice.

"Oh! You are up already! I slipped out to get some clothes and I got the ice from the room service waiter, I didn't want him to come in and disturb you. How are you feeling?"

Karen rubbed her throat and motioned to her mouth. He poured water into the glass of ice and brought it to the bed, while dumping his clothes on a chair.

"Here," he said, bringing the glass to her lips.

As Karen drank, he rubbed her back. "You are such a fighter, Karen. I don't know many people who could handle this much pain," he said. She didn't have a choice. She wanted to live.

When her throat didn't feel so parched, she tried to speak. "Dele." It came out with barely any sound. Dele didn't even hear her; he had started moving towards the bathroom. He was saying he wanted to take a bath because he was sure he had started to smell.

"Dele," she said again, but her voice was still too weak to be heard. Finally she mustered up all her strength and even though it felt like a scream, it came out just audible enough for Dele to hear. "Dele!" He turned to her immediately. "What is it? Do you need something?" he said, moving quickly to her side.

She shook her head. "I just wanted to say, thank you. Thank you." He smiled and his eyes started to get wet.

He patted her hand and squeezed it. "Karen, I love you. I am sorry it took me this long to show you. But I do."

Karen smiled. "I love you too," she said.

He hugged her. "Baby, we will beat this together okay? I will help you. You will not be alone." She let herself rest in his flesh as she contemplated her future. Dr. Livingston told her that they would try the available treatments and then hope for the best, but she had to be honest, the prognosis wasn't great. The cancer was further along than they previously thought. Most people didn't survive cancers at this stage. At her last appointment, she had asked Karen to begin to make sure her affairs were in order.

Karen told her that she wasn't most people. That day she sat straight backed in Dr. Livingston's office with her hair pulled back into a no nonsense chignon. She was wearing south sea pearls that had been passed down from her grandmother and her mother's gold watch. She had worn these pieces to remind herself who she was, that the women in her family had survived so much gracefully, and she would be no exception. So when she spoke to Dr. Livingston, she drew strength from these memories.

"Doctor, thank you for speaking honestly, but I am not your average woman. I am what people describe as formidable, and I come from a generation of formidable women with very few exceptions and if this cancer can be overcome, I will do it."

Dr. Livingston smiled and told her that she shared her faith and she also encouraged her to keep that attitude because she believed in the power of positive thinking. She had confided in her aunt about the doctor's prognosis, but she couldn't bring herself to tell Dele. She pushed the thought away from her. Dele was right. So much had happened. They had come so far. After everything that had happened in their marriage it was amazing that they would feel any love, not to talk of feeling like this. That Dele would be the one to hold her hair out of her eyes as she vomited, even as the hair shed in his hands. That he would wipe her off her spit and bathe her, who could have predicted that there could be this, Karen thought. She wondered if she was tempting fate by calling it love. Could a philanderer reform? Could an ice queen thaw? Wiser men would say no. Yet here they were. If this was possible, then the idea of her going into remission was possible as well. She just knew it. For a split second Chika popped into Karen's mind. Chika would say that this was a miracle. And for the first time in a long time, Karen hoped that there were indeed miracles. She hoped that there was God.

As Karen inhaled Dele's masculine scent, she thought to herself that perhaps a testimony would be a good way to describe their marriage story. At the beginning of the year, she felt nothing for him, she was indifferent to him. He was simply part of her landscape. Her husband. Like a tree that only served to recycle nutrients in a never used garden. He didn't matter to her and she didn't matter to him. Even when he came to be with her because he found out she was sick, she was sure it was merely out of obligation. It had shocked her to find out that he cared about her. It surprised her more to know that she cared about him. She had locked that part of herself away. She had become emotionally unavailable on purpose, and it didn't matter that she locked out love, because as far as she could tell, love equaled hurt.

Suddenly she had a rush of panic. What if this was all a lie? What is Dele was simply doing all this out of pity? What if he was still cheating? Her heart started to race at the thought and she started to gasp for air. Dele held her away from him, looking at her with concern. "Are you okay?"

When he asked, she wanted to answer his question with one of her own. She wanted to ask if he was really being true? She wanted to ask if she was the only one he was truly committed to as a husband should be? But she couldn't. How could she open herself up like that? She had already let him get too close; she couldn't give him more power over her.

"I'm fine. I just need to rest," She said.

"Of course," he said, laying her back down against the pillows and fluffing them up around her. He pulled the duvet up around her, tucking her in as if she were a child. "Better?" he asked. She nodded and leaned back into the pillows.

He stood there looking at her. Karen felt uncomfortable. She felt as if he was reading her mind and sensing her fears and insecurities. She forced herself to breathe slowly and as the air filled up her lungs, she regained her sense of control. Dele looked at her trying to decipher her closed expression. Karen looked away, feeling like a naked woman with scars that crisscrossed her body. From the corner of her eye, she saw him shrug and turn away in the direction of the bathroom. Soon she heard the shower running, and the rhythmic sound of water hitting the tiled floor lulled her to sleep. By the time Dele came out with his towel wrapped around his waist, Karen was too far gone in sleep to appreciate how lovingly he looked at her.

# Chapter 29

# Lola
## Cater to me

Lola stood in her kitchen preparing to cook. She had given the cook the day off because she felt as if she needed to feel more like she used to, more normal somehow. As she cut the onions, her eyes started to smart. John had already sent a text saying that he wouldn't be able to make it home for dinner. The text was so matter of fact. There was no care, no affection. It was if he didn't even count her worthy of a phone call or a more carefully worded message anymore. She tried to call him when she received the text, but he didn't pick up her call.

She retreated to the kitchen and as she remembered how rejected she felt, she allowed the fumes of the onions to be a catalyst for her tears. She poured the chopped onions in a bowl and walked over to the sink to wash her hands. The diamond rings sparkled as the light and water hit it. The charms on her gold bracelet tinkled as she moved her wrists. She walked out of the kitchen and went to the hallway. She looked at her image in the antique style mirror they had hanging there. She saw the face of a carefully coiffed woman. Her beautiful hair was styled in loose waves and the expensive highlights that she put in regularly gave her a slightly exotic look. Even without make up, her features were attractive. She touched the skin on her cheek and it was now soft and smooth, the result of weekly facials and regular skin treatments. She shook off her sadness and went into her bedroom to wash her face, later powdered it, applied a little lip gloss and grabbed her purse. Her boys were in the family room playing. She walked in there to meet them.

The nanny looked up from the magazine she had been perusing, and Lola dismissed her for the evening. She told the boys to go and get their shoes because she was taking them out for pizza. They screamed in delight and her older son gave her a hug, "Mummy, you are the bestest mummy!" Lola smiled. Then the thought occurred to her that she was crying and feeling unloved over her husband's behavior, but here in these little faces was so much love. She spent so much time primping for her husband and agonizing over his response, yet she sometimes neglected these little boys who longed for more time with her. She resolved right there and then to change her focus. When they got their shoes, she gathered them into a hug. "Have I told you boys how much I love you" and then she started to kiss them. "Eww!" they squealed, laughing even as they pushed her away.

Lola's heart leaped. Even if the life that she knew seemed to be slipping away, she still was blessed. She had these two beautiful boys. How could she not be thankful to God. When she returned home with her sons, she noticed that her husband's car was in the compound. He had called several times while they were out. She ignored him. She didn't want anything to spoil her mood. She and her sons were having an amazing time.

She carried in her younger son and their guard helped her carry in her older son. As they approached the front door, John opened it and took his son from the guard's arms. "Where did you go?" he queried as soon as the guard left. "Why didn't you take the nanny? Why didn't you answer my calls?" With each question his voice rose a little.

She motioned for him to keep his voice down, pointing to the boys as they walked up the stairs to the children's bedroom. He placed his son in his bed and walked out. She stayed in the room and took off their shoes, then she got them out of their street clothes and into their pajamas. She touched their foreheads as she offered a quick prayer for their lives. Then she walked into their private sitting room, where she knew he would be waiting for her.

"I asked you where you went?" he demanded as soon as she crossed the threshold.

"Since you said you wouldn't make it home for dinner, I decided to take the boys out for pizza. They had such a great time," she responded.

"Okay, but I called you, why didn't you answer?" he asked.

"Oh, my phone was on silent," she responded, an answer that he always gave to her whenever she asked why he didn't answer her calls.

"Hmm...okay." He said. And then he switched on the television.

Lola turned around to leave. "Where are you going? Stay and watch something with me," he said, his attitude softer. Lola furrowed her brow. She couldn't remember the last time in weeks that he made an effort to spend time with her. Even when they were both in the house, he preferred spending time in his office on his computer than to being with her. So she was shocked, but she didn't feel like being with him.

"I am really tired. I need to go to bed" she asked as she continued moving in the direction of the door.

"Lola, wait," he said, sounding urgent. He stood up and walked over to her. She stood still and continued facing the other direction, even though she could feel him behind her.

"Lola, talk to me," he demanded, placed his hands on her shoulders and pulled her around to face him.

She turned to face him, but she found she couldn't look at him. She had no energy for fighting and she felt as if her eyes would betray her anger.

"What is wrong? Lola, why are you acting this way?" he coaxed, touching her cheek and tilting her head up towards his face. The fighting bells started to go off in her head. He was asking her what was wrong with her? As if it was normal to have a relationship like theirs.

"John, please, I am tired and I don't feel like talking, I want to go to bed," she insisted.

"Of course, you are tired Lola. After meeting with your boyfriend. And the fact that you had the guts to take my sons along is beyond me!" John shouted.

Lola was floored. She was confused because surely she wasn't being accused of cheating. "What are you talking about John? I took the boys out for pizza!" She opened her purse and pulled out the receipt. "Here! Does that prove it to you? In fact, why don't you call them and ask them if there was any man sitting with me."

John took the receipt and glanced at it. "Okay, so this time you were alone" he said.

"John, I don't know what you are getting at, but I have never cheated on you. But can you say the same? Can you tell me that you are not still seeing that woman?" Lola snapped.

John clenched his fist, crumpling the receipt in the process. "You see, this is what I can't stand. You are always accusing me, judging me."

"You didn't answer the question!" Lola said, holding firm.

"Why bother, you will think what you want," John said. "Like I said, I am not about to compete with your fertile imagination. The days when I gave a damn about what you think are gone!"

Lola shook her head and said, "Whatever John! Do what you like" and she began to walk away again.

John caught her arm and pulled her gently. "Lola, you are my wife, why can't you understand that. You are the one I loved enough to marry." He cupped her face.

Lola took his hands off. "John, I guess that is supposed to console me, but honestly if this is love, then I don't want it. You love me so much, you never take my calls. You love me so much, you are constantly having late night meetings and weekend business trips where your phone somehow dies or gets lost or on silent. You love me so much that we hardly make love. What kind of love would you describe that as?"

"Lola," John sighed. "As usual, you are being dramatic and taking things out of context. Of course I have to take meetings. How do you propose we pay for this lavish lifestyle that you adore so much? That Birkin bag that you hinted at for weeks last year, how much did it cost? How much are you bringing to the table?" John spat out.

"It always boils down to that right?" Lola shouted in frustration,"Well, you can have the bag, I don't want it anymore."

"Lola, please, save the theatrics," John said in irritation.

"No! You wanted to talk. So deal with it!" Lola shouted.

"Okay, fine, let's talk. You want to talk about sex. Lola quite frankly, sex with you is boring," John said. "You don't excite me. You just lay there. You don't even know how to give a decent blow job!" Lola shook her head and tried to will the tears away. John always hit below the belt. If he couldn't win on facts then he tried to diminish his opponent by attacking them. "To hell with you John!" Lola said as she walked away.

This time John pulled her arm forcefully, and pushed her onto the sofa. "Sex is what you want, abi!" he said as he started to unbuckle his belt. Lola just stared at him in shock, her body frozen. As he dropped his trousers, he tried to kiss her. When she turned away her face, he used his hand to hold her head steady while he devoured her mouth. He held her cheeks so forcefully that they hurt. Then he held her down with the weight of his body.

"You are my wife Lola, mine!" he shouted as he reached under her skirt and pulled her panties off. Lola couldn't speak, she couldn't even scream. The sound of life was dying within her. When he shuddered and slumped against her, that was when she noticed that his shirt was wet with her tears.

# Chapter 30

# Chika
# And the beat goes on

Collins had moved in. Kind of. Chika loved waking up in his arms so much that she ignored the dense lumps of guilt that she had to swallow every morning as she drank her coffee. She loved everything about his presence in her apartment; from the light snoring to the morning breath. He was wonderful. They had had a rocky few days though. It all started when Collins sat her down and said he had to be honest about something. As soon as the words collected in her head, Chika's could feel her heart beat stopping. It was that dull painful sensation of loss. Her face must have revealed her panic because he reached over and took her hands and told her not to worry.

"What do you need to tell me?" she asked, pulling her hands back and placing them in her lap. She knew something was wrong. She had been ignoring the uneasy feeling that had been swimming beneath the surface of their passion since they met.

"Well," he started, staring at the wall as if unable to continue.

"Well what?" Chika snapped.

"It's about my wife," he said.

Chika blinked. "You mean your ex-wife," she said.

Collins shook his head. "Well, that's actually the issue. We are not yet legally divorced."

Chika practically screamed her next few words. "What do you mean?" She started to hyperventilate a little. She had been sleeping with a married man! Every single verse on adultery popped into her head as if she had a "condemn the whorish woman app" programmed into her brain. She leaned back into her chair and when he tried to come close, she pushed him away.

"So why are you telling me this now?" she screamed and stood up at the same time. "Why? You didn't tell me when I could have made the choice, you told me after you made me fall for you. It is all just an ego boost for you, right? And now you are going back to your wife?"

"Chika wait, calm down. Let me explain." He stood up and spoke softly.

"Just get out!" she screamed. A dish fell and shattered in the kitchen. She became irritated.

"Chika, just stop. I said the divorce is not final. That's all. She is stalling, angling for more money. I am not going back to my wife. I want to be with you."

Chika didn't know what to think. As she looked at him, she desperately wanted to believe him. He saw the opening in her face and took it. He pulled her close without warning and kissed her. Her head began to spin. When he released her, he asked, "Could I kiss you like that, if I didn't love you? Could I make love to you the way I do, if you weren't everything to me?" Chika just stared at him. He continued, "I love you Chika. With everything I am and have. I want to build a life with you. This is only a temporary glitch. My lawyers and I are working on it. I just wanted you to know. Please believe me. You have got to believe me because I can't lose you. You are the best thing that has ever happened to me."

Chika allowed herself to be carried away by the cadence of his voice. She kissed him and used her lips to seal her fears in an airtight Pandora's box. She decided to believe every word he said. She soaked them up like a piece of bread and let them change the consistency of her thoughts. This had to be love. It couldn't be anything else.

She couldn't stop smiling that next morning. He had woken her up by kissing her on the cheek, and they made love. Even though she was late for work, she walked with him to the veranda where he had breakfast laid out and an envelope wrapped up in a bow. She opened the envelope and was surprised to find blueprints of a house in it.

"What is this?" She asked.

Collins began to grin. Then he took her hand. "It will be our house."

Chika just stared at him. Her brain was firing a million synapses at the same time. "What do you mean, our house?"

He then told her it was a house he had started building in Lekki, and now he knew she would be the one to share it with him.

Chika blinked. "Collins dear. That's so sweet, but wouldn't we have to get married first?" She smiled but it faded a little when she noticed his features stiffen a little, but it passed so quickly it was almost imperceptible.

"Darling! Don't be so old fashioned! This is the twenty-first century! You are talking as if we are in 1950's. I love you and you love me and that is all that matters."

Chika just sipped her coffee, the maid never made it the right way. Today it was onyx black and bitter. She peered at him over the top of the rim of her cup, and she realized he was serious. *So this is what you are becoming?* She tried to silence the voice of sadness inside of her. *What about your values? What about your faith?* The voice became louder and more insistent. She shook her head to get rid of it.

Collins reacted. "What is wrong baby? Don't you like the house? Tell me, what you want changed and we will change it."

Chika glanced at the blueprint again and said, "The house is fine, it's just that I am running late." She pushed away from the table and stood up. He didn't get up. He was lost in the lines on the light paper. "Okay sweetie, I'll see you later."

Chika nodded and she walked away. Once she got outside, she collected herself in the warmth of the morning sun. Then she walked over to her car where the driver was holding open the door for her. She put on her sunglasses, put on her ipod and her headphones. She had to change the playlist because the first song that came on was a gospel song talking about being sold out to God and she knew she couldn't flow with that, that morning. As she settled into some Diana Krall, she felt slightly more relaxed. The voice in her head was finally quelled, although it didn't go quietly. *You can run. But eventually you won't be able to hide.*

Her phone buzzed. She looked at the caller ID. Pastor Ify! Crap. She swore softly. The car had stopped because of traffic and the magazine vendors pushed their glossy covers in front of her window.

"Kuro jo!" her driver yelled at the bodies in front of his vehicle.

One glossy caught her eye. She had forgotten that she had agreed to be their cover story. She did it so long ago, when she had just moved back. She bought the magazine and then studied the full size picture of herself. The tagline screamed:

> *A Faith Filled Life! Chika Okoye*
> *talks about living her life with Godly*
> *principles.*

As she read the article, she remembered saying the words, but today, she couldn't say that she was walking the walk. The next song came on and she was grateful for the distraction. Listening to Nina Simone's rendition of "My baby just cares for me" allowed her to ignore the queasy feelings of guilt and shame bubbling up in her stomach and start visualizing a life with Collins; her man who was not quite hers alone.

# Chapter 31

# Karen
# Just love

Karen heard the doctor speaking, but the sound was muffled. It was as if she was listening with cotton stuffed into her ears.

"I'm so sorry," the doctor was saying.

They had been fighting her cancer aggressively on all fronts and they had come for the results of a new series of tests to see if the treatments were working. Nothing was working, and the cancer was spreading at a rapid pace. The doctor had said there was nothing more that could be done. She wanted to prepare Karen.

Dele spoke, his voice cracked as if he was dehydrated. "What are you really saying Doctor? How long do we have?"

Dr. Livingston looked broken as she spoke. "It's hard to say. It could be a year, or a week, or even a day. We are going to work to keep you as comfortable as possible."

Karen spoke up. "But I don't feel that bad?" she said. "Surely there must be some mistake?"

Dele interjected. "There has to be! Surely there is another kind of therapy, some clinical trial... something?"

The doctor paused. "I wish there was. I can refer you to another doctor for a second opinion if you like? I hope I am wrong, but I know I am not, I am afraid. You need to use your time well."

Karen's head was spinning. She had come to the US to see her fertility specialist so she and Dele could procreate, only to be told that there would be no babies and infact there might be no tomorrows. Dele held her close and she just allowed her head to rest on his shoulder.

"I'll give you guys some time alone," Dr. Livingston said as she got up and left the room.

Dele just held Karen and kept repeating, "It's alright" over and over. Karen was so glad he was with her at that moment, but for the first time in her life, she was facing her own mortality and she now understood the meaning of the word alone. Even though Dele was holding her hand and rubbing her back, ultimately, she was walking down this path alone. She could die in a week. Dele wouldn't go with her. That would be it. And where would she go, she wondered? The thoughts raced into her mind so fast that they began to bump against each other and her brain felt crowded.

"I've got to get out of here," she said. The urgency in her voice was deafening, even as she whispered. Dele helped her up; she was still weak from all the chemotherapy. "Where do you want to go? Back to the hotel?" he asked.

"No. Central Park," she said.

"Your wish is my command," he said with a half hearted attempt to make her smile.

She rewarded him with a small one and squeezed his hand.

When they got outside, he tried to hail a taxi, but she told him she preferred to walk. She walked slowly; every step was a chore for her.

"Sweetheart, this is too much for you. You need to rest!" Dele started to insist.

"No, I want to walk. I'll rest when I am dead," Karen said, in dark humor. Dele didn't laugh. It felt as if everyone was rushing around them and they were moving in slow motion like the special effects in those big budget Hollywood movies. They just held hands and occasionally looked at each other. They didn't speak, but so much was said. Karen touched his fingers one by one as she thought about how she saw him fully now and accepted him and loved him. Dele kissed her forehead, asking again for forgiveness, so he could be worthy of her even in these last days. Karen leaned her head on his shoulder, while holding on to his arm. She was giving herself to him, letting down her walls, letting down her guard like she was lifting up her veil at their wedding. When they reached Central Park, Karen was exhausted. They sat on a park bench.

There was something very tranquil about America, especially when she compared it to life in Lagos. If she had to die, she would rather die here: quietly and anonymously. Sitting right here on the park bench with Dele by her side.

"Do you want to see another doctor?" Dele spoke, aware that he was interrupting her thoughts.

"No. I don't. Dr. Livingston is the best. I trust her diagnosis. I just want to enjoy whatever time I have left."

"Karen..."

"Dele, please don't say anything. It is what it is. I don't want to spend whatever time I have left dying. I want to live until I die. After all we all have to do it sometime or another. So please, let's forget what just happened for now.

"Okay," he said, holding up his hands in defeat and then clasping them again as he sighed with worry.

"Dele, there is something I would like you do for me," Karen asked.

Dele stiffened and said, "Anything."

"I want to take a horse-drawn carriage ride," she said.

He laughed out loud. "I thought it would be something far more difficult!" He stood up and acted like a footman from the royal castles of England. "At your service, milady," he said in his proper English accent. Then he knelt beside her, "I'll be right back, darling. Just rest here and I'll make it happen."

Karen watched him walk away. She remembered the first time she saw his confident stride. He was such a handsome man. She relished the sound of his voice calling her darling. He said it so much tenderness. Dele had never been tender with her. He had been so hard, cold and selfish. But then again, she never had been this vulnerable. "Was this what men needed? To feel needed?" She shook her head. She had no time to consider the psychology of gender relations, she only had time to live and be happy and that was all she wanted to do. Soon Dele ran across the grass with a thick woolen blanket that he had purchased from a vendor and when he reached her, he wrapped her in it, saying, it's getting cold. She was just about to ask him what happened to her chariot, when she heard the clop, clop, sound of a horse's hooves. She looked up and there it was. She smiled. It was just like a fairytale.

Dele helped her up and she leaned against him as they settled in, he pulled the blankets up around her and tucked her in. She looked up at the trees as they moved slowly past them. The sky was clear and a beautiful blue. She gazed at it, wondering. Dele looked up too. She wondered what he was thinking.

# Chapter 32

# Chika
# You look surprised!

Chika woke up in a cold sweat. She was engulfed in guilt and frustration. She had been dreaming about making love to Collins. She was totally beside herself; feeling hypocritical. Just the other day, she spoke to the youth group at one of the popular churches in Lagos. She had accepted the invitation to speak months ago, before she even met Collins, and she couldn't figure out a way to turn it down. She squirmed on the inside as she preached the importance of abstinence and celibacy, even while her bed was still warm from Collins' body. She told the girls how they shouldn't settle to be unequally yoked and she answered questions from her last book about loving yourself and loving God.

How much lower could she sink? She decided that she had to break up with Collins, but she knew she couldn't do it; she was intoxicated, yet she knew she had to. The relationship had turned her into something and someone that she could no longer recognize. Just last night, they were talking again about moving in together and even though living with a man without being married went against her moral code, she found herself nodding in agreement and pushing her concerns to the background as she focused on the sweetness of his affections. He said all the right things. He loved her. He cared about her. Wasn't that all that mattered? Still another quieter voice asked, if it was really all that mattered? What about God? What about truth? What about having the courage of your convictions? A scripture ran through her mind: "But I have prayed for you Peter, so that your faith will not fail, and when you have turned back, encourage your brothers". She sat up straight because the verse had popped into her head unbidden. The Holy Spirit was speaking, and she could feel the vexation.

"Aunty, ah beg, stay well now, make I finish your hair. First you dey sleep, now you wan dey move your head".

The substitute stylist was trying to curl Chika's hair, and her jerking about made it difficult. Chika apologized and tried to focus on the moment, she had forgotten that she was at work, and about to go on camera. She started to make small talk with the hair stylist and then her makeup artist, who came in shortly after. Between the gossip about which socialite was dating who and what singer had had yet another child with yet another baby mama, Chika was able to dismiss her self-deprecating thoughts, and by the time Gbenga came to get her to start the show, she felt relaxed and secure once again. She took one last look in the mirror and was pleased. Yes, God had indeed made her beautiful.

When she walked on stage, the audience cheered and her heart was warmed. She felt validated by their adulation. For some reason, she resonated with the Nigerian audience. In just a few short months, she had already superseded every existing talk show host in popularity, and they were calling her the Nigerian Oprah. People wrote her letters telling her in detail how she inspired them and it was those thoughts that she pulled her energy from when she said, "Hello Nigeria! It's a new day, a new dawn, are you feeling good?" When the crowd erupted in applause, she sat down satisfied.

"Today we are taking things up a notch! Because today we are coming to you live and direct. No leave, no transfer. Today what you see is really what you get, so it's a good thing I have nothing to hide!" She said, laughing confidently. Collins was just a hiccup and she would sort it later, this woman on this stage, was who she was born to be.

"Today we are talking about relationships, and our first guest is a woman who has chosen to live in the UK, while her husband resides in Nigeria. Yet she says their marriage works. She says they are happy like that. Quite non-traditional, wouldn't you agree audience?" Chika continued, gesticulating to paint a more vivid story. "Well, she is here today, to tell us exactly how it works. Audience, I want you to join me in welcoming Funke, she wants to retain some anonymity, so we'll call her by her first name only.

Chika clapped with the audience as a stunning woman in a beautiful multi-colored tunic and jeans walked on to the stage. No one could deny that this was an elegant, attractive woman. As she walked on, Chika wondered why any man would choose to live apart from such a woman? She smiled and shook Chika's hands. Chika directed her to sit on the ash colored sofa. She sat opposite her and smiled as waited for the audience to get settled and the camera man to give her the go ahead. The show was live so every moment had to be synchronized. At the required moment, Chika began to talk.

"So Funke, tell us why you choose to live in London and not in Lagos with your husband?" Chika asked, immediately. "I am sure that I am not the only one who sees that as odd? Most people get married to be together, so how can you choose to be with someone and not live together?"

Funke didn't answer right away, her demeanor was calm. She tossed her hair back and said, "Well, you see, I don't believe that I have to conform with the norm. I like being married to my husband and at this time, unfortunately, we have individual interests that keep us apart geographically. However, he comes home regularly to spend time with us, and every trip sometimes feels like another honeymoon. So we are still quite close. In addition to that, I have been working on my PhD for the last few years, and I just completed my dissertation, so I am preparing to move back anyway."

Chika nodded and smiled encouragingly. "But hasn't the distance put a strain on your marriage? I mean it can't be easy, maintaining the level of intimacy required for a marriage to work?" she asked leaning in to show interest.

Funke shrugged her shoulders as she replied. "Certainly it does, but it works for now, I guess. I have learned in this life, you have to make the best of whatever situation you find yourself in," she said with some measure of finality.

Chika frowned slightly; this was not turning out to be as interesting as they had thought. She would have to get this woman to open up some more. Just as she was thinking about what questions to ask her to do just that, Funke spoke again without even being asked a question. "Of course there are the occasional complications..." she said, trailing off a little at the end. Chika sat up taller and she could see Gbenga giving her the thumbs up from the side of the stage. She was excited because it seemed as if Funke was ready to get real.

"Complications? Can you tell us more?" Chika probed, hoping that her guest would open up.

Funke complied with Chika's unspoken request and leaned back and spoke with care, "Well, actually Chika, perhaps you can tell us all more, being that you are actually the one complicating my life by sleeping with my husband?"

Chika stared wide-eyed at the woman before her. Surely she hadn't heard correctly. Then she looked around at her staff, maybe they were playing a practical joke on her. They seemed just as confused. She looked back at the woman sitting opposite her on the stage and she could see from her face, that the woman was being serious.

"I beg your pardon?" Chika asked, straightening up.

"Oh, don't act innocent for your audience; they should all know that you are a complete fake. Christian ko, Christian ni. Where was your faith, when my husband Collins slept in your bed last night?"

Chika felt as if she was falling. She wanted to speak, but nothing came out. Meanwhile Funke continued like a wound up doll, "You should be ashamed of yourself. Preaching about valuing yourself and yet, you sell yourself so cheap to the first man that comes along."

Chika felt dizzy. She wondered why her director, Nkechi, hadn't stopped the show. She tried to signal to her, but she wouldn't meet her eye. Funke fanned her mouth in a shaming gesture that Chika hadn't seen since she was a child.

"Yes o! Audience, now you know the truth. Your new day, new life, madam is just a common mistress." Funke then jumped up and stood over her now. She grabbed her by the shoulders and began to shake her. She kept taunting her as she did. "Ah, ah, now you have nothing to say?"

That was when Chika woke up and pushed her off her, but Funke was not to be deterred. As Chika tried to walk off the stage, she jumped on Chika's back and started pulling at Chika's weave. She tore her blouse and streaked her makeup. Some audience members ran up on stage to help, and the camera kept rolling. Chika gave in to the pain and the shame; she allowed Funke to slap her on and on, until someone pulled her off. She cried as she remained in the fetal position and as she wept. The camera was still on. She turned her face away and tried to pray, but the words wouldn't come. She didn't know what to do. "Please help me!" she cried silently.

Someone finally shouted. "Stop the show!" It was Gbenga, who had been watching from his office. He rushed onto the stage like the prince who would rescue her.

"Clear this room out now!" He bellowed.

Finally he approached her. He picked her up and carried her off the stage. "Stop crying. It's going to be okay." He said. She looked away from him ashamed.

He carried her to the office and then he put her down on the sofa. She sat up and stared blankly. Then he picked up her purse and handed it to her. "You need to go home. Don't worry, things will work out alright." He called for his driver and ordered him to take her home.

She put on her sunglasses and tried to sleep, but the driver had the radio on and the DJ was already talking about her rise and fall, and he ended his tirade with "This is why I don't trust Christians."

\*\*\*\*\*\*\*\*\*

It had been a brutal week. Collins was nowhere to be found. The clothes he left behind, were the only evidence of their relationship. It seemed he had blocked her number. She turned her phone off because it rang non-stop with people trying to get the insider view of the scandal. She couldn't listen to the newspaper or read the blogs, because her story was everywhere. She had tried reaching Karen but she was out of the country and not responding and even Lola, didn't answer either. It seemed everyone had forsaken her. By the end of the week, the darkness threatened to overwhelm her and she was entertaining suicidal thoughts.

Sunday came sooner than expected, and she didn't feel like going to church but she needed to go. She needed to feel God's love again. She felt lost and precariously close to the edge. As she considered walking into the sanctuary, she was afraid. She could already see the stares and hear the whispers. She knew most people were not as nonjudgmental and as forgiving as Pastor Ify, so she braced herself for people's reactions. She sat on the edge of her bed looking at the clock, until she didn't have much time to put on her clothes and finish her makeup. She smiled at herself in the mirror, hoping to boost her confidence, but it didn't work. She grabbed her mp3 player and scrolled through her list of songs. She found it quickly, Tenth Ave North's, "You are more". She put it on the highest volume and as she listened to the lyrics, she pushed past her fear and shame and got dressed.

She repeated the chorus in her head over and over as she grabbed her Bible and drove to church. She held onto to the words from the bridge as she walked down the aisle to her seat. *This is not about what you've done, but what's been done for you; this is not about where you've been but where your brokenness brings you to.*

She willed the music to drown out the loud sounds of judgment she felt as people began to whisper and turn around in their seats as she walked in. She saw a woman with a large pink gele, turn and hiss aloud as she rolled her eyes in her direction. Another woman grabbed her husband close with one hand and her Bible tight with her other hand. Even though Chika tried to focus on the altar, where someone was giving a special number, she couldn't. She couldn't concentrate on the image of Jesus on the cross because she felt as if she was being sentenced in the court of public opinion. She was about to grab her bag and leave, when the choir sang a line about Christ being wounded and bleeding and dying for us all. She was convicted afresh at that moment. Maybe she needed to go through discomfort. After all, she had done something that yielded this discomfort. People would make judgments, but it was up to her to show them that she was not that woman that they thought she was. It was up to her to walk and begin to live in a way that contradicted their worst images of her. She forced herself to hold her head up. She was stronger than their judgment.

It would not be easy, this path that she had to walk. The network had already called. Gbenga was apologetic as he informed her that the executives had decided to cancel the show and that they would provide her with a handsome severance package. She sat in church listening to the announcements, wondering what her next move would be. Should she stay in Lagos, or run back overseas, away from these prying eyes and angry thoughts? She had no answers.

Pastor Ify took to the stage. She walked up to the pulpit and explained that her husband, the head pastor was away in Zambia but that he sent his greetings and his love. She then asked the congregation to turn to a chapter in Luke. "Simon, Simon, Satan has asked to sift all of you as wheat".

Chika sat straight up in her seat. Suddenly, she didn't see anyone else or hear anything else but the sermon that was being preached. This was the verse that had jumped into her head just before all this drama had started. Surely this was God. Pastor Ify began the sermon.

"You see, the Bible says Satan has asked to sift all of you like wheat. Who is *all of you?*"

Chika listened to the sermon, oblivious of the stares and whispers around her. She just focused on the words. In spite of the public nature of church, she was having a private experience. Pastor Ify's sermon went on, "Temptation is constantly around me. Just as it is around you. Jesus knew this. This is why he gave Simon insider information. He wanted him to know that he already knew. He wanted Simon to know that he already knew his frailties, already knew his failures, yet he still loved him enough to pray for him."

Chika started to cry. She wept and wept.

"He who created you, knows you and he prays for you."

"He is interceding for you."

Chika let the tears roll down her face without shame and when Pastor Ify asked for those who wanted to rededicate their lives to come forward, she got to her feet and took quick steps with boldness to the altar. She ignored everyone, including those who whispered to each other that at least, she recognized her sin.

# Chapter 33

# Lola
## Release me

Lola sat in the pews and her eyes were wet after Pastor Ify's powerful sermon. She felt as if she was finally connecting with her life. She didn't go forward for the altar call. She was surprised to see Chika walking down the aisle towards the front, although, she remembered hearing something about her being disgraced on live television. But she was so consumed by her own problems that she couldn't focus on anything else.

After that horrible night with John, she hadn't been able to eat anything for days and then she had fainted once, while at an event being held on the grounds outside. Between the heat and her lack of food, her body simply gave out. Her family called John from Enugu where they lived and he assured them that she was fine, even though he checked her into a private hospital where they kept her overnight and treated her for dehydration. After that John gave strict instructions to the cook and nanny to inform him, if she didn't eat. He told her that her would come home and force her to eat if necessary. So she ate, but only the bare minimum, just enough to live. She didn't speak much and the only times she smiled was when she was with her boys. Even John was surprised at the depths of her depression. She was catatonic.

This Sunday was her first Sunday in church in a month. John stayed home as usual. The driver drove her there, and in the plush seats of their Mercedes, wrapped up in her shawl with her oversize sunglasses, they looked even more oversize now that her cheeks were shrunken from her weight loss. She sat at the back of the church, but she felt the presence of God as if she were seated right at the altar. She cried and when it was time to pray. She prayed as if her life depended on it. She couldn't go back to living like this. Her marriage had deteriorated so quickly, though if she were honest it had started to fail long before this woman had come on the scene. Though she was wounded by his betrayal, it was John's attitude that broke her. This man, whom she had given her life, showed so little regard for her. He had become so arrogant. He had no remorse about his behavior. In the weeks that followed that night, he tried to justify his actions by blaming her. He told her that it was she pushed him to hit her, through her words and through her silences. He told her that he regretted marrying her, but he was not going to let his children grow up in a broken home. After that night, he had let himself descend into this chasm of hatefulness, and the John she knew and loved was no longer in that same body.

He didn't touch her again, but he assaulted her with his tongue every day. Sometimes she would sing in her head, just to drown out his words. Sometimes she felt as if she was floating outside of her body watching the melodramatic storylines of a Nollywood movie.

She sat there in the pew, trying to figure out what she would do. She knew at that moment that she had to leave; if only for a little while. She had to get away because staying with him wasn't healthy for her or him, and her boys. As she thought about her boys, her eyes filled afresh. She started to sob and when people started to turn to see who was weeping, she put on her sunglasses and walked out, though prayers continued.

She wasn't crying because she felt helpless. She was crying because she finally felt free; she felt like she knew who she was. And she knew what she had to do. She knew that the path she was about to embark on wouldn't be easy, but she knew it was the only way.

She was going home.

And she was moving out.

# Chapter 34

# Karen
# The next season

They had just arrived at the hotel in Boston. The Four Seasons was one of the most luxurious, but Karen was tired of hotels. She yearned for her own bed and her own sheets. She wanted to walk on the carpets that she had chosen, in a house that she had furnished. She was hungry for Jollof rice made just the way her cook did, with just the right amount of hot pepper. She was so tired, but she couldn't give up. Dele watched her all the time. She could feel him willing her to live. He had pulled every string he could, he had even borrowed a few from others and finally they had an appointment to meet with the doctor starting a new investigative trial two days later. Karen was hopeful, but she was exhausted. She was in so much pain, but she was so grateful for Dele's presence, she didn't know if she could do this alone. He had put everything on hold. He still conducted business on the internet and on the phone, but he tried so hard to keep interruptions to a minimum, while she was awake.

She often woke up to see him in the shadows working through the night. She looked closely at him. He was lying down on the bed next to her and he had fallen asleep. He had aged in these past few months since this ordeal had started. Had his hair always been that grey? Her emotions rushed to the forefront of her thoughts and her sadness pushed through and enhanced her pain, so much so that she winced. They had wasted so much time. Now that the situation was so dire was when things seemed so clear. What good was her pride? What good was his? All that energy she had used hating and detesting him, what good did it do? She was angry at herself and even somewhat at him, but even as the anger came she released it into the atmosphere and covered it with forgiveness. She was human. She had been wounded and they had both made mistakes. Who is it that has truly lived and had no regrets?

So she moved from anger to gratitude; gratitude that at the end of the day, they had this and maybe they would have even more days and hours and minutes. She sent up a silent word of thanks. She still didn't understand the intricacies of religion, but she had started to feel an openness that she couldn't describe. She had been praying, who doesn't face death and reach out for their creator, she thought. Of course she had been praying. However at this moment, all she wanted to do was say thank you. Thank you for this moment. Thank you for this snapshot of life that is so beautiful. The light streamed through the window on the other side of the room and framed Dele's face. As she looked at him, she felt as if it was a supernatural experience, she could feel how much he loved her like a warm coat keeping out all the cold. Just then, she stopped feeling the pain. She closed her eyes and smiled as she tried to sleep.

The lull wouldn't come; too many thoughts still swam in her head. She was still amazed at the way things had turned out, she never could have expected that they would be in love and it would be so glorious. Stranger than fiction, she thought. Tears began to well up in her eyes. In spite of the fact that her body was being ravaged by tumors, she felt so very blessed. She had always wondered if Dele cared enough about her to be by her side if she was ill. Her father had not shown that level of care to her mother, so she had prepared herself and even when she had the occasional malaria or so, she usually bore it with a stoic smile, never letting him know just how sick she was. She lay there watching his chest fall and rise and realized that she could count the number of times they had shared a bed in their marriage, prior to this happening.

She never thought she would experience the kind of love she used to read about in the novels of her youth. She always thought it wasn't real, a fallacy used to lure in weak women. And here she was.

Her mind wandered back to a song, one of her nannies used to sing. This particular nanny didn't last very long in her parents employ. She couldn't remember the melody but she remembered the lyrics. It was a gospel song, talking about how God deserved praise, even if He didn't do one more thing because according to the songwriter, He had already done enough. Karen never understood that song. It seemed silly to say that God had done enough, wasn't there always more to do? She remembered being a little girl and thinking that she didn't even give Father Christmas that option, her Christmas list was always long and detailed and she always got what she wanted. However as she lay there thinking about how her life had turned out, she didn't feel cheated or angry or sad that she had cancer, she looked at the man that she had married lying next to her and she was grateful that she had this opportunity to love. She finally understood what people meant when they said that their hearts were full. And as the tears kept dropping into her pillow, she smiled. She really understood and whispered to herself as she reached out and touched Dele's stubbled cheek. She let her hand linger as she whispered, "It is enough".

# Chapter 35

# Lola
# The Comeback Club

Lola was running around the neighborhood. It was early evening and Lola saw quite a few other men and women out in their jogging gear. She didn't feel self conscious like she normally would be, perhaps because she had lost so much weight or because she had reached such a low point that she no longer cared what people thought. She put her headphones in her ears and started to run in tune with the beat of the song. She started picking up speed and could feel the air moving across her face. Even though the sun was still high in the sky, Lola felt comfortable and even welcomed the sweat on her skin.

After a while, she didn't know what made her feel better, the upbeat music or the endorphins that were being released inside of her. Either way, it wasn't important as she ran up to the elaborate gate that protected their compound, Lola was singing because she felt so good. She greeted the security guard and startled the cook as she ran into through the kitchen. She didn't stop till she got to her bathroom and then she stripped and got into the shower. The hot water felt good and she decided to wash her hair. She got out of the bathroom and felt clear for the first time in a long time. She noticed that John was not in the bedroom when she got up that morning and she recognized that he probably didn't even come home the night before and she hadn't seen him all day.

By the time he rushed in with excuses, Lola had finished taking off make-up and had already sent the boys off to bed. She didn't say anything to him as he started to tell her where he had been and why he had been gone all night and all day. She knew he was speaking, she knew he was explaining, but she simply had stopped listening. He followed her as she walked back up to the bedroom. He kept trying to engage her, but she had nothing to say. She waited till he closed the door behind them and then she spoke.

"You know what John? I think it is better if we go our separate ways," she said, without a trace of fear, sadness or anger.

John looked taken aback. It was probably because of her resolute disposition, he probably expected crying and shouting. "What the hell are you saying Lola? Look, I don't have time for this nonsense! I was at meetings till very late and if you don't believe me that is your problem," he started shouting.

Lola kept silent, but she didn't flinch even when he walked close to her and started waving his finger in her face. "I'll be leaving tomorrow," Lola continued as if she didn't hear his tirade.

"What is wrong with you?" John said.

"Nothing," she said calmly.

"So you want to leave me?" he said shouting again. "How do you intend to live? You think I will still be paying your bills? You can't even afford one child's school fees!"

Lola kept a straight face, even though everything he said was true; she didn't have any money, but she also knew that she couldn't stay with him, so she shrugged in response. That shrug enraged him, he lunged for her, pulling her by the arms and screamed at her. He started calling her all sorts of names. Lola kept silent and forced herself to think of other things. When he called her a bitch, she took herself to the beach and ordered a Pina Colada. When he called her a stupid, stupid slut, she pictured herself getting a hot stone massage. Her silence continued to infuriate him and Lola thought she should try to get out of his space because as she looked at him, she could see his features begin to get distorted. His face had become transfigured by his rage. She had never seen him look quite like that before and became afraid. She started to struggle against him. He held her arms so tightly that his short nails drew blood. He released her left arm, but then he formed his right hand into a fist and slammed it into her jaw.

She was knocked onto the floor and he jumped on top of her and hit her again in the face. She felt a tooth crack and could taste blood in her mouth. He opened his fist and slapped her a few more times. Lola struggled to breathe because his weight overwhelmed her now emaciated frame. Somehow, though she could taste the blood, she didn't feel any pain. She thought that this must be what doctors mean when they say someone is in a state of shock. And shocked she was. She could never have foreseen this day. Never. Not when he asked her out that first day. Not when he proposed on one knee. She couldn't imagine that the man that shed tears as she walked down the aisle was capable of this. She had read about women who were killed by their husbands and always pictured such men as monsters. For the first time, she realized how thin the line was between creature and man. It took only a few flaws in character, a few bad decisions and a few justifications, a few compromises and suddenly, even the most charming man could find himself threatening death with guttural sounds and heavy fists. Even though her mind disconnected to the pain he was inflicting on her, she was still conscious enough to try to protect herself and there were moments when she tried to fight back, though with her small frame, she wasn't making much impact. At first she was screaming, but started to whimper, softly and weakly. Finally he stopped, got up and stood over her. He looked at her for a minute and walked out. She lay there like a torn rag doll. She stopped making sounds, but the tears kept running down her cheeks. She couldn't figure out how she had allowed this to become her life. She tried to get up, but everything hurt. She thought about how bruised her face would be. Her arms hurt from fighting John and even her thigh muscles were strained. So she just lay there and eventually, her tears gave way to sleep.

She was awakened when she felt his arms around her as he

lifted her up and placed her on the bed. He got a cloth and dabbed at her face. "I am so sorry," he kept repeating. He stopped trying to wipe away the blood and spit and just sat next to her, waiting for her to open her eyes. The light was streaming in from the window so Lola realized that it was dawn. She remembered a verse from the Bible: though weeping endure for the night. Joy cometh in the morning. If it was morning, where was her joy? She lay as still as possible and forced her eyes to stay closed. She just wanted him to go away. She didn't want to see him and didn't want him to touch her. It wasn't even a conscious decision; it came from an instinctual place as if her spirit had identified him as a predator. His phone started to buzz and he left the room to answer it. When he left, she opened her eyes. She looked around quickly and located her bag. She winced as she reached for it and then she dialed the only person she felt comfortable calling.

# Chapter 36

# Chika
## Mighty to save

Chika woke up filled with a sense of urgency, so she sat up in bed contemplating this feeling of unease that she felt. Looking at her clock, it read 5:18am. She lay back down again, trying to ignore the feeling that she needed to do something right away, but the feeling intensified almost as soon as her head hit the pillow. Chika gave in, threw her legs out from under the covers, walked over to her desk and turned her laptop on. She opened her word processor and began to type some words on the screen. It was a book title. A book that she knew she had to start writing immediately. *Ashes: How I burnt my life down and found God.*

She stared at the black lettering on the white screen. Was she really ready to tell her story? The question echoed in her mind in the quiet of night. How could she bare her soul to everyone and open herself up to criticism? She sighed and snapped her laptop shut. She could not do this. She would not. It just would hurt too much to relive everything that had happened. She couldn't go to any social function without hearing people chatter about her. She didn't even feel comfortable in church because she could feel the judgmental stares of the self righteous members, and she knew what they were thinking; she knew because she used to be one of those women. One of those saved people without a back story. She had been good all her life, never slipped, never fallen and so she just knew she was good and couldn't understand how people made such selfish, yet self destructive choices. Now she was one of the fallen ones—the ones who wore the messed up badge. She saw them all the time in church. The husband whom everyone knew had cheated on his wife and had a baby outside; the woman who had stolen from the coffers of the ministry she was supposed to serve; the mother who had raised sons to be criminals. Now she too, wore some sort of marker of failure. Chika sat at the desk, feeling chained to her oppressive thoughts. At first she tried to rationalize it in her mind. She didn't know that Collins was still with his wife, so it wasn't really her fault, she had been lied to. But the lie didn't sit well with her soul because she did know. She always knew. She knew that it was wrong starting a relationship with someone who was not completely removed from someone else. She knew it was wrong to be intimate with him and more than anything, it was wrong to let the yearnings of her flesh take away from the warnings of her spirit. So at the end, she had no one to blame. No one to let her off the hook, and at the end, it was just her and she had to face her God, just as she was.

She opened her laptop again. As the screen came to life, she read the title words again. The last two words stood out to her— "found God". She contemplated them and wondered if she had found God. She looked up at the ceiling and found no answers. Chika started laughing. What did she expect, handwriting on the ceiling? What would God say? "Hi! Here I am, you found me!" She laughed all the more, when she thought about the fact that she would likely take off running if she saw some handwriting on the wall. As she laughed, she leaned back in her chair. It felt good to laugh and it felt even better to laugh as she contemplated God. She suddenly felt like she was not alone. She felt a presence, more like a sensation, a feeling that it would be okay and that it was okay to laugh and even more amazing, she felt as if God was laughing with her.

She remembered listening to a speaker at church, some months back. It was a young woman who was talking about recovering from the pain of being abandoned by her husband. She had come through and had written a book about her journey and one of the most remarkable things Chika remembered about her speech was when she talked about getting into relationship with God. She said she had started to experience God on another level, as the lover of her soul. Chika was started to understand the concept of a relationship with God. She stopped feeling so ashamed about the mistakes she had made and she started to allow herself to accept God's love. She leaned even further back on the chair and let her head hang over the back. She closed her eyes and started to feel warm, even though the air conditioning was on and she felt connected to something larger than she could articulate. She felt release. She sat up and looked at the screen. She lifted her hands to the keyboard and started to type. She would share her testimony and she would face the world knowing that even though she was one of the fallen ones, she was also one of the redeemed.

Suddenly the phone rang, Chika answered it immediately wondering who could be calling this early.

"Hello?" Chika said.

"Hello Chika, it's Lola. Please I really need your help. I'm in trouble." Lola pushed the words out of her mouth quickly before she lost her nerve.

"What's going on?" Chika asked cautiously.

"It's my husband," Lola said, starting to cry. "He's beat me pretty badly and he won't let me leave."

Chika gasped. "Oh no. I'll come right over."

"Thank you," Lola said.

"Don't worry, it's going to be alright okay?" Chika said.

Chika sprung into action. She knew it would be madness for her to go to Lola's house alone. If her husband had become violent, he would be even more volatile once he realized she had exposed him. So she called Gbenga, the only reliable male acquaintance she knew.

"Hello, may I speak to Gbenga please?" she said.

"Gbenga on the line, who is this?" he said, his voice gruff.

"Gbenga, it's me, Chika," she said.

"Oh!" he said, his tone softening. "Chika! How are you? I hope you are okay these days?"

"I am. Pressed down, but not destroyed," she said.

"Amen o!" he said laughing. Chika interrupted quickly.

"Gbenga, I need your help."

"What is it?" he responded.

"Can you meet me at a friend's house? She and her husband are having an altercation and she sounds really battered. I am heading there now," Chika said, while pulling on her shoes.

"What! No...don't go alone. Hmm... I am actually around the corner from your house. I stopped at that supermarket near you. I'll come and get you. Wait for me."

"Okay," Chika said, sounding unsure. "But please hurry."

"No worries. I'll be there shortly."

Chika waited for him impatiently. She was worried about Lola. Lola had tried to be her friend, reached out to her numerous times, and each time Chika saw her she looked more and more drawn. Chika never asked if everything was okay; never tried to be there as a friend to her.

"I may have the gift to speak what God has revealed, and I may understand all mysteries and have all knowledge. I may even have enough faith to move mountains, but if I don't have love, I am nothing," she thought. She had been too self-absorbed and too focused on showing the world just how good she was that she missed an opportunity to help someone. She felt so guilty. She had really made a mess of things. The one person who genuinely tried to connect with her, well, she treated her so poorly. Chika started to pace the room, feeling stressed and helpless. What if John was pummeling her right now? Where was Gbenga? She picked up her phone to call him again, but she didn't dial because she knew that he was doing his best to get there.

She thought about calling Lola, but thought that might be a bad idea. She wanted to do something, but she didn't know what to do. Then she remembered that there was one thing she could do that could really make a difference, she could pray. And so she did. A simple four word prayer from the deepest parts of her heart and spirit: "Please God. Help Lola."

Just then the doorbell rang. Chika yelped with relief. She opened the door and gave Gbenga a big hug. He looked taken aback, but he wrapped his arms around her just the same, and a warmth rose up between them that they both noticed, but the hug was over as soon as it began.

"Let's go," he said. His voice deep and husky.

Chika turned to lock her door and her cheeks started to flush because she could feel his eyes on her. They rushed to the car and drove out in the direction of Lekki, but within minutes, they hit bumper to bumper traffic. Chika and Gbenga both groaned. Chika started to crane her neck and get agitated.

Gbenga noticed her fidgeting and grabbed her hand. "Calm down. Your friend will be okay. Alright?"

"Thank you," Chika said. "You are sweet to encourage me."

"Well, if you keep picking at my leather seats, I'll have to get them reupholstered!" he said. They both laughed, trying to release their tension.

"How are you really? I've been thinking about you."

Chika sighed. That was a loaded question and there was no straight answer.

"Honestly... it changes moment to moment. But by and large, I would say, I am better than I was yesterday. I have had a lot of growing up to do and I have changed in many ways. I can only hope it's for the better."

"Wow!" Gbenga said, "you sound like a different person!" he exclaimed.

"Well, I got served a large dose of humble pie and then a mirror to really see how judgmental and self righteous I really was."

"Mmhmm," Gbenga murmured.

"And it was painful, but honestly now I think I actually have a real relationship with God and so I am grateful," Chika said.

"Well, sometimes it takes hitting rock bottom in order to really build a firm foundation," Gbenga said.

"I guess so," Chika agreed.

"I am glad you called. I wanted to call you, but I didn't want to intrude," Gbenga admitted.

Chika smiled. This man was so kind. "Oh, it would have been all right for you to call. After all, if not for you, I might have been really physically hurt by that woman."

"She did get quite out of hand," Gbenga said, sounding irritated. "No matter what she thought was happening, physical violence is never warranted."

"Well, I can't really blame her. To her, I was trying to break up her happy home," Chika said.

"Were you?" Gbenga asked looking at her. "I am sorry to ask, but I..."

"It's okay. You should know. I didn't know he was married," Chika said. "Well...that's not technically true. He told me he was separated and that they were filing for divorce." Chika's voice broke a little. "I knew better. Separated is still married. I knew better," she said, shaking her head and lowering her eyes in shame.

Gbenga nodded. "Maybe. Some men are very deceptive." He shook his head.

"I was so stupid," Chika said sadly. Gbenga would probably be disgusted with her.

"Well, maybe so, but who among us hasn't been guilty of making poor decisions. Just this morning, I made the ill advised choice of having yam, plantain and fried eggs. Something my waistline could really do without," he said winking at her, and then he reached over and touched her cheek and smiled. "The important thing is to own up to your mistakes and take steps to be a better person. And as far as I can see, you are doing that, so kudos!" Gbenga said smiling.

Chika was quiet. She didn't expect his reaction. She was

ready for judgment, but now she didn't have anything to say because the only words she had prepared were in her own defense and now that she sat there without an accuser, there was nothing to say. Just then, the traffic cleared as if through magic and the road was free to drive. Gbenga put the car into gear and started to race towards Lola's house. Just as they got close to Lola's house, Chika found her tongue.

"Thank you for understanding," she said. Gbenga kept his eyes on the road. But he smiled.

"You know something Chika. I always liked something about you," he confessed.

Chika raised her eyebrows because it always seemed to her that he was avoiding her in the early days when they started to work together. Once, she ran into him sitting outside smoking and she began to lecture him on the health and moral ills of smoking. She remembered him rolling his eyes and simply walking away from her, while she was still speaking.

"Really, I don't remember that. You always seemed a bit irritated by me," she said.

"Oh, I was! You were quite irritating with your holier than thou attitude." He smirked as he thought about it. "But in spite of all that, I liked you. Something about you anyway. I always felt that if you would just stop wearing your religion as a coat and let your humanity be seen, then you would be such an amazing woman."

"Oh really!" Chika said, sounding a bit perturbed.

"Come on now, don't get all upset! I thought we were speaking frankly?" he said, trying to glance at her and still focus on the road.

He almost sideswiped an okada for his efforts. The okada driver's curses filtered in through the open windows.

"You see, when you were on camera, funny enough, I felt that was when you really came through to being yourself. I remember the show with the prostitute. I couldn't take my eyes off the screen," he remarked.

"She wasn't that attractive. Her life had hardened her. But she had such a sad story and a truly good heart."

"I wasn't looking at her! I was looking at you. I remember watching you as she told you about being raped at ten by her father's younger brother and you had tears in your eyes. I couldn't stop staring at you. You were luminous."

"Because I was crying?" Chika asked cautiously.

"No, because I could see your heart!" Gbenga said sharply. "Why would I want you to cry?"

Chika again fell silent.

# Chapter 37

# Lola
# The way through

Lola was sitting up on the bed. John was sitting on the other edge. "Lola, I am sorry," he said. Lola said nothing. She could still feel his weight as if he were still on top of her. She no longer wanted to talk, she just wanted to leave, but she was afraid to get up and provoke him.

"It's just that you make me so crazy!" he said. "Why do you push me so much? Can't you see that things would be better if you just realized when to stop? You push me to the wall and then I react."

Lola licked the wound in her mouth. When he hit her face, somehow, she must have bit down on her cheek.

"Haven't I been a good husband? Haven't I provided everything you need?" he said, getting agitated again and standing up. His voice rose as he spoke. "I admit I haven't been perfect, but that woman means nothing to me. Nothing" he shouted as he looked at her. Lola looked away, she couldn't bear to hold his gaze.

"Why are you looking away as if I am a monster. Look at me!" he demanded. She acquiesced. "Can't you understand it is nothing. Just sex. She... look Lola, you are the one I married. The one, I still want to be married to. Why can't that be enough?" he asked.

Lola snorted involuntarily. "You don't believe me!" he said. "Oh so now, I guess, I am a liar? You know what? You are the problem in this marriage. You. You can stay in that corner and play the victim, but you are the problem. You wanted everything. You had to keep up with the joneses. You had to have the best cars, the best house, have your kids go to only certain schools. Don't you think all those things come at a price?" he said screaming. "Don't you? You nagged me till I became this person and now you look at me as if I am a monster! I only hit you because you pushed my buttons."

Lola just looked down at her sheets and shook her head. She couldn't believe what he was saying and the shocking thing for her was that he believed it. Though there was some truth in his words. She had been too eager to fit in and she thought the path to that was in having the right things and living in the right neighborhood, so she did push him. But she didn't want or ask for this. Nothing she could have done could have warranted this treatment. This was too much. He did this on his own. She would not allow him make her both a victim and a villain. Each of them had to take responsibility for their own actions. When she looked at him again, her defiance was evident in her eyes.

"There you go again. Looking at me like that. You are always criticizing, always nagging. Lola you are a nag! If you don't know it, know it now. You are a horrible, disgusting nag. Why wouldn't I go outside, when I can't get peace in my own home? Every man I know has someone on the side, so that perfect person you are looking for, you won't find it." He continued to rant.

"You want to leave me and try to disgrace me," he said as he came closer to the bed. "I won't let you. Do you hear me? I won't let you. I'll kill you first!"

Just as he approached the bed, someone kept blowing their horn at the gate. John walked over to the window. Lola took that opportunity and fled into the bathroom and locked the door. He ran behind her and demanded that she open the door.

The guard let in Chika and Gbenga. Chika could hear them shouting as they came up the stairs. John stopped banging on the door and went out to meet them. Lola opened the door and followed him quietly. He met them at the staircase.

"Why are you in my house?" She heard him ask them.

Gbenga responded. "Guy, look we don't want to make trouble, but your wife called Chika."

"And so? Because she called you to lie, you came to intrude on my privacy?" John began to roar.

Lola ran out right then. "Don't believe him. It's not a lie. Something is wrong with him. He will kill me!"

John took three quick steps back and slapped her so hard she fell backwards to the floor. Chika screamed and ran to her. Gbenga ran to John and struggled to hold him back as he advanced towards Lola. Lola looked up at her husband and though she could only see him through a haze, he looked like a charging bull. She heard Chika say, "Oh my God! She is bleeding at the back of her head." Then Lola passed out.

# Chapter 38

# Chika
# Amen

Chika sat in the hospital waiting room and tried to pray. She couldn't clear her mind enough to speak to God. Whenever she started, she only got as far as "Father..." All she could think about was holding Lola's head in her hands. Even though she had washed her hands, she still felt the stickiness from the blood. John was alternating between pacing the room and talking to Gbenga. He would shake his head and shout loudly, "She has to be okay."

Chika looked at him, enraged. She wanted to beat him like he beat his wife. Lola's face, arms and stomach were bruised and he stood there wanting someone to feel sorry for him; wanting someone to tell him that it was not his fault. He had the nerve to say that the devil must have taken over him. Chika said that if that was the case, how could she be sure that said devil had left the building? She knew she shouldn't talk that way, but she was incensed. What kind of nonsense was this? She was overwhelmed and couldn't even clarify her emotions; it was all jumbled up inside her, swirling. She felt angry and frustrated. She saw Gbenga trying to calm John down and she couldn't hold back any longer. She let herself go and started spewing the anger that was rising inside of her.

"How could you?" Chika screamed. The other patrons of the hospital turned to stare. "Now you want her to be okay, when you were hitting her as if you were pounding meat, you didn't want her to be okay then?" John put his head in his hands. "How could you treat someone you loved that way?" Chika said, finally lowering her voice at Gbenga's request. "How could you? Was everything you ever said a lie? You don't hurt the people you love! You just don't!" She turned and walked over to the window and began to cry. Gbenga walked over to her, took her in his arms and she sobbed into his shoulder. Her make-up left a smudge of brown and plum. John had collapsed into a chair and was staring at the ceiling. Chika found herself beginning to feel sorry for him. He was a mess, she thought, but then again, she mused, so was she.

The doctor finally came out with some news. She wasn't conscious, but the worst was over, she would be fine very soon. A woman who was sitting on a bench close to them, stood up and shouted "Praiseee the Lord!"

It startled them. Chika and Gbenga laughed together, and nodded saying, "Amen" simultaneously.

# Chapter 39

# Karen
# Beyond understanding

The last few hours had been the most exhausting of her life. She sat in her hotel room and dialed numbers that terminated all over the world. She had to say goodbye. The call to her Aunt in Ibadan had been the most difficult.

"Stop saying that!" Her aunt insisted. "Speak positively! God can change this situation! Stop confessing negatively."

Karen was irritated by her commands. How dare she tell her what to say and how to feel? She wasn't the one whose life was ebbing away in increments. She wanted to shout at her, to tell her off, but as she sat there holding the phone, listening to her aunt attempt to shout her cancer away, she realized there was no need to. Her aunt was simply trying to reconcile the news the only way she could. Plus she couldn't waste any breath on denial.

"Thank you Aunty," she said. "I understand," she finished softly.

"Karen!" Her aunt cried out. "Karen, wait!" Karen flinched at the pitch of her voice. Her pain had shifted it. Even as she paused, she was filled with regret. Why hadn't she taken the time to be closer to this woman? Her mother's only sister. Karen thought back to a time when she was only a child and her mother was plum cheeked and beautiful. Aunty Linda used to visit and bring her chocolates from London. Karen remembered the funeral when Aunty Linda tried to comfort her even as she watched her mother lowered into the ground. Her aunt was crying, she sobbed loudly, even as she reached for Karen. Karen shrugged her hand off her shoulder. She would not be weak. She was angry at her mother. She left her alone because she was weak. Now as Karen listened to the anguish breaking her aunt's voice, she understood pain, and she saw agony from a different perspective. She wished she was in London with her aunt so she could return the embrace that was offered so long ago. She finally acknowledged that nerves of steel couldn't necessarily trump the cords of love.

As she called various people, leaving instructions with some, revealing the whole truth to others and in some cases, simply waiting for the lull in the conversation so that she could say a casual but final goodbye. She had tried to call Lola, but her cell phone had been switched off for hours and Chika's simply rang with no answer. She was relieved in a way. She couldn't bear to tell them for some reason. She thought that maybe it was because they would remind her of the possibilities that could have existed for her.

Dele walked back into the room. He had a gift wrapped box in his hand. Karen looked at it and asked what it was, coyly. He smiled and she laughed and grabbed it from him. She wanted to cry as she tore open the package. After all these years, finally she felt loved. In the box was a large satin envelope, and inside the envelope, a rich red velvety card with embossed gold lettering. It was tickets on a cruise ship. The Matador, the world's most luxurious. Karen looked up at Dele after reading the words in the elaborate packaging.

"We have to fly to Greece and then we travel the world!" he said looking at her as if something in her expression might say more than her words. But Karen held nothing back; there was no longer any need to, when she spoke, it was in liberty.

"Wow! Well, the doctor says I should feel well in a day or two, once the chemo is completely out of my system. I guess I should say, Bon voyage!"

Dele leaned down and tried to kiss her. It was supposed to be romantic, but Karen just started laughing. He looked at her quizzically, and she raised her eyebrows and said, "Really?" He laughed with her. "I just went with what I felt!" he said sitting down on the bed. Karen laughed even more. They fell back on the bed together and then he kissed her. They just lay there for awhile and Karen had started drifting off to sleep when he spoke.

"Karen," he said. She said nothing, just waited for him to continue, but she moved in acknowledgment of his voice. "I want you to see another doctor. An old friend of mine found another revolutionary new trial. I don't think we should give up yet, just because getting into this trial didn't work out. We need to go see the doctor in Cleveland, but they might be able to get you in," he said, rushing through the words like they held magic that might dissipate as they were said. Karen was afraid to hope for the possibility.

Dele reached for her hand. "Say yes."

Tears accompanied the breath. He lifted his head up and looked at her. She nodded. His shoulders fell with relief and he kissed her. She held on to him and tried to lose herself in the sensation of his mouth, his breath, his life. This was all she had ever wanted. In that moment, though she still didn't really know or fully acknowledge any God, she prayed. "Please. Please. Please."

# Chapter 40

# Lola
# The business of living

Lola unpacked her clothes. She was still sore in places and had bruises from the beating. That night when he was on top on her, punching her face, she thought she would die, and she was so sorry for the life that she had lived. She had done nothing. Even her sons, she wasn't sure what memories they would have. When she came out of the hospital, she was grateful for the pain because it reminded her that she was alive. Now, she was grateful for every breath, though it hurt with every inhalation because her ribs were bruised as well. There was nothing that John could say that would make her risk death again. The only thing she knew for sure was that from that moment on, she intended to live.

She had moved into Chika's guest room temporarily. Chika had offered to let her sublet the whole flat in a few months because she planned to go back to London. She thanked her, but she wasn't sure if she would be able to afford the rent. She smiled at the irony of life; the handbag she was holding could have at least covered a few months of rent. As she sat there looking over all her expensive laces, her gold and other trappings, her eyes glazed over. The year was ending differently from how it had begun. She had the trappings of wealth, but she had never really been rich.

Her former life as she knew was officially over. The crazy thing was that there were those around her who thought she was foolish to make such a decision. Her aunt had come with John to see her and to plead with her to take him back. She said that he had come to his senses. John got on his knees and begged Lola to return home. He offered anything she wanted. He even called his mistress and cursed her in front of Lola. She was not moved. She no longer loved him. She felt as if she no longer knew him and she didn't care to rediscover him. She was too focused on trying to figure out herself. When he saw that she wasn't responding to her pleas, he threatened her with her sons. He said he wouldn't let her take her sons. She teared up just thinking about them, but Lola knew this was the only way. She would never go back to that marriage. In due time she would fight for her sons, for now, they were fine. John was not an abusive father, distant perhaps but not abusive and at the moment she couldn't be useful to them anyway.

It made her break down, when she considered how she had failed her boys. She had let them down in the worst possible way. She wondered if they would ever forgive her for leaving them behind. She hoped they would understand her motives one day. She needed to start over. She needed to figure out who she was, in order to be a better mother to them. So even though John didn't know it, his threats suited her just fine. Plus they cemented her belief that he was no longer the man she had loved. She was resolute. She was not ready to divorce him, but she needed to live apart for a while before she could make any more decisions.

The pressure to stay married was enormous though, even her parents had intervened. They called her. Initially they wanted to tar and feather John, but it didn't take long for her father to change his tune. He told her that she should be reasonable, after all, no man is perfect and that he was indeed sorry. Her mother pointed out that she had no money and no source of income and asked her what her plan was. When she replied, "I don't know" her mother hissed and counseled her to return to her home before some other woman took her place. Lola shook her head. She had no words to express what she felt and she didn't think her mom would take too kindly to a guttural scream. John finally told her that he would give her what she wanted. She could stay by herself and figure out her life. He sneered at her and told her he would not support her lifestyle, so she better get used to living off her own sweat.

He seemed surprised when she nodded. He couldn't understand her sense of confidence. But Lola did not feel confident. She was scared, but she knew she had to face life anyway. When John stood up to leave, she walked over to him and took his hands in her hands. She had expected to curse him, to hate him, but she didn't. She felt sorry for him, for both of them. They had started out so well to end up so badly. John had not previously been an abuser, in all the years they had been together, he had never touched her before this season, but over the years as he compromised one value after another, it was like his soul was slowly being changed. Just as hers was. They were becoming less and less like themselves and more like something else. She remembered a sermon given once by a visiting speaker in church. He talked about the realities of your environment. He shared the results of a research study. This study was done on a particular patch of land. The soil in that land had certain unique properties, certain minerals and elements. Every plant that they tested growing in that soil had those same minerals and elements inside of it. They took plants from other places and planted them in that same soil at various times, and all the plants showed different levels of the same minerals and elements. They had changed. It would be easy to just point her fingers at John, but she knew she had a hand in their demise as well. So when she finally spoke, all she could say was "I'm sorry too".

He stared at her as if trying to understand her words and to Lola's surprise, he began to tear up and Lola again, felt compassion for him. A more cynical woman would have called it manipulation, but she knew it was more than that. He knew he was wrong. He knew he had failed. He also was grieving the loss of who he could have been. They stood like that for a few minutes, while her aunt sat quietly, murmuring to herself. Lola thought that perhaps she was praying for a miracle. Lola smiled. The miracle wasn't her going back to John, the miracle had already happened.

The worst had happened and they were still living. She watched John's back as he walked out of the flat that night and she knew then, that she would never again walk into his arms for an embrace. She held back her tears for the duration of time that it took for them to walk out of the door and close it. Then she wept until she had no more strength left.

The truth was it wasn't about John; she had to deal with herself. Here she was almost middle aged with no money and no source of income. Living at the mercy of a woman she hadn't even known for more than a year. She put the blouse she had been folding down and lay back on the clothes strewn bed. She took a deep breath. The time for crying had passed, now she would have to figure out what to do next.

# Chapter 41

# Chika
# Coming out

Chika sat in Gbenga's flat watching Arsenal battle with Man United. Well, she kind of watched while also perusing her magazine. If you asked her who scored last, she wouldn't have been able to tell you. Gbenga looked over at her every so often and smiled. She had been honest with him about her sports apathy when he invited her over to watch the game, but he insisted that she come anyway because he enjoyed having her there. However, he asked that she not distract him by asking questions if she really didn't care. She smiled back. She liked Gbenga. He was not suave but he could be sweet and he seemed incredibly genuine. He was a good friend to her and she was grateful for him. Sometimes she wondered if he felt something more for her. Often she would catch him looking at her in a way that suggested that something more was bubbling under the surface and it worried her. She didn't want to lose his friendship, but after Collins, she felt more than a little gun shy.

They had spent a lot of time together since helping Lola that day. Sharing her pain had bonded them together and as Chika got to know him better, she liked him all the more. They shared common values. He practiced compassion and integrity. One Saturday, he took her to a grilled fish place by the beach and there they talked about religion for the first time. He admitted that he didn't go to church regularly, but he knew his Bible well and considered himself a spiritual follower of Christ. When Chika asked him what that meant, he said he had had a number of negative experiences in churches so he was yet to find one that fit him, but he believed in the Bible and he practiced the tenets of Christianity as best he could. He reached for his cigarette as he spoke and Chika raised her eyebrows. He noticed her expression and shrugged. He took a drag on it and said, "Like you, I am a work in progress."

Now he leaned back and picked up the phone. Chika watched his muscles in his arm tense slightly as he put the phone to his ear. "I am ordering Chinese delivery, what do you want?" He was ordering from Yang's Chinese. She loved their fried rice so she asked for a small bowl. He added his own requests and placed the order. He smiled as he put the phone down, when Chika asked him why, he admitted to having a corny thought. "Are you the yin to my yang?" he asked laughing. Chika laughed too but her eyes betrayed some worry. Gbenga saw it and asked her what was wrong. She didn't know what to tell him so she said nothing, but he heard her loud and clear just the same. He sat up and looked at her, "Look, Chika, I'd be lying if I told you I wasn't attracted to you. Of course I am, but I also know you have been through something really traumatic and you need time and space to heal, so relax. Right now, all I want to be is your friend okay? Plus I might be just too much man for you!" he added while rubbing his chest, which made Chika burst out laughing.

Chika was so relaxed with him, she really enjoyed the man that he was. Why couldn't she have met him first, she thought. Then she wrinkled her forehead as she realized that she did meet him first but she hadn't paid him any attention. Instead she had fallen for Collins, Mr. Smooth talker with his expensive shirts and fancy words. She recalled her last meeting with Collins. It was by chance because after the encounter with his wife, Collins who had professed to love her more than his own life, had avoided her calls and emails as if she were a bill collector. Chika had been upset about it because she felt she needed some closure. In fact one night after recounting the ills of her relationship with Collins for the umpteenth time, Gbenga who had been her weary audience told her he had had enough and she needed to move on. She told him she just wanted closure and he rolled his eyes. "You women and closure. The closure is that he has closed his mind and heart to you, now do the same. That's all the closure you need. And if you ask me why men behave this way one more time, I might burst a blood vessel. All men do not behave this way. Men who have issues do. However for some inane reason, most of you women seem to be attracted to the ones with the most baggage!" he exclaimed in frustration.

After that conversation Chika started to get over Collins, so she was unprepared to run into him in the supermarket, a few days later. She bumped into him by the fresh produce. His expression was one of shock and fear. Chika looked him over, he looked none the worse for wear. Even though she had gone over all the things she would say to him in her mind, when it finally came down to it, she had nothing to say to him. She just stared at him. It was the strangest thing, when she looked at this man that used to make her feverish; she was no longer impressed. It was as if a haze had lifted and now she could see all his cracks and imperfections, the beginnings of a slight paunch, ashy skin. She was amazed that she had once thought he was so desirable. He also said nothing, but he didn't walk away, he alternated between staring at her and looking around furtively. It took a minute but Chika finally got why, he was there with someone else. In seconds, she caught a glimpse of his wife talking with someone, just a few yards away. She quickly turned to leave and then he reached out and grabbed her arm. She yanked it away and hissed like an angry cat.

"Don't touch me!" she snapped. He withdrew quickly and started walking away from her, towards his wife, and Chika was left holding a rotting onion.

Gbenga was right, Chika thought, she still had quite a bit of healing and growing to do before she could consider getting back into a relationship. She leaned back in the chair and sighed.

Gbenga looked over at her and smiled. "Are you okay?" he asked. She nodded, but she was thinking, "No, I am not. But I will be".

# Chapter 42

# Lola
## "Standing"

Lola had been sitting on the bed for a long time. The sun that was high in the sky, had started to set gloriously and the sky was filled with reddish orange hues accented by the occasional purple. Lola leaned forward and looked out of the window. She smiled and looked back at her phone. The red light was blinking signaling that the record function was on. Lola opened her mouth and began to sing.

*Standing,*
*In the midst of the storm,*
*When everything seems wrong,*
*And I'm barely holding on.*

Lola sang, even as the tears ran down her face, but every word came from deep within and she felt healed even as the words left her mouth. She had never thought of herself as a song writer, but the melody and lyrics, poured out of her without hesitation.

*Yearning,*
*For the break of new day,*
*new mercies, new favor*
*Lord, please make a way.*

She stopped and exhaled. Feeling even sadder. What would her life be like now? What would she do? She had no job, no money, no prospects and now she would have no husband. *Lord please make a way!* She lay on the bed and started to cry again but the melody kept swirling around in her mind.

When she opened her mouth again, she had no idea what she was going to sing but she felt her spirits lifting with each note.

*Who can say what tomorrow will bring.*
*All I know is I will still sing.*
*I will still sing.*

She sat up as she sang, and then before she moved to the next part, she actually stood up, lifting the her hands up and closing her eyes as she began to worship.

*I will sing,*
*of His grace and His love, His kindness.*
*I will sing*
*Of His power, His strength and His will*

She squared her shoulders, threw her head back and sang with everything inside of her. Her voice dropped a few octaves lower as she released the sounds soulfully.

*Smiling,*
*For my life's in His hands.*
*I know He has a plan,*
*I know He'll see it through*

*Dancing,*
*For I know who I serve*
*and it gives me the nerve*
*to start again.*

By end of the song, she had started to feel strong and she sang the song again with more enthusiasm and at the top of her voice. It was a bluesy, jazzy rendition and she gave every lyric life. When she finished singing, she heard a knock at the door. She was mortified, she had forgotten where she was, forgotten that she was staying over at someone's house, so she was apologetic when

Chika opened the door in response to her "come in". "Chika, I am so sorry! I got carried away." She heard noise coming from behind Chika. "Oh, no! Do you have guests?" She continued, not giving Chika a chance to respond to her at all. "Oh, I am so embarrassed. Sorry!"

Chika held her hand up. "Please stop saying you are sorry! Your song is so beautiful, I have never heard it before. In fact my friend wanted me to come and ask you what the name of the CD you got it from was?" Lola started laughing. "Actually I just made it up." She said smiling widely. Chika threw her hands up. "No way!" She shrieked. "I knew you had a great voice, but I didn't know you had songwriting skills as well." Lola just stood there grinning, she felt really good and she didn't want to say anything to chase away the feeling, so they just stood there for a few moments.

Suddenly Chika grabbed her hand and pulled her to the door, saying, "come and meet my friends!". Lola started to resist, she felt quite unpresentable, she was wearing an old boubou and wasn't wearing any makeup. "Oh, I'm really not ready to see anyone. I look a mess!" She protested. "Nonsense!" Chika insisted. "Just come" she said while practically dragging her to the door.

Lola was surprised to see more than one person in the living room. Chika made the introductions quickly. She already knew Gbenga but she would be meeting the other two people who also worked in media for the first time. They immediately began to compliment her on her voice and the song. Ade, who worked at a radio station and also in the music industry, asked her if she was planning to record the song. She shook her head while staring at him incredulously. *What in the world was he talking about*, she thought, *He is probably just using it as an excuse to run game*. She sat down warily and watched him closely as he talked. "I would like to introduce you to a friend of mine who is looking for a new gospel artist for his label, I think he would love your sound."

He said. Lola shook her head. She still remembered the feel of that disgusting tongue in her ear. "No thank you, I already met with someone and I am really not interested in that life". Chika asked her why and she proceeded to share the story but leaving out the names of the key players. Gbenga guessed who it was immediately. "Are you talking about Boyo?" Lola didn't say anything but the widening of her eyes confirmed his suspicions. He continued talking after noting her physical response. "You can't let one bad experience stop you from moving forward. You clearly have a gift and for the record, men like Boyo exist in every industry, there is no running from them, you just have to learn how to deal." Lola listened and considered the wisdom in his words. "Maybe" She responded. Chika latched onto the possibility in the two syllables. "Indeed. Lola, I believe that this is the path God wants you to tread, I am sure you will do amazingly well." She said, smiling at Lola encouragingly. Lola returned the gesture. "Maybe" She said. "Maybe".

# Chapter 43

# Chika
# Returning home

The sun was beginning to set, and for the first time in a long time, Chika started to feel like herself again. Ade and Daniel had left and Lola had retired to her room. She and Gbenga sat in silence. After a while, Gbenga asked if she would like to go for a walk. Chika said yes. Soon they were walking on the street like teenagers who had nowhere else to go to share their love, but they did not talk about love. Gbenga was grilling her about her plans to leave Nigeria. Chika did not say much of anything. In frustration, he insisted she say something definitive. She shrugged her shoulders and asked what he wanted to hear. She was leaving. That was all there was to it. She needed to create some space to think and feel whole again. To heal and to grow from her mistakes, space to be introspective and fully understand the drivers behind her decision making. Gbenga insisted that she could do that in Lagos.

She shook her head, "I can't," she continued shaking her head and repeated. "I can't, I need to leave."

He asked her when she would be traveling and was shocked when she said that it would be in a week. He started to say something, but Chika excused herself to answer her ringing phone. As soon as she heard what Lola had to say, she told Gbenga she had to go.

# Chapter 44

# Lola
# Getting through

Lola sat on the floor, staring at the walls around her. What they were saying was simply impossible. Karen could not be dead. How could that be true? She kept dialing Karen's phone and the disembodied voice kept repeating that the call couldn't be accepted at this time. She had received a few texts from Karen while she was in New York, but she had been so wrapped up in her own drama that she kept putting off responding and now, Karen was dead. Gone. Just like that.

Chika was curled up in the chair on the other side of the room, rocking herself back and forth. She had not stopped sobbing since they got the news a few hours ago. Dele had returned to Lagos from New York and asked them to come and meet with him. They had known that Karen was undergoing treatments, so they thought maybe she was still in the US, while he came back to retrieve one or two things. They thought they were being asked to run some errands for Karen. On the way to meet him, Chika joked that it was so like Karen to have them summoned to the palace. They had both laughed in the back of the car, and even cried out "jinx" after they said, "Queen Karen" together.

They were ushered into the sitting room by the steward, who looked subdued, but they didn't think too much of it when they gave him their drink orders in response to his offer for refreshment. As soon as Dele walked into the room, they knew that it was not just a bad day for the steward. Before he spoke, they could both tell that something was very, very wrong.

Dele had always been that man who took great care with his appearance, everything, right down to his nails was always well groomed. When he walked in, his hair was uncombed and he was unshaven. He looked so unkempt and when he started to speak, his voice cracked. Chika jumped to her feet and guided him to a chair to sit down. He sat down.

When he was able to produce words and told them the news. He was instantly overcome and broke down, weeping in front of them. His family members must have been listening from the outer room because his mother and his sister ran in and started crying too. Chika dissolved into tears, but Lola just kept shaking her head saying, "It's not true."

One of the relatives put his arms around Lola and tried to comfort her. Then Dele lifted his head and stopped weeping. He made no effort to wipe his face. He told the others to stop crying. He told them that she went in her sleep. He said they had been lying next to each other in the hotel and he felt her touching his cheek, and so he woke up and he could tell she was crying. He asked her if she was in pain, but she said no that she just wanted to be held so she could fall asleep. So he did, and then fell asleep. In the morning, when he woke up, she was gone. As he told the story, his mother started to scream and his sisters started to sob again. He went to his mother to try and calm her and got her to sit in a chair. Lola watched her sit hunched over and couldn't take her eyes off her shaking legs.

Dele walked over to a table and said that Karen must have made peace with leaving because she wrote various people letters and they were included. He handed them envelopes and gave them hugs and then excused himself. Lola couldn't imagine the pain he was in. She shuddered when she thought about the fact that she would never see Karen again.

# Chapter 45

# Chika
# So long a letter

Lola's envelope now sat on the coffee table in Chika's living room and she didn't think she could bring herself to read it. Lola looked over at Chika, who was quiet now, but tears rolled down her eyes. She asked her if she was ready to read her letter. Chika shook her head. She still clutched her envelope in her hand. Lola nodded because she understood Chika's reluctance. She realized that it must have been unfathomably hard for Karen to write it, and if she had taken the time to do so, the very least she could do was to read it. So she stood up and gave Chika a hug. They held each other for a very long time and cried together. Then she told Chika "I need to go and read my letter." Then she picked up the envelope and went quietly to her room.

After Lola left, a palpable quiet descended on the room. Chika felt like all the blood was rushing to her head, and she had to hold her forehead for a moment. Karen was one of her oldest friends, and the only person she could count on to tell her the truth always; the only person who wouldn't judge her. She had really missed her during these past months. She hadn't wanted to call and intrude on her fertility treatments. She remembered telling Karen that she had started dating Collins. She didn't lecture her, though she did raise an eyebrow and ask, "I thought you didn't live your life that way?" Without allowing Chika to respond, she shrugged and said, "Well, I guess if you like it, then I love it, but I still think you deserve better." Then she ordered champagne and dismissed the conversation, and squeezed her hand. "If it makes you happy, it works for me."

The memory made Chika smile a little through her tears. She was going to miss Karen. She took several deep breaths and indulged in a few more memories, and then she was ready to open the letter. She opened the envelope with care because it was already wet in places from her tears and read the words.

*Chika,*

*This note will not be long because I have so many to write, and even though I hope that you will never have to see this, I have a feeling that I will never again feel the dense heat of Lagos again.*

*I wanted you to know that I am so grateful for our friendship. I know I have never been particularly emotional, but right now, I feel so overwhelmed at the beautiful memories we have shared, I guess cancer does that to you. You have always inspired me with your determination to live fully dedicated to God. I didn't always understand it, but I admired the strength of your convictions.*

*I read about you recently (yes, even I, read the gossip blogs every now and then) and I heard about you and Collins. Ah well, I knew it wouldn't end well, but we all have our lessons. I certainly have had mine. I have so many regrets. But this is not a note about regrets. It is a note about life, love and everything in between. You always tried to encourage me to pray. And guess what, I did. I didn't use any fancy words and Lord knows, this whole time, I haven't even looked at a Bible, but I did. And you know what; I do believe God answered me.*

*I forgave Dele and he forgave me. If you can believe*

*this, we have been almost on a second honeymoon. Well, call it our first because we never really had a real one. We had great pictures, but no love. This time, we have no pictures, but I hope Dele has enough memories to last him a lifetime; I know mine will last me through eternity.*

*So back to you, my darling. I hope you are not beating yourself up over that whole Collins mess. What's done, is done. And I hope you are not getting ready to run back abroad. I know you. You probably can't bear anyone to see you as anything less than perfect. Even back in school, you couldn't bear it when you didn't get the highest score. Well, listen Chika, get over yourself. You screwed up, so what, guess what you are human. Now get about the business of getting back to who you were meant to be. Maybe this is what your true message and work will be about; you were always telling me that the work of Christ is about redemption. Well, my dear, start singing that redemption song.*

*If you are reading this, then right now, I am somewhere in the atmosphere and my body is decaying. I certainly hope I go to heaven, but the truth is I have no idea. I know I feel God's presence and I hope that's a good thing, but I don't know. I know I am grateful to have the last days that I did. I am grateful to have had the experience of redemption in life. I am grateful to have finally begun to live, even as I started to die.*

*My dearest friend. I love you. Do what you were born to do. And yes...goodbye.*

Chika's wept aloud as she read the letter. Karen had such a kind soul. What kind of woman takes the time to encourage a friend even as she herself is dying? She leaned her head back and looked at the ceiling.

"Rest in peace Karen," She thought. "Rest in peace."

# Chapter 46

# Alpha and Omega

A year had passed since Karen's death and Dele had set up a foundation to honor her memory. It was a foundation to provide therapy for cancer patients and their families.

Lola clapped and stood proudly with everyone else as they saluted Dele for giving a heartfelt speech about how going to therapy with Karen changed their lives. He talked about how it made him a different man and how he still had to do the work of forgiving himself for almost completely missing out on the gift of love that God had given him.

Lola knew he received a standing ovation not just because of the wonderful speech he gave, but because of the man he had become. He was not only a new man but he had become an agent of change in Nigerian society.

Lola looked over at Chika and they both smiled. She had given her own speech earlier and had given away copies of her best selling new book. She was a bonafide celebrity now. Her return to TV was actually triumphant and her new show, executive produced by Gbenga, who was happily standing to her right, could certainly be described as change your life television.

Chika squeezed Lola's hand and whispered in her ear, saying a quick prayer and telling her not to be nervous. Lola nodded but inside she had a whole rabble of butterflies so she took slow deep breaths to try and calm herself. She was anxious because this was her first time being presented as an artist to a real live audience. She felt some measure of confidence because she had the number one hit gospel song on the radio but she still worried if these people would think she was good enough and if she would do Karen proud. The truth was she wanted to run home and hide under the covers but doing this was a necessary step in the right direction as Chika said, it was time to step into the spotlight and let the world share in her shine, so when Dele asked her to sing at this event because it would be good exposure especially with her full album coming out soon, she had no choice but to say yes. However now that the moment was upon her, even the warm smile Chika gave her couldn't make her feel better.

Her head started to pound and her skin started to feel tight and all the deep breathing didn't seem to be helping. She was officially freaking out. Lola knew that Chika could see her shaking and she was never more grateful for their friendship than then, because Chika leaned over and asked her a question that distracted her and pulled her out of her head and right back into the present moment where she needed to be. Chika asked "So tell me, what did Karen really say to you in her letter?"

Lola smiled when she remembered the piece of paper that she still kept in her bedside drawer and she sighed releasing every toxic emotion that was at the root of her fear as she remembered her dear friend. She looked at Chika and finally said, "She wrote just two sentences. Lola, I love you and you need to know that you are enough. Now love yourself and live your life!". Chika laughed as she heard the words, trust Karen to wrap her affection up in a command. She shook her head in that poignant moment. And they both started to laugh again and said "Queen Karen!" in unison and just right then the announcer called Lola up to the stage to grace the room with her God given voice.

# A note from the author:

This story may make you cry…it may make you angry…and hopefully, you will find moments to laugh as well. Much like life, these women are complicated. Much like you and I, they were on a journey to find themselves. I hope you find yourself as well as you read and draw strength from their stories. There was an article referenced in the book about being happy and finding purpose. I write similar articles, as well as teach and support women in their journey to soulful success. I host events and workshops and do one on one coaching. To learn more about my work with women like yourself, please visit my website, www.refreshwithekene.com

I hope many of you will read this with friends and have evenings were you discuss the themes in this book over wine and great food. I thought I would include some discussion questions for just such occasions.

Suggested discussion questions:
1. How would you describe Karen, Chika and Lola? What did you find remarkable about each of them? Did anything about any or all the women resonate with you?
2. Why do you think Lola lost herself? Do you know women who have?
3. When we first meet Chika, do you think she is an example of many christian women? Why do you think she is the way she is?
4. Why do you think Karen and Lola stayed with their husbands?
5. Would you consider Lola a good mother? How did you feel about the choices she had to make later in the book?
6. What do you think about the men in story, Dele, John, Collins and Gbenga?

7. What did you feel when Karen and Dele rediscovered themselves in therapy?
8. What would you have wished for Karen, Lola and/or Chika?
9. What are the biggest takeaways from this book for you?

Thank you so much for reading and I hope to meet you at one of our Refresh events in a city near you.

# Gratitude

With all honor and glory given to whom from whom all blessings flow

To David, for holding it down when necessary, so I can live out my dreams but pushing me to do more when necessary as well.

To Sina for being my biggest why and inspiration.

To Audrey for being such a blessing, a stew specialist and listening to my stories.

To my siblings... For being and being and being, through thick and thin!

To my mother - for defining resilience and determination

To my father - for being a thinker.

And there are so many more I could mention. You know my heart and I know yours.

Thank you.

www.ingramcontent.com/pod-product-compliance
Lightning Source LLC
Chambersburg PA
CBHW070755280626
47162CB00016B/900